Another One Gone

Also by Paul Breen

Runner's Path
A Sudden Interest in Shakespeare

Another One Gone

A Seamus O'Neill Mystery

Paul Breen

Dutch Hollow Press

ISBN 979-8-9862083-6-7 (paperback)

ISBN 979-8-9862083-5-0 (ebook)

ISBN 979-8-9862083-7-4 (hardcover)

Book Cover Design by ebooklaunch.com

For Dave and Betty Gifford, who farmed for many years in Pierce County, Wisconsin

Chapter 1

June 2000

It was test day. Seamus O'Neill hit the alarm clock's snooze button and rolled off his mattress. Crawling into the kitchen area, he grabbed the countertop and pulled himself up. With the faucet at full blast, he ducked his face into the sink and water splashed against his cheek. After easing the stream, he drank several mouthfuls.

The clock said 7:20 AM. His boss, John Ryder, was scheduled to arrive in twenty minutes. O'Neill stripped off his clothes and stumbled into the bathroom. He turned the shower on, stepped inside, and the icy stream slapped his skin. Rubbing soap through his hair and body, he turned around three times then slammed the faucet off. As he dried himself, the alarm flipped back on, catching the last few notes of Bruce Springsteen's "Hungry Heart."

Returning to the main room, he dressed and pulled the half-empty flask from his pants pocket. The scent of bourbon was unmistakable, and the metal felt cold as he set it on the kitchen counter. The apartment buzzer rang as he stared at the container. He assumed Ryder was outside, so he gave the liquor one more look and buzzed the outer door open. Within a few moments, there was a knock at his apartment door. O'Neill slid into his shoes and exited.

"You're actually ready?" Ryder said.

"Course. Told you I would be."

Ryder shook his head and let out his squeal of a laugh. "Like that means anything."

O'Neill descended the stairs, opened the front door, and stepped into the sunlight. Once his eyes adjusted, he spotted Ryder's black Chevy S-10 across the street. "Did you bring the article with you?"

"You haven't seen it?"

"No. Thought I'd wait and look at it in the office. Figure I might as well get paid if I'm going to read about your crime solving skills. But I'll read it on the drive if you got it."

Ryder snorted and unlocked the truck. Reaching into the back seat, he pulled a newspaper from his briefcase and dropped a single sheet on the passenger seat. "I'm getting it framed. I'll put it behind my desk."

O'Neill picked up the newspaper as he slid into the seat. The story took up a third of a page in the *Wisconsin State Journal's* Daybreak section. The page also included an advice column and a wedding directory. Above Ryder's story was the verbiage "Know your Madisonian" and the subtitle, "John Ryder Continues Family Crime Solving Tradition." A picture of him sitting on his desk with his arms folded accompanied the article. A summary profile listed Ryder as single, thirty-nine years old, and the owner of the Ryder Detective Agency. The story said his hobbies were "following the Packers, Badgers, and Brewers."

"You sound like a deep guy," O'Neill said as the truck pulled into traffic. "Why didn't you bring up the Bucks?"

"What am I supposed to say? I should have mentioned fishing, but it didn't occur to me until later."

"You mention me," O'Neill said after reading the first few paragraphs. "You say, 'I should recognize my partner, Seamus O'Neill. Detective work involves more teamwork than most people realize.' Aw, you call me your *partner*." He smiled widely. "Is this you offering me part ownership of the business, assuming I pass the test?"

"Hell no. I was using the term in a more egalitarian way."

"Egalitarian? Do you even know what that means?"

"Oh, quit whining. I was trying to be nice by mentioning you."

"I know," O'Neill said, almost to himself. "Just giving you flak. Do you think appearing to be a high-flying private detective will get you dates?"

"That's not why I agreed to the interview, but who knows?" He shifted uncomfortably as the truck lingered in front of a stoplight. "What do you think of the picture?"

"A chubby bald guy sitting on a desk with his arms folded. At least the shirt looks clean."

"That should teach me to ask you a serious question. Did you eat this morning?"

"No time."

"The state's private detective exam is scheduled for an hour, so you should have something in your stomach. Lucky for you, I planned." Ryder reached behind the seat and pulled out a McDonald's bag. "The McMuffin is mine; the sausage biscuit is yours."

"Thanks." O'Neill unwrapped the biscuit and took a bite.

"Now remember, this test is multiple choice and mostly common sense. Make sure you answer every question. If you don't know the answer, guess. If you run out of time, just fill in everything. A one out of four chance is better than no chance."

"Don't worry," O'Neill said between bites. "I'm good at multiple choice; I'll be fine."

"You better be. And remember, I paid for your application and the test; but if you fail, you pay for the retake. Got it?"

O'Neill nodded, but he was not worried. Tests didn't bother him and, though he had worked for two years at the Ryder Detective Agency, the idea of being a private detective still didn't seem real. For most of those two years, he had assumed that a smattering of misdemeanor charges from his youth would prevent him from getting a license. There were also rules about excessive drinking that could be problematic. But Ryder, working with staff from the Wisconsin Department of Regulation and Licensing, found a path that allowed O'Neill to obtain a license. The process required a passed exam, sponsorship from a business, and letters of support from law enforcement and local government. Ryder sponsored the application and wrangled letters of support from their alderman and two City of Madison Police Department Detectives they had worked with: Robert Leidel and Phil Garcia. O'Neill's task was to pass the test.

State officials also required Ryder's sponsorship to declare that O'Neill would not perform investigative services for the agency until they issued him a license. The bureaucrats claimed that O'Neill's previous investigative activities had put the Ryder Detective Agency's license at risk. Ryder's letter stated that, until licensed, O'Neill's duties would be limited to "office work, computer support, and routine research."

"It's about ten till eight," Ryder said as he pulled his truck in front of the City-County Building. "I'll park in the ramp. Call as soon as you're done, and I'll pick you up."

"Thanks." He pushed the door open and got out of the vehicle.

"Seamus, you didn't bring your flask, did you?"

"Course not; it's at home." He finished the biscuit and ascended the steps.

Entering a building which housed the City of Madison Police Department made him nervous. Inside, he showed the exam notice to a woman at the front desk. She signaled him through, pointing at the elevators and a stairwell. He chose the stairs, exiting on the third floor.

The building held both city and county government offices and meeting rooms, including a jail where he had been a short-term resident more than once. He arrived at the exam room, waiting as a brunette woman wearing a pantsuit and holding a clipboard checked people in. After allowing the teenager in front of him to enter, the woman motioned O'Neill forward, and he handed her the notice.

She glanced at her watch. "Can I see your driver's license?"

O'Neill showed her his brand new State of Wisconsin Identification Card. "I was told this will work."

"This is fine." She checked him off her list and gave him one sheet filled with numbers and circles and one with his name printed in a large font along with the number forty-seven. "Hand the numbered one to the proctor. She will pass out the questions in a few minutes."

Getting a job with Ryder had been O'Neill's first move in a life which had been stuck in idle for ten years. The test was another step. A chance for him to move to the next stage, whatever that might be.

He took the sheets and ambled into the test room.

Chapter 2

The state tested monthly, so O'Neill expected there would only be two or three test takers and a proctor. But there appeared to be at least a dozen people waiting to take the exam. He knew that most Madison-area private detectives monitored shoppers and managed retail security, so he imagined the people walking around Wal-Mart or Kohl's in a few months, busting shoplifters. Except for one man, those taking the test were younger than him, with several appearing to be college-aged. He gave the sheet with his name to the proctor, and she pointed him to an open chair.

At eight o'clock, the woman handed out pencils and pamphlets that included the exam questions. O'Neill had not taken a test since getting kicked out of Edgewood High School sixteen years earlier, so he should have been nervous. But after fifteen minutes, he was halfway through. Most of the answers were, as Ryder said, common sense. A few involved state statutes and an understanding of how state, county, and city governments were organized. He guessed when he wasn't sure, and after half an hour, he finished. He went back through the questions, changing only one answer. Forty-five minutes into the test, a man who looked to be in his early twenties brought his exam to the proctor and left the room. O'Neill followed, muttering a thank you and nodding to the brunette in the hallway.

Outside the building, he took out his cell phone and called Ryder. Within minutes, the truck pulled into a loading zone.

Ryder reached over and unlocked the passenger seat. "How'd it go?"

"Aced it." O'Neill hopped inside. "You know, you didn't need to wait. I could walk home from here."

"I wanted to make sure you finished without incident. And since I'm here, I might as well drop you off. You can come into the office this afternoon for a few hours. But remember, you are not working on any cases until you get your license. That should take at least a few weeks. Since I sponsored you, they'll notify me about whether you passed the test."

"What do you want me to work on if I come in?"

Ryder looked into the rearview mirror before pulling into traffic. "Read the email I sent you with potential cases; you can help me evaluate which to choose. It's crazy. I'm trying to wind up that Schmidt case, and I just signed a long-term agreement with Riser Training for regular background checks. Besides that, we've got feelers out related to three missing person cases and a cold-case murder. We even got an inquiry about a computer crime. Who knows what yesterday's newspaper article on me will pull in? The publicity is great, but I can't keep up with all these potential clients. We've got to analyze them and decide which to pursue. My concern is less about the jobs themselves and more about the clients. I mean, will the client pay invoices or not? Shit, I can't wait to hire a secretary or someone to help manage this stuff. Until you get your license, you'll focus on administrative duties. You can continue to take the lead on background checks. Once you pass and I hire an administrative assistant, we can work on multiple cases at the same time."

"If you got money for a secretary, you got money to give me a raise, especially since I'll be a legit detective." O'Neill closed his eyes and tilted the seat back.

"Can't say I'll ever think of you as a *legit* detective, but I have been thinking about compensation. I will give you a raise when you get your license, though I won't pay a higher rate for doing background checks, picking up coffee, cleaning the bathroom, or updating Windows. I'll pay more when you're working as a detective. We'll talk about that later. For now, look at the cases and clients. Tomorrow, we'll go through them and I'll decide which ones to take. If you get those things done, you can organize files."

"Hey, can I ask you a dumb, totally unrelated question?"

"Sure, if I can give you a dumb answer."

"I'm thinking about buying a bed. You know, so I have more than just a mattress."

Ryder tilted closer. "You want to sleep in a proper bed like a normal human being? I thought you were fine with sleeping on a mattress on the floor."

"I'm figuring it might make it easier having an actual bed in case I bring a woman to my place."

Ryder giggled as he parked his truck in front of O'Neill's apartment. "What happened to *that's rock & roll*? You told me that line works with women, or at least it stops them from high-tailing it out of your room when they see the dump you live in and that you don't have a bed."

"I'm not in a rock band anymore and I'm thirty-three years old. Women have different expectations than they did back in the day."

"Oh, I get it." Ryder pounded his hand on the dashboard. "The line worked on drunk headbangers after a show, but not on normal women. And you are afraid of what our tall detective friend will think if you bring her to your apartment."

O'Neill shrugged his shoulders and muttered a few unintelligible words.

"You're right to be worried. Detective Meyer won't give you a second look if she sees that apartment. A professional woman has higher expectations than a groupie."

"That's what I'm figuring."

"Don't assume it will make a difference. Meyer's going to hear stories about you. A police detective won't get into a relationship with someone like you. You got too much baggage and you drink too much."

"Let me worry about that," O'Neill said. "So, what kind of coin are we talking about for a bed? That would be a frame and a mattress."

"What size bed?" Ryder asked.

"What sizes are there?"

"Twin, full, queen, and king. You probably got a twin now, which is suitable for a ten-year-old kid or a little guy like you, provided you don't share the bed with a woman."

"Twin isn't big enough for two? It's always worked before, though I could always put a knee on the floor or whatever."

"No, a twin isn't big enough for two. Ideally, you'd go queen, but those are expensive and one would take up a good portion of your tiny apartment. Go full. You could probably go through the classifieds and find someone selling a set for a hundred bucks. If you buy new, you're looking at six hundred bucks. My guess is it's two hundred for the frame and two hundred for each mattress."

"I need two mattresses? Isn't one enough?"

"No, you idiot. One's a box spring and the other's cushier." Ryder looked at his watch. "You coming in later today or not?"

"Depends. I'm going to ask my sister to help me choose a bed. I don't want to do it on my own."

"You have a sister?" Ryder's eyes widened and his jaw dropped. "What's her name?"

"Lena."

"Lena?"

"Yeah, Lena. What's wrong with that?"

"Nothing, but I thought it would be Sinead or Fiona or some weird-sounding Irish name that would go along with your weird-sounding Irish name. What's the story?"

"Nothing that complicated. My dad got to name me and my mom got to name my sister. Mom had an Aunt Marlena who she liked, I guess."

"Okay. Sorry I asked."

"Anyway, if she can go out bed hunting with me today, we'll do that. If not, I'll be in. Though I might just come in for an hour if shopping doesn't take that long."

"Good enough. You gonna need your bonus cash?" Ryder said, referring to some money he was holding for O'Neill.

"Yeah, unless I get everything real cheap. I'll let you know how much it will cost and how much cash I'll need."

"Great. The suspense is killing me."

Chapter 3

O'Neill scaled the apartment building's steps, shut his door, and locked the deadbolt. He leaned against the door, pulled out his cell phone, and looked about the room. A guitar stand stood at one side of the window holding two acoustic guitars and a banjo. A folding chair was on the other side of the window, and his mattress was pushed against a wall, while a sliding closet door dominated another wall. His kitchen area was on one side of the entry door, and the bathroom on the other.

The double window had blinds but no curtains, and the only thing on the walls was a University of Wisconsin calendar open to the month of June. His nineteen-inch television sat on a milk crate beside the chair. A boom box and a trio of CD racks were at the foot of the bed next to a half-full bottle of Old Crow Bourbon.

He staggered into the kitchen area, ducking his mouth under the faucet for twenty seconds. After collecting the empty beer bottles that dotted the counter, he stuck them into his lone trash can. Deciding it would be best to take the empties out of the apartment, he carried the trash to the basement where they kept the building's recycling bin. He dropped the bottles into the bin one by one as if saying goodbye to each.

As he walked up the stairs, he pulled out his phone. Ryder had assigned it to him a few weeks ago, and he used it regularly. He clicked his sister's name in his contacts list and she answered after four rings.

"Lena?"

"Yeah, Seamus," Lena O'Neill said. "Glad you called. What's up?"

"I was wondering if you could help me out with something." He hesitated as he searched for the right words. "There's this woman I like, you know. And she's a professional-type, and I'm nervous about inviting her to my apartment cause, you know, it's not decorated and I don't have a bed or anything. And, of course, it's an efficiency."

"You need money?"

"No. I got money for this. I'm thinking I want a bed, probably a full-size one if that makes sense to you. And I thought maybe a chair or a sofa or something. And perhaps a picture or something to go on the wall. I don't want to put up posters or whatever like I'm a teenager."

"Seamus, you're talking a lot of cash."

"Ryder, my boss, thinks I could buy a used bed with the frame and everything for a hundred bucks. I'm assuming the same is true for a chair or a sofa. No idea how much it would cost to buy a picture or something."

An exasperated breath filtered through the phone. "You don't want a used mattress if you can avoid it. Last time I did, it stunk and came with questionable stains. How much money do you got?"

"Ryder's holding eight hundred and nine dollars for me."

"Holy cow," Lena said. "Where'd you get that type of money?"

"Back in '98 I got a bonus on a case, but Ryder held it so I wouldn't blow it. I started with fifteen hundred and he's given me cash for legit stuff, like my security deposit and first month's rent. He'll give it to me for something like a bed."

"Okay. Buy the bed first, then see what's left. We could probably go to Goodwill or St. Vinnie's for a sofa or a chair or two. As to the wall decorations, I could give you a few of my drawings for the cost of the frames."

"You've been drawing?"

"Yeah. Drawing, painting, hiking, and running are my outlets. There are a few that might work. I frame them myself, so it's just the cost of the frame and any matting. Could be anywhere from ten to twenty-five bucks. So, who's this woman you're thinking about?"

"Her name is Erin," O'Neill said in a quiet voice. "She's a cop, believe it or not."

"You and a cop? That's crazy."

"She's also tall."

"Okay, so what? You said you're no longer on Lake Street, right?"

"I'm on Doty Street, more toward the Capitol. Would you have time to stop by? Then you could help me decide what to do next. Would today work? You said it's your free day?"

"Yeah, I'm off, but since I have a dental appointment, I brought Dawson to daycare," Lena said, referring to her four-year-old son. "I will be clear after that and I could leave him there for the afternoon. We could check out your apartment and then go shopping. I'll go online this morning and figure out what sales are going on."

"That would be great." O'Neill gave her his address. He said goodbye, but before hanging up the phone, she interrupted him.

"How are you going to pay for the bed?" she asked. "Don't bring cash."

"I have a checking account now and a checkbook, so I'll write a check."

"You have a checkbook? That's progress."

O'Neill spent an hour and a half in the office reviewing potential cases and conducting client background checks. He wanted to do anything to kill time until he could go to The Great Dane Brewpub for one of the two drinks he would have for the day. He arrived at the bar at twelve thirty, sat on a barstool in front of the taps, and milked a Scotch Ale. When his phone rang, a spike of energy flowed through him. Lena said she would be at his place in ten minutes, so he stared at his drink knowing it would be his last until six o'clock that night. He savored the final mouthful before heading home.

It was about a twelve-minute walk, so he hurried. As he got to his block, his sister's blue Chevy Corsica pulled to the curb. The engine sputtered, and he noticed that much of the paint had come off its trunk, revealing a dirty gray frame with a spattering of rust.

"Lena!" O'Neill yelled as his sister slammed the car door and started for the building entrance.

She stopped, turned toward him, and waved. Tiny, she told people she was five-foot two and weighed one hundred pounds, but both were a stretch. She wore jean shorts and a blue Dane County Parks shirt with white lettering. Tattoos lined one arm.

"Seamus," she said as he approached. "I still can't get over the hair. I forgot to ask you when I saw you last. Why did you cut it? I don't remember it ever being so short."

"Three or so weeks ago, my shower broke." He touched his head and rubbed the hair, which was now approaching half an inch long. "Shaved my head since I couldn't wash more than once a week. The landlord just fixed it. Got a shower today and the hair's growing back."

"I hardly recognize you without your mane." She leaned forward, and they hugged. As usual, she was chewing gum.

"Speaking of which," O'Neill said, patting the top of her head. "When you gonna give Ronnie Wood his hair back?" Her hair was naturally dark brown, like his, but she dyed it black for as long as he could remember. He walked toward the building and spoke about the neighborhood as he opened the outer door and scaled the stairs. After unlocking his door, he waved her into his apartment. "What do you think?"

She laughed and shook her head, then stepped into the kitchen area and opened the refrigerator. There was beer, Diet Mountain Dew, American cheese, bagels, tomato soup, and mustard. She turned toward him and shook her head. "The place looks abandoned." She rummaged through the cupboard. "Most people would say there's not enough storage space, but it's more than you need to keep potatoes, saltines, and two sets of dishes. And those glasses have got to go. They look like you pulled them out of a dumpster, and the wine glass has a fracture." She walked into the bathroom and opened the medicine cabinet before turning on the shower. Finally, she went into the living area.

"I like the wood flooring, but you gotta get the smell of beer out of here." She opened the window, chewing her gum louder for a few moments. "It's way better than your last place, but you need an actual bed and something else. When you stand in the doorway, it looks like an empty room in a frat house where the band sets up."

"Back before they turned this into an apartment, it was two separate kid bedrooms. Guess the rental company added the bathroom and moved the wall. At least I have a window."

"What I said earlier still makes sense. Get a bed with a frame, a chair or a loveseat, and an end table to set the TV on. And then we could put a few pieces of art on the wall. Curtains would help, but that's for another day. Also, a guy at my work said his mom will give us his old frame and headboard for free. That will save a few bucks and allow us to buy mattresses that will last. We'll also buy sheets and pillows and can get a few things at St. Vinnie's."

O'Neill nodded, and they headed toward the door. "If we buy it today, how will we get it here and when?"

"We can pick up the frame and headboard today. It's three long pieces of metal that fold up, and the headboard is wood. I think we can fit them in my trunk. If not, we'll have to figure something out."

"A bedframe without a mattress won't do much good, will it?"

"No. You'll have to wait till they deliver the mattresses. This week, American TV & Furniture has a sale that includes free delivery. But they probably won't deliver it until next week. They'll also take away your smelly old mattress for free. What's the rush?"

"I'm going running tomorrow with Erin," O'Neill said as he opened the door.

"Erin? She's your cop girlfriend?"

"Wouldn't call her my girlfriend. I hope she will be, but maybe I'm being unrealistic. I mean, she might think that dating me is slumming. But I don't have any chance with the place looking like this. I won't invite her over until it's set up a bit."

"Assume it will be no earlier than next week." She backed out of the room, seeming to avoid looking at the guitars and the banjo.

O'Neill pulled out his keys, locking the door as they exited. Once in Lena's car, they talked as she drove through downtown Madison. At the furniture store, she chose a full-sized mattress set, using up most of his money. They found a recliner, an end table, dishes, and silverware at St. Vincent de Paul, and spent more than they planned on sheets and pillowcases at K-Mart. They took the table with them but would have to come back another day to get the chair.

"We're off to pick up the bedframe," Lena said. "My friend Fred's mom lives on a farm near Verona, maybe twenty minutes from here. Fred told his mom we'd be there around three." She pointed at the McDonald's across the road. "We have enough time to grab a burger."

They pulled into the drive-through and O'Neill ordered a hamburger and a large Diet Coke. "I'm limiting myself to two beers today," he said to his sister. "Thought a soda would help keep my mind off anything stronger."

"You? Only two drinks? That's awesome." Lena paused as she handed the cash to an attendant. "I'm glad you're cutting down."

"Haven't done it yet, but that's the plan. It's something I need to do, I think, to keep moving forward. Besides, it's the only way I can run tomorrow. Going running is my date with Erin. She runs most days. On Wednesday mornings, I join her. Last week was the first time. I barely made a mile."

"How far does she run?"

"Five miles on the days she's off, less when she has to work. She runs circles around me, which is embarrassing since I ran in high school and she didn't. But she was in volleyball and basketball, so she's athletic."

"Another reason to stop drinking. I run at least twenty-five miles a week. No way I could do that if I still drank." She took a bag from the attendant and relayed the soda to her brother.

"Never said I would stop drinking," O'Neill said as the car lurched forward. "I'm simply limiting myself to two drinks on Tuesdays. Two for Tuesday; that's my new motto."

Lena didn't respond. Instead, she unwrapped her hamburger and started the drive to Verona.

Chapter 4

Lena woke O'Neill with a pat on the shoulder. His eyes opened, and he realized they were on a country road. Newly cut hay lay in the field outside the driver-side window, while crops covered the view from the passenger side. Lena ordered him to turn off the radio and said they had been driving southeast of Verona for twenty minutes, but she couldn't find Fred's mother's home or even the road on which the farm was located.

"What's that sign say?" she asked as they approached an intersection.

He leaned forward as if getting a foot closer to the sign would help. "Gifford Road."

She paused, then accelerated through the intersection. "Shit. If Echo's not the next one, I'm taking a right and heading back to Highway M. We'll have to go into town for directions."

They passed a farmhouse on their left. "Do you want me to call this woman?" O'Neill said. "Remember, I have a cell phone."

"Idiot me didn't bring her number. If we find a phonebook, I can look up Fred's number and we can call him. I'm used to having a map when I drive the truck at work. But I almost never drive outside Madison."

The sun was high in the sky, and the aroma of the newly cut hay was intense. The blacktop seemed to steam as the car came over a crest in the road and the back of a red tractor came into view. It was pulling farm equipment, lumbering slowly down the road. Lena took her foot off the pedal, but they quickly closed in on the vehicle.

"What the hell?" Lena muttered as she pumped the brakes. "This dickwad's over the center line. Idiot!" The tractor was four or five car lengths ahead of them when she jerked her vehicle across the double yellow line.

The road ahead was flat, and O'Neill didn't see any vehicles coming toward them. Then he fixed his gaze on the farm vehicle. The huge tires rolled slowly, and a yellow triangle was affixed to its backside. In the driver's compartment, he spotted the steering wheel and his eyes widened. The left side of Lena's car plopped off the pavement, continuing on the gravel berm and kicking up dirt and dust as the car passed the tractor. O'Neill stared at the vehicle's cab until they had driven past. Despite the dust, he was sure no one was inside the tractor.

"What an asshole!" she said once they were clear. She steered back into the right lane and sped up.

O'Neill undid his seat belt and twisted around so he could watch the tractor through the rear window. "No one is driving that thing." The farm vehicle disappeared as they descended over a crest.

"What do you mean?" She wiped a hand across her face.

"No one was in that tractor. Did you see anyone driving?"

There was a pause. "I was too busy trying to not crash into the damn thing to give it a good look. But, now that you say it, you might be right."

A red pickup came toward them, and Lena flashed her lights as the truck flew past. O'Neill twisted around again as the pickup disappeared behind the knoll. "Let's hope that guy..."

A horn blared and tires squealed, followed by a distant bang.

"You hear that?" he said.

Lena looked into the rearview mirror, lifted her foot off the gas, and flipped on a blinker. "Hold on!"

Adrenaline rushed through O'Neill's body as Lena slammed on the brakes and completed a Y turn. Dust fluttered in the air. Neither of them spoke as they roared toward the incline. O'Neill leaned forward and tilted his head, imagining the driverless tractor appearing in front of them. Instead, they saw the tractor, its tires still turning as it crossed between utility poles and continued into a cornfield. On the other side of the road, the pickup lay on its side. The truck's tires were spinning but, unlike the tractor, the vehicle was not moving.

Lena pulled to the road's shoulder, flipped on the car's flashers, and jumped out. She rushed toward the tractor, so O'Neill ran to the truck.

The vehicle's undercarriage was facing him, laying atop rows of foot-high corn. There was dust, but he didn't see or smell smoke or fire.

He placed both hands on the bottom of the pickup's driver-side door, which was facing skyward. The truck felt warm. He reached for the door handle, and the frame tilted slightly. Running to the front of the vehicle, he saw a gray-haired man behind the steering wheel. The passenger side was dug into the ground, and a seatbelt held the driver in his seat. The man's eyes were closed, his mouth was open, and blood drained from his nose. O'Neill banged on the windshield, but the man did not respond, so he looked about for something to break the window with. Then he remembered he had a phone. He flipped it open and dialed.

"Dane County 911," a female voice said. "Please give me your name, location, and the nature of your emergency."

"Seamus O'Neill. I'm on Dance Road in, I think, the Town of Verona, just west of Gifford Road. A tractor crashed into some guy's pickup, and the truck is on its side. An old guy is behind the wheel looking dead or knocked out. I can see blood."

"Is it Chance Road?"

"Yes. That's it."

"Is there smoke or fire?"

"Lots of dust and stuff, but no smoke." O'Neill coughed. "The truck's engine isn't running, but something's leaking underneath, though it smells like oil rather than gas. Should I try to pull the guy out?"

"Negative. Don't move the injured man. Emergency personnel will be there within minutes. They will extract him from the vehicle. Please stay on the line until assistance arrives. What about the other vehicle?"

"There's no one in it. Least I don't think there is." He walked around the truck and saw his sister across the road, climbing down from the tractor cab. "An ambulance is on the way!" He yelled to her.

"Is there someone else with you?" the dispatcher asked.

"My sister, Lena. She ran to the tractor while I went to the pickup."

Lena looked both ways before crossing the road. "No sign of the driver," she said as she ran to her brother. "I put it in neutral and turned it off."

"911 is on the phone. They said someone should be here soon."

"The tractor driver must have jumped out." Lena's gaze bounced across the farmland. "How about the pickup driver?"

O'Neill led his sister around the truck. "The 911 lady told me to not move him."

She went to the windshield and crouched down. "Can I talk to the dispatcher?"

He handed her the phone and walked back to the edge of the blacktop. There were cornfields on both sides of the road, and a barn and two silos were visible to the west. Telephone poles lined one side of the road. In the distance a line of trees separated one field from another. A cluster of trees was to the northeast, followed by what appeared to be a driveway.

He placed his sunglasses on the top of his head and looked through the fields, expecting to spot the farmer lying between rows of crops, but there was nothing. He heard a distant cry and, looking to the east, he saw a man running on the road. O'Neill waited as the man came closer.

"Dad!" the man yelled. He broke out of his run and rested hands on his knees. Placing a cap atop his abundant blonde hair, the man looked at O'Neill, then took off toward the tractor.

O'Neill crossed the road, following the man. "Were you driving that thing? We didn't see anyone inside."

The man hopped onto the tractor step and opened the door. He was burly and wore jeans, boots, and a plain white T-shirt. A mustache and a five-day beard made him appear mature, but there was something in his manner and the way he moved that led O'Neill to think that he was younger than he looked. The man jumped off the tractor. "My dad was driving this. Where is he?"

"No idea. We came up behind the thing. It was in the center of the road going super slow. I don't think anyone was driving it. We passed it and, a moment later, that red pickup blew past us. They must have crashed, or else the pickup went off the road trying to avoid hitting it."

"My dad was in the field in that tractor just a few minutes ago." He walked in a circle, gazing across the fields. "Where the hell did he go? Dad!"

"Could he have jumped out earlier? The tractor came up from the same direction you did." O'Neill pointed to the east. "Maybe he's behind those trees."

"There's a house there. A new house. I would have seen him."

There was a siren in the distance. "Do you know the guy in the pickup?"

The man froze for a moment, as if needing to change his focus from the tractor to the truck. Then he jogged across the road with O'Neill trailing.

"That should help," Lena said to the dispatcher. Then she looked up at the men. The blonde man approached the truck's windshield. "Who are you?" she asked.

"He came running up the road," O'Neill said.

"My name is Randy Cooper. I was raking hay with my dad on the other side of Gifford Road. A few minutes ago, I noticed he wasn't in the field, and I heard something and thought I saw smoke or dust." He cupped his hands against the window and peered inside the truck. "That is Ben Hefty. He doesn't look good."

Chapter 5

The siren grew louder, then flipped off. O'Neill returned to the road's shoulder as a Dane County Sheriff's cruiser parked across from Lena's car. The lights shone as a deputy got out of the vehicle and hurried to the pickup.

The deputy cupped his hands against the front window, peering in as Cooper had done. After a moment, he started toward the road. "Everyone, please move away from the vehicle." He walked backwards, and the others followed. "Wait here." He spoke into his car radio, then ran across the road toward the tractor.

Despite the deputy's instructions, O'Neill followed, explaining that they didn't find anyone in the tractor.

"He must have walked off," the deputy said as he directed O'Neill back to the road's edge. "Who saw what happened?"

O'Neill went into a brief explanation of what he had seen. The deputy told them to stay where they were as he returned to his vehicle and a pair of sirens grew louder. He reached into his Crown Victoria Interceptor and spoke into his radio. After another minute, a red Verona Fire Department truck pulled in. The firefighters, donned in light yellow jackets, evaluated the pickup as additional deputies arrived.

One deputy, a young woman with brown hair and reflective sunglasses, joined O'Neill, Lena, and Randy Cooper. She introduced herself as Deputy Anna Peterson. O'Neill assumed she was going to take their statements, but it became apparent that her role was to keep them away from the vehicles. She also had Lena move her car further from the accident and across the road, since that was the lane that the deputies had blocked off.

A pair of firefighters attached a strut to the pickup's subframe while the three witnesses spoke to Peterson. They anchored the vehicle to the firetruck, and soon a window broke.

"How long will it take to pull him out of there?" Lena asked Peterson.

"Fifteen minutes, though they won't go too far until the ambulance gets here." She paused and motioned down the road, past a host of road flares. "Speaking of which, here she comes."

Windows continued to break on the pickup as the ambulance parked. The deputy first on the scene spoke to the emergency crew. He then approached the witnesses, pausing as he wiped his forehead with a handkerchief. "I'm hoping to talk with you three." He looked at O'Neill and then at Randy Cooper. "I'm Deputy Franklin. You three aren't together, are you?"

"Nah," Cooper said. "I live up on M, just a mile from here. My dad and I were in the fields when I realized he was gone."

"What do you mean, 'he was gone'?"

"I was in the field back that way," he said, pointing down the road, "and Dad was in the other one. I was in our Case IH while Dad was in that one," he said with a nod, "the 1086 International Harvester. When he was in the field, he was within sight the whole time, but he suddenly wasn't there. That was odd, though I kept going. When I turned around again, I still didn't see him, so I went to the edge of the field. I heard a horn and what I thought was a collision. I still couldn't see him, so I jumped off the tractor and rushed to the road. There was a dust cloud, so I ran toward it. That's when I saw the 1086." He pointed at O'Neill. "And this man was on the side of the road. He brought me over to the pickup."

"When was this?"

"Maybe ten minutes ago. I was here four or five minutes before you arrived."

"So, this is your dad's tractor," the deputy said. "Where is he now?"

"That's what I want to know," Cooper said. "He must have jumped out. Maybe he hit his head. He's not lying somewhere on the road, is he?"

"No, he's not on the pavement, and we have deputies checking the nearby fields and houses. We'll find him." The deputy's gaze moved to the O'Neills. "What's your story? Were you two in the blue car?"

"Yeah," Lena said. "That's mine. I was driving."

"And what's your name and address?"

"Marlena O'Neill." She handed him her driver's license. "The address is current."

"Okay." He wrote her name and address on a small notepad. "Go on."

She motioned to her left. "We drove from that direction, looking for the Purdy farm on Echo Road and got kind of lost. We came up on the tractor. It was sort of in the middle of the road. I slowed down and barely got past without bumping into it. Then we got back into our lane and the truck was coming toward us. It was moving fast and going to where we knew the tractor was. Seamus said something about hoping the truck didn't crash into it and then we heard a horn and squealing tires. I flipped the car around and came back. That's when we saw all this."

"Have you had anything to drink today?"

"Me? Nope," Lena said. "I haven't had a drink in over three years. Test me if it makes you feel better."

"No, that's fine." He looked at O'Neill. "How about you? Name and address."

O'Neill dug out his brand new State of Wisconsin Identification Card. "The address is current."

"You two married?"

"Brother and sister," O'Neill said. "What Lena said is how I remember it. Except that no one was driving the tractor, even when we passed it."

"When you got to the crash?" Franklin said. The sound of drilling interrupted them, and he glanced back at the truck. "They're taking off the roof. Once they have that off, they'll use a flat board to minimize the movement of his spine while they extract him from the vehicle."

"There was no one driving when we passed it," O'Neill said. "I could see into the cab. No one was in it. I'm almost sure the tractor was empty."

Franklin looked at the farm vehicle and then at O'Neill. Finally, he turned toward Cooper. "I thought your father was driving it?"

"He was," Cooper said.

"Just telling you what I saw," O'Neill said.

Franklin looked at Lena. "Is that what you saw?"

"I was trying to pass it without getting pushed off the road, so I didn't look closely. But I think Seamus is right. I don't think anyone was in the cab. What I know is that, when we got to the accident, the tractor was still moving. I jumped in, put it into neutral, and turned it off."

The deputy's eyebrows scrunched together. "You know how to drive a tractor?"

"I work for the Dane County Parks Department and I drive mowers, forklifts, and other equipment. It took me a minute to figure out how to stop it, but once I got it into neutral, it stopped. After that, it was just a matter of finding the key and turning it off."

"Okay, okay." He turned toward Cooper and held the pen close to his notepad. "Why would your dad have gotten out of the tractor while it was moving?"

"I can't imagine why." Cooper took off his hat and ran a hand through his hair as he glanced up at the clear blue sky. "The tedder he was pulling was folded up, so he was going down the road. Don't know why he would be in that low of a gear."

"Have you or your father been drinking?"

"Not me. And my dad? No way." Cooper stuck his hat back on. "I was with him all day. We worked around the yard and cut hay in the morning and went inside for lunch. We got the equipment set up and did a few chores before going back into the field. He didn't have anything to drink besides water mixed with Red Bull."

"The energy drink?"

"Yeah. It's his caffeine fix since he doesn't drink coffee."

"It sounds like a lot doesn't make sense," Franklin said. "We need to find your father. I think it would be best if you went home while we work on that. Maybe he got hit on the head and he walked home and is waiting for you. Even if he's not there, you're better off there in case he shows up. Is anyone else at your house?"

"I don't think so, but my sister might be back from Madison. She's at some event. Regardless, I need to get back into the field yet today. My dad will give me hell if I don't finish." Cooper's lips quivered as he looked at the sky. "The forecast is showing rain tomorrow. We'll need to ted again and rake and bail."

"Ted?" Franklin said.

"Flipping the hay over after it's cut, which allows it to dry faster." Cooper's head was shaking. "Dad can't have just left. I didn't quite finish, so he probably didn't either. I got time in the fields yet."

"No rest for farmers," Franklin said as he looked up at the afternoon sun. "Deputy Peterson will take you home. She can wait at your house for as long as you need."

"How about us?" O'Neill said. "Can we head out? We still got to find the Purdy farm."

"I have a son to pick up at daycare," Lena said. "And Fred's mom is probably wondering where we are."

"Fred Purdy?" Cooper said. "I know him. I'll call them when I get to the house, and I'll tell Mrs. Purdy why you didn't make it to her place. It will give me something useful to do."

"We were picking up an old bedframe and a headboard. Tell her we could pick it up another day if that works. And tell her we apologize for the inconvenience. My name is Lena O'Neill. I work with Fred in the Parks Department."

The young farmer nodded. "Can I get your number?"

Since she didn't have a cell phone, he called O'Neill as they stood on the shoulder of the road, and O'Neill entered him into his contact list.

Lena exchanged a glance with her brother. "Let's wind this up. I need to get Dawson from daycare."

O'Neill nodded as he stared at the driverless tractor sitting aimlessly in the cornfield.

Chapter 6

After giving brief statements, the siblings hopped into Lena's vehicle and headed west. They took the first right and were soon on Highway M. Lena sped through Verona, aiming to avoid a late charge by picking her son up before five o'clock. O'Neill rested his head against the side window and was quickly asleep. She woke him in downtown Madison, telling him he would have to walk the rest of the way. He left her a twenty-dollar bill for gas, lunch, and her inconvenience.

Once home, he shut the window and looked anxiously at the clock. It was a little after five, so he had a long hour before he could have a drink. He picked up his guitar and killed time playing nearly every song from the Rolling Stones' *Beggars' Banquet* album. Most of the songs went well, and he played loudly, as if he had an audience.

Although he didn't have any clean towels, he got into the shower at five thirty, passing another fifteen minutes before drying off with a T-shirt. At five forty-five, he headed to the Main Depot. It was only a ten-minute walk, so he took a long route, arriving at six o'clock.

"Yo, O'Neill," the bartender said as he came inside.

O'Neill nodded and scanned the Tuesday evening crowd. Someone patted him on the shoulder as he sat on a barstool near a regular wearing a Citgo shirt and a Mautz painter's cap. His name was Ted, but O'Neill called him Blatz because he often wore a blue Blatz shirt.

"Bob and I were just talking about you." Blatz gestured at the television behind the bar. The sound was turned down in favor of a Tom Petty song. "The news says the coast guard is trying to find that Sheila E boat again that went missing on Lake Michigan. I said we should have you find it since you're our local detective."

"The boat is the *Linda E*," the bartender said. "Sheila E is that drummer who plays with Prince."

Blatz adjusted his hat. "Oh yeah, that's right. At least I got the E part right."

The Linda E was a boat that had been missing for several years. O'Neill remembered the incident partly because the three-man crew was from the Milwaukee area. The disappearance had gotten a significant amount of press.

The bartender stepped in front of O'Neill. "My thought is a boat or a barge ran into it and the crew that hit them either didn't realize it or they didn't want to get in trouble."

"Hard to find anything underwater, isn't it?" Blatz said, looking at O'Neill.

"Suppose so." O'Neill said. An empty stool sat between them. "Course it will help if they know exactly where to look. Let's hope they find it so the families can have some closure. Closure is good." He looked up as the television showed murky photos of an underwater wreck.

"Is that it?" Blatz asked.

"Course not. There are a ton of wrecks at the bottom of Lake Michigan. It won't be hard to find a sunken boat. The trick will be to locate the right one and identify it as the Linda E. There's always a chance they'll get out there, find a wreck, then a week later figure out it's some other fishing trawler." He looked up at the bartender. She was a woman in her late forties with blonde hair that he thought was dyed. He had seen her before, but couldn't recall her name. "Pour me a pint of the Blonde Doppelbock. Fill it to the top."

The bartender flipped the tap, and a mug caught the flow of straw-colored liquid. O'Neill stared, and thoughts of the sunken boat dissipated as foam formed atop his doppelbock. He leaned forward and inhaled as the beer glided in front of him.

"Excellent stuff," she said. "Smells like toasted bread."

O'Neill's sniffer was not good enough to detect toasted bread in a tap beer, but it smelled good. He wrapped his hand around the glass and thought of the tractor rumbling driverless through the sea of corn. After another gulp he pulled out his phone, thinking he should call Ryder.

"When did you get a phone?" Blatz asked.

"A few weeks ago. It's for work."

"Looks like mine." Blatz took out his own phone. "A Nokia, right?"

O'Neill nodded and clicked on Ryder's office phone. After five rings, the call went to voicemail and he hung up as he stared into his nearly empty glass. After two more gulps, his last drink of the day was gone. So, he left the bar and took a meandering route home.

He spent the next several hours on his mattress watching television. He was limited to the five local broadcast stations, so he watched thunderstorms on *Savage Planet* followed by a documentary about flightless birds. Yet his thoughts were dominated by his refrigerator that held a half dozen beers, the cupboard that held a half full bottle of Old Crow, and a driverless tractor in a field of corn. He didn't know how he would make it to midnight, but suddenly the flightless birds were gone and the clock said it was four in the morning. He realized he must have fallen asleep, so he congratulated himself, walked into the kitchen, and took two gulps of bourbon from the bottle. Closing his eyes, he savored the burning sensation then visited the bathroom and returned to bed.

He tried to fall back to sleep but couldn't. Perhaps he was too excited about his upcoming run with Meyer, or maybe he was simply relieved that his first two-for-Tuesday was history.

Two hours before he was scheduled to meet Meyer for her Wednesday morning run, O'Neill was ready. He spent the first hour watching an episode of *Perry Mason* and the second strumming his guitar. When it was finally time to leave, he took a sip of bourbon and walked to Law Park, arriving ten minutes early. As he sat on a patch of grass, he stretched and eventually spotted Meyer's tall figure in the distance.

The City of Madison Police detective was dressed in black shorts and a gray shirt with orange lettering. Her long black hair was pulled into a ponytail, and she waved as she waited for the light to change. He could see her eyes above the head of the man standing in front of her. Once the light turned, Meyer passed the man and O'Neill admired her legs, which went on forever. As she approached, he looked away and leaned forward, stretching his calves.

"Good morning, Seamus," Meyer said, walking up to him. She looked relaxed and playful. It was a look from her he wasn't used to seeing.

"Morning, Erin," he said as she lined up next to him and stretched. "Looks like you are in a good mood."

"I'm off work, and it is a beautiful day. It's a little blustery, but there's nothing like a sunny June day for a run."

Twisting back, his gaze was even with her waist. She reached forward, touching her fists against the ground and reminding him it wasn't only her legs that were long. She turned toward him, revealing the orange-lettered University of Illinois shirt. The shirt didn't surprise him, since he knew she had played college volleyball for The Fighting Illini.

"Going five miles again? Same route from here to the Sheraton Hotel and back?"

"Yeah. It's a tad over five."

The last time they ran, O'Neill put her pace at under seven minutes a mile. His plan was to keep up with her for a mile and a half. At that point, he would let her go and eventually turn around. He would walk for about seven minutes, which would put her near the turning point. From there he would jog slowly, figuring she would catch him within the last half mile. His secondary goal was to beat her across the imaginary finish line.

"Let me know when we hit a mile and a half," he said.

"You think you can make it that far? You didn't make a mile last week."

"That was last week," he said. "Course I can make a mile and a half."

Chapter 7

After a dozen steps, Meyer went into a run and O'Neill mirrored her pace, staying tight to her shoulder. The path through Law Park kept them thirty feet from Lake Monona on their left and twenty feet from John Nolen Drive's oncoming traffic. The left side of the trail was meant for pedestrians, while the right side was intended for bicyclists. A man in a baseball cap ran toward them, nodding at the pair as he passed.

"Working on anything interesting?" Meyer asked, her gaze fixed forward.

He swallowed hard. "Ryder's trying to decide on cases. He's feeling overwhelmed. I'm gonna help him evaluate which to take next, but I can't do any investigating until I get my license."

"When do you take the exam?"

"Took it yesterday. Think it went okay. Ryder should have the results in about a week."

"That's awesome. Once you're licensed, I'll be able to talk to you if we cross paths at work without fear of getting reamed out."

"I'll pump you for all sorts of information."

She glanced at him as if she wanted to make sure he was kidding.

"Something strange happened to me, though," he said. "Yesterday, I was outside of Verona, and there was an accident between a tractor and a pickup truck."

"Outside of Verona? With Ryder?"

O'Neill wanted to tell her all about the tractor with no driver, but he didn't want to have to explain that he was with his sister getting a free bedframe as part of a long-term plan to get Meyer into bed with him. "Yeah. Me and Ryder," he lied. "We're trying to figure out what cases to take."

They ran side-by-side for a few minutes as bicycles rode past. O'Neill briefly dropped behind her as they overtook a trio of middle-aged men in sweatpants and baseball hats. The route turned closer to the lake as they passed the Monona Terrace Convention Center and its parking lot. He sensed a pair of runners behind them, and Meyer picked up the pace.

"How about you?" he asked. "You working on anything interesting?"

The two men passed them, and Meyer didn't speak again until they were far ahead. "I finally tied up my part of the Newman case," she said, referring to the case on which O'Neill and she had met. It had involved a missing man whose murdered body he had helped her locate. "As you know, it won't go to trial, so I won't have to deal with that. There are a few things I'm assisting on and a series of robberies of area businesses that I'm leading on. But nothing you would think of as interesting."

The pair approached Monona Bay, which was where O'Neill dropped out the prior week. The bay was across the street on their right. Anglers lined both sides of the bridge, their rods dangling over the railing. O'Neill thought the bay was roughly a half mile long, so he set his goal to keep on Meyer's shoulder until they reached its other end. As they crossed the halfway point, she told him in an even voice that they were past the one and a quarter mile mark. Finally, they closed in on Olin Park, which sat at the end of the bay. He felt as if he was sprinting, trying to finish a race.

"Mile and a half," she said.

O'Neill stayed with her for another thirty feet until they were firmly in Olin Park. "Catch you on the rebound," he said, breaking stride.

Meyer nodded, and he watched her hips sway as her arms pumped, pushing her forward. His gaze slid down her long legs and, after a few moments, she was far ahead. He stopped, leaning palms on his thighs. After a break, he turned and started the return trip.

His gaze fell upon the lake as he walked along the trail, which bisected Monona Bay on his left and Lake Monona on his right. He didn't know how deep the water was, but he rarely saw swimmers. He wondered how many baseballs, golf balls, and beer cans sat in the lake, never to be seen again.

Halfway across the bay, O'Neill wiped sweat from his forehead and started to jog. Bicyclists continued to fly past, and he glanced back a few times, making sure Meyer wasn't already closing in on him. Once across the bay, a flock of ducks flew overhead, and he looked back, seeing Meyer at the edge of Olin Park. He sped up, hoping she wouldn't catch him until they were in front of the convention center. A minute later, as he came closer to the building, he heard footsteps. She soon passed him, and he spent the next quarter of a mile on her shoulder. It worked for a while, but as they entered Law Park, he settled behind her, staring at her long legs and swaying hips.

Meyer was twenty feet ahead of him when she slowed. After another thirty feet, she stopped, turned, and waited. Coughing and wheezing, he stumbled toward her. She was smiling, obviously enjoying the easy win. He dried his face with his shirt. As she stepped closer, she lifted her University of Illinois shirt and wiped a bead of sweat from the tip of her nose. He glimpsed her stomach, her belly button, and her sports bra. Suddenly he wasn't thinking about his breathing or how glad he was to be done running.

"Made it a mile and a half, like I said I would," O'Neill said between breaths. He moved closer and, simply wanting to touch her, brushed a hand against her shoulder.

"You gonna make it two miles next week?"

"Maybe in two weeks."

After recovering and stretching, Meyer recommended a walk to cool down. Though he would have preferred lying down, he agreed. They crossed the street, walking along the road toward the State Capitol. As they approached an intersection, Meyer suggested they stop at Badger Candy Kitchen to get water and a coffee. While she knew he didn't drink coffee, he obviously needed water.

When they arrived, Meyer suggested he wait outside. She came out after a few minutes, holding two small clear-plastic glasses filled with water and a Styrofoam cup. Getting to his feet, he took a glass, drinking it in two gulps and throwing the empty into a nearby trashcan.

"The other one is for you too," she said, handing him the water. "I inhaled three inside, so I'm good. You want to walk me home?"

"Course."

They discussed his private detective test as they walked toward Meyer's apartment. The topics soon lightened and by the time they crossed the street, they were discussing their favorite childhood cartoons. As they turned the corner, her building came into view, and his focus changed.

"Any chance I could check out your place? Curious about what the inside is like."

There was a pause before Meyer replied. "You can come in, but only for a minute." She pivoted toward him and switched the now empty coffee cup into her other hand. "Don't get any ideas."

He searched for a suitable reply, but none came. Instead, he gazed at the twelve white pillars that sat in front of the three-story apartment building. He knew Meyer's unit was on the first floor in the front.

Following her up the steps, he waited as she unlocked the outer door. She went inside, and two women passed, muttering greetings and looking curiously at him. Meyer stood at the door, struggling to put the key into the lock. He leaned against the wall and she smiled at him as she switched keys, finally pushing the door open.

O'Neill entered what he assumed was the living room. A hallway went far back along the inner wall. Staring into the darkness, he saw an oven, a kitchen sink, and a back door. The walls were plaster, and wood planks braced the ceiling, though he thought they were decorative. A sofa with two end tables sat facing a television. The door to the porch was to their right and further past was a closed door. He thought there was a lot of square footage for one person, though the layout was long and thin, not much wider than a shotgun house. It felt claustrophobic despite the southeasterly sunlight coming through the windows.

"What do you think?" Meyer said as she picked up her cell phone from a counter.

"Is that your bedroom?"

"Nope. There are two bedrooms and a small storage room, but I use this one as an office." She returned the phone to the counter before pushing the door open. O'Neill peered inside, seeing a computer on a desk. There was a bookcase with family pictures and a smattering of books and magazines. A television was in one corner with a jigsaw puzzled covered card table in front of it.

"I love puzzles," O'Neill said. "Haven't done one for fifteen years, but I always enjoyed them." He turned toward Meyer. "Where's the other bedroom?"

She pointed to another door. "It is smaller than this one and only has one window, but it is on the side of the building rather than the front, so it doesn't get as loud." She walked down the hallway and showed him her kitchen and bathroom.

"You got a tub. That's nice." He ran a hand along the basin, acting as if it was of considerable value. "I haven't had a bath since I was in high school. Every place I've stayed in just has a shower. When I was in a band, there were hotel rooms and places with tubs, but I never got around to taking a bath." O'Neill walked about, turning on faucets and looking behind the shower curtain.

"Shouldn't you be getting to work?" Smiling nervously, her gaze dropped to the floor. "Plus, I've got errands to run, the mirrors need a shot of Windex, and the toilet bowl needs cleaning."

He looked at her standing in black shorts and her University of Illinois T-shirt, but his thoughts came back to the brief view he had of her bare midriff. The last thing he wanted to do was to leave, but he nodded and slipped past her, walking toward the door.

"You're off on Sunday, right?" he said.

"That's the schedule. Doesn't mean it won't change."

"I will run with you again next Wednesday, if that's still okay, but we could do something on Sunday, too. Maybe we could go swimming at B.B. Clarke Beach. That's only a short walk from here."

She laughed. "I am not about to be anywhere in this city in a swimsuit. You know how it is with cops? If anyone spots me, I'll get comment after comment. I'd never live it down."

"We could leave town sometime. I remember going swimming at Devil's Lake. That was fun."

"Perhaps some other time."

"Or we could go out and get something to eat. Maybe we could see a band."

Meyer leaned against the wall next to the door. "Seamus," she said after a long pause, "I'm not going bar hopping with you. I'm not a big drinker like you."

"That's my reputation, but it's mostly left over from my days in rock & roll bands. I'm growing out of that, you know? We could do dinner."

She bit her lower lip. "Okay. But dinner only. And Saturday night would be better. I'm off at three, so I would prefer to go early. You okay with Italian?"

"Course." It would be their first date that didn't involve walking or running. "My band practices on Sunday, anyway. Does Porta Bella work?"

"That would work. How about I meet you at your place at four thirty? We could walk from there to the restaurant."

"That would be perfect." He looked at her for a moment, remembering the one time they had kissed. Her lips looked soft, and he wanted to kiss them long and hard, but decided not to risk it and settled on her cheek. Even on his tiptoes, the peck landed on her jawbone. He dropped to his heels. "Goodbye, Erin. I'm looking forward to Saturday." He hurried out the door before he could try to kiss her again.

Chapter 8

The basement washing machine demanded two quarters for a load, but O'Neill only had one, so he walked down the street to the Doty apartments. The building's laundry room had a change machine. After getting four quarters, he went home and started a load, which included nearly all his clothes and towels, regardless of color. Sitting on his mattress, he played the tin whistle, changing to guitar after flipping his clothes to the dryer. He showered quickly, drying off with a clean, warm towel.

He took a sip from his flask before sticking it inside his clean Levi's next to his Sweetone tin whistle. Grabbing sunglasses, he hurried down the stairs and was soon on the street. Clouds were thickening over Madison, interrupting the blue sky as he started the twenty-minute walk to the Ryder Detective Agency.

While walking along Regent Street, someone in a red Camaro honked at him, so he waved. Looking up at the sun, he estimated it was after eleven o'clock, and the clock behind the counter at Sal's Subs verified his guess.

After picking up a loaf of day-old bread, he walked up the Ryder Detective Agency steps and was surprised to find the office door locked and the window sign flipped to "Will Return." He pulled out his key, stepped in, and turned on the lights. After booting up his computer, he heard a noise in the back room. He got to his feet, took his tin whistle from his pocket, and held it tight in his right hand. He thought tin whistles were decent self-defense weapons.

As he approached the storeroom door, he realized the sound was snoring. He put the Sweetone back in his pocket, opened the door, and flipped on the light. "Hey, Boss."

Ryder's eyes opened, and he sat up on the storage room's black foam sofa. He wore dark shoes and his usual white shirt and tie. "Turn off the light."

The room went dark. "Thought I was the one who slept back here."

"I was working late on the Stein report," Ryder said, letting out a yawn. "Plus, I had a nine o'clock call and I wanted to refer to my files, so I had to come in. Afterward, I laid down for a quick nap." He looked at his watch, spun his hefty body to the side, and stood. "Thanks for waking me."

O'Neill left the backroom and returned to his desk. He was reading headlines from the *Wisconsin State Journal* when Ryder came out. Rather than walking to his own desk, the big detective sat in the lone chair in front of O'Neill.

"How did your Two for Tuesday go?" Ryder asked after a brief silence. "Did you make it? And did you make your run?"

"Yeah, everything went fine. I made a mile and a half and covered about three miles, including the parts I walked."

"Meyer does five miles, right?"

"Yeah. I'll try to go a little further next week."

"Did you hold to two drinks yesterday?"

"Yeah, believe it or not."

"Good for you. But remember, you can't use that as an excuse to go on a bender today, okay?"

"Right, Dad." O'Neill flipped through the paper when an article caught his attention. "Hey, they got a story on the accident."

"What accident?" Ryder asked.

"My sister and I were on a country road near Verona and we came upon a crash between a pickup and a farm tractor. It was the weirdest thing. No one was driving the tractor."

"What were you doing in Verona?"

"Picking up a bedframe."

"Oh, yeah. Seamus is getting an actual bed. It's like he's a real boy."

O'Neill gave him the finger then turned his attention to the newspaper article. The story included a photo of the farm vehicle plowed into the cornfield.

Man injured, another missing following head-on truck-tractor crash

A 67-year-old Dane County man was in serious condition on Tuesday after the truck he was driving crashed into a tractor on Chance Road in the Town of Verona, the Dane County Sheriff's Office said.

Ben Hefty, the truck driver, indicated that he came over a hill and the tractor was coming toward him driving in the middle of the road. The tractor was reportedly in motion, but Hefty and another witness claimed it did not have a driver. The tractor's owner, Vernon Cooper, was operating the tractor earlier in the afternoon, but was not found at the accident location.

Officials suspect that Cooper, 44, lost control of the tractor and fell or jumped off prior to the accident and may have been injured. A Dane County Sheriff's official indicated they were unable to locate Mr. Cooper despite a thorough search of the area and of Mr. Cooper's farm. They are requesting anyone who knows of Mr. Cooper's whereabouts to contact their office. Cooper is described as 6 feet 2 inches tall, 210 pounds, with brownish-blonde hair, a mustache, and blue eyes. He was last seen wearing a red hat, gray shirt, jeans, and beige boots.

"Look at this," O'Neill said, as he tossed the newspaper across his desk. "The guy who was in the truck says no one was driving the tractor. That's what I saw too."

The paper crinkled as Ryder's paw snatched it. He held the local section in an outstretched arm, muttering a few sounds.

"What do you think?"

"The farmer could have been drinking or hungover and had to puke or something and didn't turn the tractor off by accident," Ryder said. "Or maybe he got sick of doing the same thing day after day and made a break for it. Maybe they'll find him living in a motel in Las Vegas or something."

"How did he just disappear? Remember, I was there. If he was meandering around drunk, why didn't I see him and why didn't the sheriff find him?"

"How should I know? Were there woods, houses, or barns nearby? Were there places along the road where he could hide?"

"Nothing obvious, but suppose he could have hidden if he wanted to. Still seems strange."

"Perhaps he got picked up as a hitchhiker. I'll only care if someone pays me to care. The sheriff's office will probably resolve this in the next twenty-four hours." Ryder yawned as he got to his feet. "Let's talk about what you're working on today. We got half a dozen background checks needing processing and a few more that we've got all the data on, but they need to be pulled together for the report. Also, the testimonials page on our site isn't working. Get that fixed. Finally, there are four potential clients that I want you to do background checks on. Fix the website first. Oh, and I got a call from some Microsoft rep about something with our licenses. I left the contact information in your inbox." Ryder walked toward his desk. "Call him when you have a chance."

O'Neill opened Internet Explorer and navigated to the Ryder Detective Agency's webpage. "Don't know what that error message on our testimonial page is about."

"I don't care what it's about, only that it's fixed."

"Yes, Master."

"Then push on the background checks and, if you have time, we'll go through our potential cases. In the meantime, I'm going to revise the Schmidt report. I sent them a draft, but they're supposed to have comments to me by noon, so I'll go through them and finalize. I'd like you to proof it before I pull the trigger. We'll see whether that will work."

The website problem only took a few minutes to solve, though O'Neill was annoyed since it related to a mistake he had made when adding a testimonial a week earlier. That meant the page had been down for a full week and he had not realized it.

He then started credit checks and driver record requests for nine background checks and queried the State of Wisconsin Circuit Court System. This was only a part of the process, but it was the most routine. O'Neill also verified employment and other contacts, but before he finished, his cell phone rang.

"Seamus, it's Lena."

"Hey, what's up?"

"I got a call from Detective Martin Becker with the Dane County Sheriff's Office. He wants to meet with both of us about the accident we witnessed."

"Sure. He can drop in at Ryder's place if he wants or we could drop in on him at the City-County Building. Ryder would probably like to meet a Dane County detective. He says getting to know detectives is good for business. Usually, he's talking about Madison PD, but I suppose it's true for county cops too."

"What detective are you talking about?" Ryder launched to his feet and was quickly in front of O'Neill's desk.

"Detective Martin Becker," O'Neill said, holding a hand in front of his phone. "Dane County Sheriff's Office?"

"Name rings a bell, but I don't think I ever met him."

"I didn't want to go to the cop shop," Lena said, "and figured you wouldn't want to go there either. We agreed to meet in Verona. My supervisor said I can go right now during work. I even get to be on the clock."

"Getting off with pay? Nice boss."

"We're part of Dane County just like the sheriff's office, so my supervisor is okay with it. Becker wants to talk to both of us, though, so I told him I would check to see if it would work for you, too. We're meeting at Fireman's Park. I think he's assuming I work in the Verona area. I'm supposed to be there at two, so I'm leaving now. Do you want me to pick you up or not?"

"Let me check with my overseer." O'Neill held the phone against his chest. "Can I go to Verona to meet with Detective Becker about the accident we saw? Lena's driving."

"Yes, you can go. But you're not on the clock."

"Lena's boss is paying her for the meeting."

"The government can do that sort of thing, but I'm running a business. You go on your own time."

"Okay, I will go on my own, oh mighty one."

Chapter 9

O'Neill estimated it would take his sister about fifteen minutes to drive from her job at Babcock County Park to his office on Regent Street. He slipped his flask and tin whistle inside the desk, and told Ryder he would be back in ten minutes. After a short walk, he saw the tall spinning top with "Regent Liquor" written on it.

He patted the ice machine outside the liquor store and passed two empty kegs. Inside, he found the vodka section and chose a 375 milliliter plastic bottle of Fleischmann's Royal. At the cooler, he grabbed a Diet Mountain Dew and rushed to the checkout, where a bearded man wearing a purple dastar waited.

After paying, O'Neill took a gulp of vodka then struggled to stuff the bottle into his pants pocket. He jogged to the office to be at his desk when Lena arrived. It shouldn't have mattered, but he wanted her to see him working a genuine job.

"Where'd you go?" Ryder asked.

O'Neill strolled over to his desk, put the soda down, and pulled out the liquor. "Bought a few things for my trip."

"Don't take vodka to a meeting with a sheriff detective, you idiot."

"Don't worry. People can't smell vodka on your breath."

"I know that. The point is, don't get drunk."

"Course I won't get drunk." O'Neill took a nip and stuffed the bottle back into his pocket. "I only had two drinks all day yesterday and only a few sips of bourbon today. Just don't want to be stuck for who knows how long without options."

Ryder shook his head. "If you need a drink, have one after you meet with this Becker."

"Meeting with the cops isn't the issue, Lena's the issue. Can't drink around her because she used to drink too much, but she doesn't drink anymore, you know?"

"No. I didn't even know she existed before yesterday, so I sure didn't know she was a boozer. Though I should have guessed, since she's related to you."

There was a knock on the door, and both men jumped to their feet and looked at each other. O'Neill was the first to move toward the door.

"Have her come in so I can meet her," Ryder said as he straightened his tie.

O'Neill opened the door, and Lena stepped in, giving him a brief hug. She wore a Dane County Parks T-shirt, boots, and green pants that looked like they were army surplus. Ryder's gaze seemed to focus on her tattooed arm.

"So, this is your office?" she said as she pulled away from her brother. She maneuvered down the entryway step, chewing gum as she walked.

"Yeah. This is my boss, John Ryder." O'Neill waved an arm as if opening a path between the two. "He owns this place."

Ryder slipped around his desk and took two steps toward the O'Neills. "Not really. I own the detective agency, but I lease the building." He nodded as he shook her hand. "Good to meet you."

"Likewise." She turned toward her brother and blew a bubble that popped. "We should go. We're supposed to be there at two and I'm parked a few blocks back. Time's tight."

Lena and Ryder exchanged pleasantries while O'Neill pulled out receipts from their shopping trip. He left them with Ryder who said he'd leave a check on O'Neill's desk. After grabbing the Diet Mountain Dew, he stuck the whistle into his pocket. Shuffling his sister onto the staircase, he followed her down the stairs.

"You're right," Lena said as they got to the bottom of the steps. "He looks like an ex-cop."

"A bald, fat ex-cop."

She nodded, and they walked in silence for two blocks before she pointed at an off-white Ford F-150 with a Dane County Parks emblem on its side.

"You get a company vehicle? Cool."

"It's even got a map." She blew a huge bubble as she unlocked the truck with her fob.

O'Neill sat inside and, as he closed the door, the scent of decaying plants overshadowed the smell of bubblegum. "What do you think this is going to be about, anyway? Does this detective just have more questions or did he do background checks on us and he thinks we're somehow involved?"

Lena started the pickup and pulled into traffic. "Involved in what?"

"I don't know. This farmer guy's disappearance."

"Why would he think that?" she said. "Nothing I did was violent. I wouldn't make someone disappear. Not even when I was a junkie. Is there something you've been busted for that would make them worry about you?"

"Nah. But you know how cops are. If you get busted for anything, they assume you'll do anything." He put on his sunglasses, closed his eyes, and rested his head against the window.

"Just tell the truth, Seamus, and everything will be fine. But don't do that."

"Don't do what?"

"Don't sleep with your head touching the window. This is a Dane County Parks vehicle. The public will think you're a parks employee. They'll see you sleeping in the truck and call in and complain."

"Screw the public."

Lena hit his shoulder. "I'm the one who'll be in trouble."

"Geez." He straightened up. "Can I adjust this seat somehow so it will lean back? You know me. A moving vehicle makes me sleepy."

She explained how the seat adjusted and O'Neill played with the levers before finally leaning back without touching the window. All was silent except for Lena's chewing and the rumble of the truck's engine.

O'Neill's eyes popped open as the pickup came to a stop and he jolted forward. He adjusted his sunglasses, which had slid to the bottom of his nose.

"That's got to be Becker." Lena nodded toward a Ford Crown Victoria parked in a row in front of them. "Let's go. But Seamus..."

"Yeah?" After yawning, he wiped drool from his chin.

"You can bring the Diet Dew, but leave the booze in the truck."

She got out, slamming the door. O'Neill pulled out the vodka, took a gulp, and screwed the lid on. The driver of the Crown Victoria exited his vehicle and walked toward Lena. O'Neill left the bottle upright in the passenger seat.

A shelter was at the edge of the parking lot and picnic tables sat under and near the building. Dandelions and grass surrounded the structure. Behind it, trees lined a bike trail that the city had converted from a railroad line. A pair of thick, low-lying clouds passed overhead, creating a shadow that moved across the pavement. O'Neill followed as Lena and Becker walked to a nearby table.

The sheriff detective was in his mid-fifties with a balding head, a dark mustache, and a face that looked as if it had spent too much time in the sun. He opened a black briefcase and pulled out a yellow folder, which he laid on the table.

"I appreciate both of you meeting with me." Becker sat on the table's bench. "Have you recovered from the accident?"

O'Neill sat beside Lena and opposite the detective, staying away from the bird droppings that spattered the bench. "We weren't in the accident," he said. "Lena avoided the tractor when we passed it. We turned back because we thought the next guy hit the tractor and we wanted to help. Just being good Samaritans and all that."

"Yes, I understand," Becker said. "I just meant that being at an accident scene is exhausting. Especially for the public." Becker's eyes locked onto Lena. "First off, let me be straight with you two. I'm sure you have nothing to do with Vernon Cooper's disappearance. However, you have interesting backgrounds. While it's clear that you've both turned your lives around, I have to ask a few questions."

The O'Neill's exchanged glances.

"This *accident* you witnessed is now a missing person's case. You both have records as juveniles and adults, including drug charges. Meanwhile, you two were at what we might call the scene of the disappearance, so I think it's prudent to document what you were doing there."

"Sounds like we're suspects," Lena said.

"No," Becker said. "Persons of interest."

"What's that mean?" she asked.

O'Neill rolled his eyes. "It means we're suspects."

Chapter 10

Detective Becker paused as a pair of minivans pulled into the lot, parking side by side. The rear doors popped open and a dozen high school-aged boys emerged carrying stacks of orange cones and two footballs.

"We're suspects?" Lena stopped chewing her gum, and her eyes widened into circles. "We were meeting the mother of a coworker of mine to pick up a bedframe for Seamus. My friend's name is Fred Purdy. I don't know his mother's name, but you can talk to them. We weren't doing anything illegal."

"The farmer's kid at the accident knows the Purdys," O'Neill said in a rising voice. "The guy was going to call her so she knew we weren't going to make it to her place. We don't know shit about what happened to the farmer who disappeared."

Becker lifted his hands off the table. "Calm down; I believe you."

"We weren't buying or selling drugs or anything," Lena said. "We were picking up a fucking bedframe."

"That's what I needed to hear. You were on personal business and have no involvement in illegal activities and were not involved in something related to Mr. Cooper's disappearance."

"Of course not," Lena said.

There was a pause, then Becker's squinting eyes shifted to O'Neill. "You work for a private detective agency. Did your activities relate to *an investigation* of yours?"

"Our trip didn't relate to an investigation or a case and we weren't doing anything wrong," O'Neill said. "Like Lena mentioned, we were picking up a bed."

"A *bedframe*," she said.

"Okay. You needed a bedframe. That's a long drive though from downtown Madison to rural Verona. That's what, fifteen miles?"

"Yeah. I need a bed cause there's this woman who..." O'Neill stopped, glancing at Lena. "Why am I telling this story again? Yeah. I need a bedframe because I don't have one and this one was free. You can come over and take a picture of my mattress on the floor if that makes you happy."

"No, no," Becker said, waving his hands in the air. "I believe you and didn't mean to make you defensive. I'm just documenting that Vernon Cooper's disappearance didn't relate to anything involving either of you, including Mr. O'Neill's job working for a private detective."

"We were there because I got lost," Lena said. "It's that simple."

"Let's get to it then, okay? I want you to take me through what you saw. Once again, when our deputies were at the scene, they viewed this as a vehicular accident, so they took a standard statement. Now it is a disappearance, so the level of detail we are interested in has increased, so please be as specific as you can. Miss O'Neill, perhaps you can start?"

"I was driving, of course. We got lost looking for Mrs. Purdy's farm." A bubble rose and popped. "I remember we were on this road..."

"Chance Road," O'Neill said.

Lena detailed their sighting of Vernon Cooper's tractor and their hearing a crash. O'Neill added several comments and facts while Becker wrote in his notepad.

"What did you initially see when you came to the accident?"

She popped a bubble before answering. "The tractor had plowed into the cornfield on our right, but it was still moving. The truck was off the road to our left, but my first thought was to stop the tractor, since Seamus doesn't know how to drive a car let alone an old International Harvester. Besides, it looked like no one was inside the thing. After stopping the car, I ran after the tractor." She closed her eyes. "It was barely moving, so it wasn't hard to catch. I wanted to grab the sidebar and get on the step, but I wasn't sure if I could open the door while standing on the step, so I grasped the handle and let the door swing open. I snagged the sidebar and got onto the step. I tried to slide into the seat in one motion, but the gearbox stopped me, so I grabbed the top of the steering wheel and lifted myself over the gears."

Becker's brow shot skyward. "Getting into a running tractor sounds dangerous."

"The corn was only a foot high and the ground was not muddy, so it wasn't hard to run in the field. But those huge tires worried me. I didn't want to slip and get run over."

"You said you opened the door. It was closed when you got to the tractor?"

She nodded.

"What did you do inside the tractor cab? And what exactly did you touch?"

"After I got in, I didn't close the door. I remember that because it never latched and continued to flop around." Lena stopped chewing and stared forward. "I felt for the key but didn't find it, so I looked for the clutch, trying to figure out the gears. While I've never driven a tractor before, I've driven heavy equipment. I knew enough to hit the clutch and drop it into neutral. That stopped the wheels. Then I found the throttle. It was low, but I slid it to off and finally found the ignition. I touched those controls, but that's all, though my hands may have touched other gearshifts as I was trying to figure out what was what." Her chewing resumed.

"You did good for someone who has never driven a tractor. What else was in the cab?"

"Nothing I can recall. Wait. There was, I think, a cupholder with a mug or a thermos or something in it on the right side of the cab. Otherwise, it was just an old stinky tractor. I don't remember anything else other than red levers, and the seat was black and ripped in several places with duct tape covering the tears."

"Did you touch the thermos?"

"No. Don't think so. If I did, maybe a hand brushed against it, but I don't remember touching it. Don't see why I would have."

"What color was it?"

"The thermos? It was..." She closed her eyes and tilted her head back. "Silver or metallic, I think."

Becker paused and scribbled on his notepad. "Did you smell anything in the tractor? Booze maybe?"

"No. I didn't smell booze. Don't think I smelled anything other than the field and the stinky inside of an old tractor."

Becker nodded. "What did you do once you stopped it?"

"I took a moment to catch my breath. Then I jumped down and ran toward the road while looking for the driver. I didn't see anyone, so I rushed to Seamus and the truck. He gave me the phone and I talked with the 911 operator. Pretty soon after that, the Cooper guy arrived. Then I heard sirens, and a cop showed up."

"How about you, Mr. O'Neill? You already told me about the tractor without a driver. What did you see when your sister pulled onto the side of the road?"

O'Neill's phone rang, so he plucked it out, silenced the call, and stuck it back into his pocket. He explained how he rushed to the truck after the accident and dialed 911. The part Becker seemed interested in, however, was their interaction with Randy Cooper, the son of the farmer who disappeared.

"Did Randy look tired?"

"I remember him leaning down, dropping, and getting a few breaths in. It was as if he had been running for a while. He's young, but he's a big guy who doesn't look like the jogging type."

"Did Randy Cooper get into the tractor?"

"The door was open." O'Neill looked at the sky as he remembered. "The guy got on the lower step and looked inside. He didn't sit inside."

"Could he have reached into the cab without you noticing?"

"Don't think so. He just got on the step and, once he saw no one was inside, he jumped down."

Becker made a few more notes and after some small talk, he thanked them for their time.

"Have you found any other witnesses?" O'Neill asked. "Neighbors or other people driving through the area?"

"No, though it's still early. The closest thing is a local who drove down Chance Road about twenty minutes before you came along. He didn't see anything unusual, just the two Cooper tractors operating in separate fields."

"Too bad. Do you suspect foul play?"

Becker chuckled and shook his head. "It's a continuing investigation, but there's no evidence of anything nefarious."

"No one with a grudge against Vernon Cooper or his family?"

"There are two siblings who have issues with Vernon, but they have alibis. They couldn't have been involved in the disappearance. That much is a fact."

"In my experience, alibis can be less solid than they initially appear."

The Dane County Sheriff's detective leaned forward, and the lines on his forehead whitened. "Mr. O'Neill, I've been validating alibis since before your sister first ran away from home. I appreciate that you've got some limited experience, but I didn't fall out of a tree yesterday. Besides, the Coopers have a history of disappearing. That's probably all that happened."

"What do you mean?"

Becker chuckled and shook his head. "One Cooper disappeared while plowing the same field back a hundred years ago. I remember hearing the story when I first came to Dane County. It was like he was gone in a puff of smoke. And Vernon's grandpa disappeared multiple times. One time, they came across him in Miller's Supermarket wearing only his long underwear. The last time, they found him dead in a ditch along Highway M. The old guy had apparently run away and had a heart attack."

"Are you suggesting the Coopers are unstable?" Lena asked.

Becker lifted a leg over the bench and got to his feet. "Just pointing out a pattern."

They shook hands as the teenagers started their touch football game and a sedan pulled into the parking lot. Becker lumbered toward his car, so the O'Neills headed for Lena's truck. She unlocked the vehicle and O'Neill opened the door, grabbing the vodka from the seat. As he got into the pickup, he took a quick nip and shoved the bottle into his pocket.

"Suppose we were a little defensive," O'Neill said as the doors shut.

"Definitely," she replied. "He seems to think Randy Cooper was driving the tractor, or he thinks Vernon had a nervous breakdown and ran away."

"He certainly sees those as possibilities," O'Neill said as he pulled out his phone. "But if Vernon made a run for it, why didn't we see him? Becker pushed us on what Randy did, so my guess is he's thinking Randy may have had a role in his father's disappearance." He clicked on his voicemail and listened to the message.

"Speak of the devil," he said. "That was Randy Cooper."

Lena stopped chewing. "He called you?"

"Apparently he picked up your friend's mom's bedframe. He said we can stop by his place to claim it."

She looked at her watch. "That was nice of him, but I got to head back to work."

"Oh, come on. You're on the clock and this will save us a trip. It's not too far out of the way and his farm is on Highway M, so you can't get lost. Besides, your boss won't know how long the detective meeting would take."

"Okay. But make it fast."

He smiled. "Let's go meet with Detective Becker's number one suspect."

Chapter 11

O'Neill called Randy Cooper, and they agreed to meet at the Cooper farm. He said it was on the right after Gifford Road and there was a blue Harvester. Though he didn't know what a Harvester was, Lena pointed the farm out as soon as it came into view. She turned into the driveway and they spotted the farmer sitting on the foot runner of a white GMC Sierra truck.

"Guess that's the Harvester," O'Neill said, pointing to a large blue silo with "Harvester" painted in white letters.

A black dog barked as they pulled between a detached garage and a mustard yellow two-story farmhouse. The house looked to be an early 1900s construction, but appeared well maintained. Lena parked the pickup near Cooper's vehicle and hopped out. The dog ran in circles in front of her.

"What's his name?" she said as the animal barked.

"Bernie," Cooper said.

Lena said the dog's name and kneeled on the concrete in front of the garage. Bernie licked her face, and she rubbed both hands down his back. O'Neill got out of the truck and walked toward Cooper. The dog ran to the two men before returning to Lena.

"What a baby. He's an old dog, but you wouldn't think so when someone he likes shows up. I'm sure you remember me from yesterday. I'm Randy Cooper."

The men shook hands. Cooper's grip made O'Neill forget that the farmer's son looked like he could still be a teenager. He was at least six-two and O'Neill thought the farmer might weigh more than he and his sister combined. He had shaved since the previous day, but the blonde mustache remained, as did the Case logoed trucker cap.

"This is my sister, Lena. I'm not sure whether you two met yesterday."

"Briefly," she said as she played with Bernie. "Good to see you again, and thanks for picking up the bedframe. I'm sorry about this business with your father."

"Yes. Thanks." The farmer eyed the Dane County Parks vehicle. "You work for the parks?"

"Yeah. Detective Becker from the sheriff's office asked us to stop over for another interview. My boss let me skip over from work, since it's our department's policy to cooperate with other county agencies. He wanted to talk with Seamus as well, so I brought him along since he doesn't drive."

Cooper turned toward the sun and his left eye closed. "You don't drive? That's strange."

"That's Seamus," Lena said.

"Did Detective Becker give you an idea if he's making progress?" Cooper asked. "I talked to him early this morning. He was getting oriented to things."

"He wanted more detail than he got from our earlier statements, but he didn't really take a new statement," O'Neill said. "Didn't give us much sense of how the investigation is going."

Cooper shook his head. "He took another one from me. It took a good two hours at their office in downtown Madison and I had to sign it at the end. My uncle came over and raked the hay this morning. Becker was going to meet with him too." He motioned toward the field that adjoined the barnyard. "I'm going to do this field after we're done."

"Do you have any idea what happened to your dad?" O'Neill said.

"No. I can't imagine. At one point, I thought maybe he got hit by a car while riding, got a concussion or something and fell out. That might explain why he would leave the 1086 in gear. But the only sign of an impact on the tractor or the tedder is from Mr. Hefty's truck. The only other thing I can think of is that he was talking to someone and they reached up and pulled him out of the tractor."

"Is there someone who would do that? An enemy?"

Cooper frowned as if he had no interest in discussing his family's enemies.

"Sorry." O'Neill glanced back at Lena, who was throwing a stick for Bernie to chase. "I don't mean to get into your business, but I work for a private detective and we regularly investigate disappearances." He pulled out a business card and handed it to the farmer. "You don't need to talk about it if you don't want to. Suppose my job and my experience make me curious."

"You're a private detective?" A smile appeared on Cooper's face. "You don't look like any private detective I've ever seen."

O'Neill touched his earring. "Yeah, I hear that a lot. Technically, I'm not a detective; I just work for one."

"But Seamus is the brains of the operation," Lena said as she walked toward the men.

"Really?" Cooper didn't look convinced, but as he stared at O'Neill, his shoulders dropped as if admitting defeat. "People assume Dad had a mental breakdown and ran away. I'm sure that's what people are saying, and that's obviously what the sheriff's office thinks. They'll say it runs in the family. It's just another Cooper gone."

"There have been other disappearances?" O'Neill knew the answer, but wanted the farmer to tell the story.

"You really want to hear this?" Cooper said.

"If you're willing to share it."

"Okay. Well, my great-great-grandpa and his brother settled on this land back around 1900. This was his place," he said, motioning toward the house, "and his brother Stephen's place was on Chance Road. Family lore is that Stephen was always a bit of a moody sort and, anyway, he disappeared one day. He sent his daughter to retrieve a bucket of water, but when she returned, all she found was the horse and plow in the middle of the field. My great-great-grandpa searched for him, but they never found him. It was always a bit of a mystery, Stephen's disappearance from Cooper's Chance."

"What's Cooper's Chance?"

Cooper chuckled. "Stephen named his farm. He called it Cooper's Chance."

"Why do people connect a story from a hundred years ago with your dad?" O'Neill asked.

"Maybe they aren't. Maybe it's me being paranoid, but people are suspicious and like to talk. There are always stories, and my grandpa had issues as well. He had a reputation for drinking too much and being eccentric, especially as he got old. The last time he wondered off, they found him up on Highway M, dead in a ditch from a heart attack. People around here assume that all of us Coopers are off-kilter. And Dad was under a lot of stress. He has always been a worrywart and things have only gotten worse in the last few years. He was anxious about the farm, and then there's the anniversary."

"Anniversary?"

"It's a long story," Cooper said. "But someone my dad was close to died five years ago today. People probably think that played into his mindset. I bet they assume the anniversary combined with the financial stress led to a nervous breakdown."

"If he had a breakdown, wouldn't you have seen him walking away from the tractor?"

"Yes. I should have."

"Can you tell me what happened? Or do you think he simply walked away?"

Cooper lifted his hat, raked fingers through his hair, then returned the cap to his head. "I don't think he ran away, but I can't ignore the possibility." He looked downward, then straightened up and pointed away from the highway and toward Chance Road. "My father and I were tedding two tracts. The one I was on is twenty acres, and the one my dad was on is across the road. It is twenty acres as well, but some areas in that field aren't tillable. It's the field where Stephen Cooper's homestead was located. The same field where Stephen disappeared a hundred years ago."

"Are the fields next to each other?"

"There's a twenty-acre tract of soybeans between the two hayfields. Soybeans are what we plant on most of our land. We have two hundred and forty acres."

"Is tedding when you flip the hay over after it's been cut?" Lena said.

"Yeah, it helps the hay to dry." Cooper moved to the side so the sun wasn't in his eyes. "It's something we've been doing the last few years after my dad got a tedder for cheap at an auction. He found it to be useful. Sometimes we call it raking, but tedding is the correct term."

"Would you mind showing us the field?" O'Neill said. "There was corn where the crash happened, but that was further away, past Gifford Road."

"Yeah, the crash happened near old man Purcell's place. The corn is his." Cooper glanced at his watch. "You really want to see it?"

"If you don't mind."

"Okay, but I don't have money to pay a private detective. If you're curious, I'll show you. If you're hoping to get a job out of this, you're out of luck. Besides, the sheriff's office thinks they'll resolve things in a day or two. And if Dad did have a breakdown, he might come out of it and call."

"I'm not looking for work. Just got a curious nature. Promise."

Cooper smiled, and it made him look like a teenager. "Being that you're a detective, it won't hurt to get your perspective, especially if you don't assume we're all crazy. Let's put this bedframe and the headboard in the back of your truck, then I'll take you to the field."

Chapter 12

O'Neill grabbed a metal beam with wheels connected to it while Cooper lifted the wood headboard and set it in Lena's truck bed. She took another beam, with Bernie underfoot. Once they had the frame arranged, Cooper and Lena got into his vehicle. O'Neill climbed into the pickup's cargo bed. Though he had never been in the back of a truck, he thought it might give him a good look at the topography of the surrounding farmland.

Bernie ran down the driveway as the pickup pulled onto the highway. O'Neill slid sideways, grabbed the edge of the truck bed, and waved to the dog. Moments later, they turned at Gifford Road. The vehicle moved slowly, stopping after only a few hundred feet. Cooper leaned out the window, pointing at the farmland. "I was in this field on this side of that tree line. You can see the cut hay. Those are soybeans in the next field." He motioned forward. "My dad was in the tract on the other side of the road."

O'Neill was relieved he did not smell manure. Instead, the cut hay dominated his senses. He looked at the area, taking in the soybeans that separated the hayfields. The land was generally flat, so he could see the second hayfield across the road. The truck lurched ahead, stopping as it approached an intersection. Cooper and Lena got out, so O'Neill followed. A stop sign sat at the crossing.

Lena looked at the cut grass lying peacefully in the field. "Are both hayfields planted with alfalfa?"

"Yeah," Cooper said. "You can just call it hay if you like. But yes, that is the field my dad was tedding yesterday and my uncle did earlier today. Once we're done talking, I'm going to do that one again, since it looks like the day will end up dry. Our land is on both sides of Chance Road. The soybean fields to the west are owned by Mr. Purcell. Past that field, he's got corn. That's where the crash was."

"Walk me through what happened."

"We mowed hay in the morning. My dad always took that plot," he said with a nod, "the old Cooper's Chance. We finished at twelve thirty or so and went back for something to eat and to get the equipment ready. We started tedding at two or so, going back and forth parallel to Gifford Road, so I would see my dad when driving toward him. It varied a little since there are some dicey areas in the field he was in, including a cluster of trees around where the old cistern and windmill are. It was like any day in the fields. Dad was on the 1086, while I was on the newer Case IH. His tractor is bigger than he needs for tedding, but he loves it because it's reliable."

O'Neill didn't know what a 1086 was, but he wrote it down, then stared into the fields. "How much traffic does this road get? The one that the tractor ended up on."

"Not much at all. A truck or car comes by every four or five minutes."

"How about on that day? Was there traffic around that time? Any parked vehicles?"

"Nothing parked. Think I heard a honk once, but that was maybe half an hour before dad disappeared. I'm sure a few vehicles went past, but I wasn't really paying attention, so I don't recall."

"But you could see the road?"

"When I'm going that direction, sure," Cooper said. "And if you're wondering, I didn't see the 1086 going down Chance Road."

"You obviously couldn't see your dad's tractor when you were going away from him." O'Neill pointed at the field where Vernon Cooper vanished. "How long would have your dad been out of your sight?"

Cooper's brow scrunched downward. "Each twenty-acre field is an eighth of a mile by an eighth of a mile. It probably took me three or four minutes to go from one end to the other, including getting turned around."

"So he was out of your sight for three or four minutes," O'Neill said. "Would you mind giving us a ride to where the accident was? And Lena, would you look at the odometer thing and let me know exactly how far the accident was from the intersection?"

She nodded, and the three started toward the truck, walking side-by-side with Cooper in the middle and O'Neill on the pavement. A red-winged blackbird chirped loudly as it swooped between trees that lined the road.

"Are you the only son?" O'Neill said, breaking the silence. "Thought you mentioned sisters."

"Yeah, two older sisters, but no brothers. Jenny has been home since school ended and Annie works in town, but lives at home. Jenny does the books and both help a little on the farm, though neither drive tractor."

"Does your mother live with you as well?"

"My mom died three years ago in October. Cancer."

"I'm sorry," Lena said. Her gaze dropped to the road's dirt shoulder. "Our mother died from cancer, too."

Cooper looked sideways at her, and his pace slowed. "How old were you when it happened?"

"Nine. Seamus was thirteen. The twenty-year anniversary of her death is in August."

Cooper nodded, and they walked silently to the truck.

The pickup's engine roared to life and O'Neill tried to imagine the two farmers in the fields on their tractors. At the intersection, they waited as a semi barreled past. Then Cooper turned the truck right.

Corn was planted to their left, and they went past a farmhouse which had a Harvester. They passed the area with the lump of trees and a driveway that O'Neill remembered from the previous day. For the first time, he spotted the house tucked at the end of the long driveway. The pickup slowed and pulled onto the shoulder of the two-lane road.

O'Neill stood on the truck bed. Smashed corn and areas of bare dirt were on their right, marking where Ben Hefty's vehicle slid off the pavement. Tractor tire marks on their left showed where the tractor had driven into the field. To his left, he could see the farmhouse they had passed. Another farm was in the distance. The road's shoulder was mostly grass and weeds with a few inches of dirt skirting the pavement. The corn on both sides of the road was already approaching knee-high height.

Cooper got out of his vehicle, slamming the door. O'Neill glanced both ways before grasping the bed's edge and vaulting onto the blacktop. The truck's body was hot to the touch, and he could feel heat coming off the pavement.

"Over three-tenths of a mile," Lena said. "That's how far we are from the intersection."

O'Neill noted the distance, then followed the farmer across the road while Lena waited in the vehicle.

"Purcell should thank you two for getting the 1086 stopped," Cooper said. "Who knows how far it would have gone through his field if your sister hadn't stopped it?"

O'Neill crouched down and noticed the tire marks on the blacktop. "What would have happened to the tractor had it not collided with Mr. Hefty's truck?"

"The road continues to curve, and it had already crossed lanes," Cooper said. "If Dad really wasn't inside, the tractor would have crossed fully into the wrong lane and then driven along the shoulder. It probably would have rolled over as it edged off the shoulder. A tractor has a higher center of gravity than a car or a pickup, so it's more prone to a rollover. It wouldn't have made it much further."

"It would have tipped over?"

"Yeah."

"But it didn't tip over. Why not?"

"The collision with Mr. Hefty changed its direction, so it drove straight downhill and into the field." Cooper pointed to the tire tracks. "Tractor rollovers rarely happen when driving downhill. Instead, they happen when going alongside a hill, a ditch, or an embankment such as the shoulder of a road."

"Okay," O'Neill replied. "What I still don't get is why the tractor was moving when we got here. It's not like anyone's foot was on the gas."

Lena got out of the pickup and slammed the door. "Keep in mind that Seamus has never been in a tractor and has never even driven a car."

"You have never driven a car? Man, that's weird." He shook his head and smiled. "The 1086 has a manual transmission and uses a clutch which you engage to change gears. There isn't a gas pedal like a car, though there is a hand throttle. You just set it; you don't need to hold it down."

"The tractor was in low gear and the throttle was almost off," Lena said.

"That would mean it was just crawling along." Cooper looked at her. "Maybe two or three miles an hour. Does that sound right to you?"

"Yeah," she said. "I could have walked at a slow pace right along with it."

O'Neill stepped off the road into the area where the corn wasn't growing and crouched down. They were estimating the tractor's speed based on Lena's memory of walking alongside it. He wanted the exact speed since it would tell him how long it took for the tractor to go from the intersection to the spot of the accident. After a brief discussion, Cooper said he would talk about it with his neighbor, who had driven a 1086 for twenty-five years.

A semi approached from the west, so they stepped off the shoulder, descending into weeds and the edge of the corn. O'Neill looked to the ground, trying to make sure he wouldn't tip backward. The vehicle roared past and there was a "ping" as a grain of sand belted his sunglasses.

Once the truck passed, Cooper took his hat off and rubbed his curly blonde hair. "As I got close to the accident, I could see the pickup on one side of the road and the tractor on the other. My reaction was that something might blow up, like in the movies, so I rushed to the cab, thinking I needed to pull my dad out before the tractor blew. As I got close, I realized the cab was empty. I was relieved because I thought he got out. But I couldn't see him, so I assumed he got hurt in the accident, stumbled out of the cab, and was nearby. I ran around looking for him in the cornfield. I could see a long way since the crops were only a foot high, but I couldn't find him."

"We were searching around here, but he probably never got past the hayfield," O'Neill said. "Is there a spot back near the hayfield where he could hide?"

"At Cooper's Chance? Why do you think he got off back there?"

"The tractor crashed over three-tenths of a mile past the intersection," O'Neill said, "which is also the end of the hayfield. There was no reason for him to drive away from his own farmland. There was no reason to go past that intersection and I know I saw the cab empty when Lena and I drove past. If it was going two or three miles an hour, it would have rumbled down the road for nearly ten minutes before the crash."

Cooper lifted his hat and turned around. "I hadn't thought about that, but you're right. There was no reason for him to go past Gifford Road. He probably got out earlier. If he did, it would have taken a bit for the tractor to get up here to where the crash occurred."

"You must not have even noticed that he wasn't in the field for at least one lap."

The farmer was nodding. "Yes, you're right. He must have folded up the tedder back by Cooper's Chance then gotten onto the road. It's straight there, so he could have gotten off or gotten pulled off, leaving the tractor going down the road. If so, maybe he hid back around Cooper's Chance."

"That would make sense," O'Neill said. "But what do you mean by *folded up* the tedder?"

"When in operation, the tractor pulls the tedder, which is roughly eighteen feet wide." He spread his arms out. "That's too wide for road travel, even for a short distance since both lanes on a road are only about twenty-five feet wide. Folding up the tedder brings the width down to about ten feet."

"The road curves about halfway down the hayfield." O'Neill's sunglasses dropped from his head to the bridge of his nose. He pushed them back and forced a smile. "If the tractor got onto the road before the curve, it would have veered off before it even got to the intersection. That means the tractor started no earlier than at the beginning of the straightaway in front of Cooper's Chance."

"What are you suggesting?" Cooper asked.

"I'm saying that's where your dad disappeared."

Chapter 13

Cooper waved to a passing car, partially covering his face as dust blew past. O'Neill wanted to see the culvert near Cooper's Chance, though it was only after Lena gave an unenthusiastic approval that they returned to the farmer's truck. They drove to the top of the crest, where they did a Y-turn. The pickup sped up, going faster than before, and O'Neill sat nervously with his back to the cab, feeling each bounce as the truck rumbled down the country road. After passing the intersection, he took a nip of vodka, and the truck slowed and veered onto the dirt shoulder. A puff of dirt engulfed the vehicle as it stopped.

O'Neill estimated that the road curved twenty feet from the culvert. He leaped out and followed Cooper down a rainwater path that led to a silver pipe under the road. The weeds were thick, but the farmer ignored them and leaned against the culvert as O'Neill inched closer.

The pipe was five feet in diameter and, unlike some culverts he had seen, there was no grate. Several inches of water sat in the tunnel, and a red-winged blackbird flew upward, landing atop the nearest telephone wire. Soybeans lined one field while the newly cut hay of Cooper's Chance was on the other.

O'Neill climbed back up to the blacktop. He jogged to the beginning of the straightaway, then walked, taking long steps, all the way to the intersection with Gifford Road. Cooper and Lena followed.

"How many feet do you guys figure, from the culvert to the intersection?" O'Neill asked.

"Two or three hundred?" Cooper said.

"I'll go closer to two hundred," Lena said.

O'Neill ran back toward them. "I counted it out at about seventy-five steps." He stopped in front of them. "Assuming a yard for each step, that would be two hundred and twenty-five feet. So, add in the three-plus tenths of a mile from the intersection to the accident, it means the tractor was on the road for about nineteen hundred feet, which is pushing four-tenths of a mile."

"Okay." Lena opened her phone. "Seamus, I know you want to look at the tractor, so let's do that quick so I can get back to work." She walked toward the truck, and they followed.

When they pulled into the driveway, Bernie ran alongside. After a moment with the dog, Cooper led the O'Neills to a huge white shed. The blue Harvester towered behind it. A red barn and a pair of smaller sheds sat nearby. He instructed them to wait as he went in through the shed's side entrance. The overhead door opened, and they stepped inside, finding a four-wheel drive all-terrain vehicle, two tractors, and a variety of farm equipment.

Cooper flipped on a light and approached a red tractor. "The 1086 is in better shape than I expected. The axle is bent, though it doesn't seem like a lot." Cooper motioned toward the front of the vehicle. "One headlight was broken. I replaced it, but it still doesn't work, so there's something else going on. Also, the grill is cracked and there's oil leaking. You can hardly tell, but that's because it leaked out when it was with the sheriff."

Lena hopped onto one of the two steps on the tractor's side. She seized the handle, pulled the door open, and swung herself over the gearbox and into the tractor's lone seat. Cooper opened the other side door and put a foot on the first step, lifting himself so his head was higher than hers. The farmer's weight tilted the tractor toward him. O'Neill hesitated, but stuck his foot on a step on the side opposite of Cooper, raising himself so that he and Lena were at roughly the same height.

The cab's inside showed wear. Its seat was torn in multiple places, revealing yellow cushioning partially covered with lines of duct tape. The dashboard and flooring were black, but a layer of dirt coated every crevice and corner.

"The seat is more comfortable than you might think," Lena said. She shifted sideways to reach a red pedal and rested one hand on the steering wheel while pretending to move the lever at her side. "I drive a lot of equipment at work, though nothing this big. And I've not driven a manual before. I think everything at my work is hydraulic."

"The 1086 uses hydraulics to control what it is pulling," Cooper said, pointing at the controls. "Hydraulics fold and unfold the tedder, but the transmission is manual." He paused and shook his head. "You wanna hear something crazy? Detective Becker thinks Dad crashed this so we could collect insurance money."

"Couldn't you just sell the tractor?" she said.

"That's what I told Becker. I agree we might do a little better with insurance money, but we're talking a few thousand dollars difference. It's not enough to make him crash a tractor that he loved. Dad's a worrier, but he's not unstable. Why would he leave with nothing more than his keys and his wallet? Nothing else was missing. No personal items, no extra money, no nothing." Cooper's head was shaking. "If he was making a run for it, he would take supplies with him."

"What did your dad leave in the cab?" O'Neill asked. "Did the sheriff's office give you a detailing of it?"

"Yeah, it's on the receipt I signed. It's inside, but it was just a pen, a notepad, and a thermos. They still have them, but they said I can pick them up in a few days. Deputy Franklin said there weren't fingerprints on the thermos. It was mostly empty with just a little water and Red Bull left inside. That's why they won't keep them long."

"Red Bull energy drink?" O'Neill chuckled. "You mentioned that on the day of the accident. I'm surprised. I thought farmers drank coffee and it was people your age who drank Red Bull."

"My dad used to be a huge coffee drinker, but quit ten years ago at his doctor's request. She said he was overdoing caffeine and it wasn't helping his stress. It took a few months, but he gave it up. After my mom died, he was struggling to get out of bed. I got him to try the Red Bull. Twice a day, he would fill his thermos with ice water and add a bottle of Red Bull. That's all he drinks when he's in the fields. There's less caffeine than a cup of coffee. And since he mixes it with the ice water, it's even less potent."

"You said there were no prints on the thermos?" O'Neill asked.

"Yeah. None. Becker talked about that, too. He said they found plenty of fingerprints inside the tractor cab, just as he expected. Most were Dad's, though mine were in there, as were your sister's. I gave them my fingerprints and they got dad's from his bedroom. He said Lena's were on file, whatever that means."

"Was your dad wearing gloves?"

"No. Becker confirmed that, since there were fingerprints on the wheel and the levers and everything. He said that if Dad was wearing gloves, there would have been smudges on the wheel and areas with no prints."

"Why weren't his prints on the thermos?" O'Neill asked.

Cooper shrugged his shoulders. "Maybe he never touched it."

"Was the water left over from the morning?"

"No, I filled it up that afternoon before we headed into the fields," he said. "As we got ready to go back out, I made coffee for myself. Dad brought it in, and I packed it with ice, added water, and dumped in a can of Red Bull. Dad was still in the bathroom, so I stuck it in the 1086's cupholder." He pointed to a spot inside the cab. "I put the thermos right there. It is odd if he didn't drink from it."

"Were you wearing gloves when you set the thermos in the tractor?" O'Neill asked.

"Me? No. I have some in my cab, but it was too hot for gloves. I certainly wasn't wearing any when I got my coffee and filled up Dad's water."

"Would your dad have wiped off the container for any reason? Did he keep a rag or anything with him?"

"The sheriff's office didn't find one in his cab, though he could have had a Kleenex in his pocket or something. I don't know why he would wipe off the thermos unless there was a spill. The sheriff's deputy I spoke with wasn't too concerned." Cooper shook his head. "They asked me about it a few times, but they apparently don't think it matters."

"Earlier, you mentioned an anniversary," O'Neill said. "Becker brought up something about someone's death, but didn't give any details. What were you referring to?"

Cooper remained on the tractor step. His gaze jumped between the siblings, settling on O'Neill. "My dad had an affair six or seven years back. It was before they diagnosed my mom with cancer. The affair was with this woman named Amy Ring, who lived a mile or so from here with her husband Bobby and their two kids. I don't know how long this affair went on, but Bobby Ring Senior found out about it and that wasn't good. Bobby Senior, you see, was trouble. He threatened my dad, started a fire in our barn, keyed my dad's truck, and even shot out its front window. The cows got out once after someone cut open our fence. My dad was sure it was him. This was back when we milked."

Lena tilted forward. "Sounds like someone with major anger management issues."

Cooper nodded, then his gaze dropped downward so far that it looked as if his eyes were closed. "Exactly five years ago today, Bobby Senior came home drunk and shot his wife Amy in the head before shooting himself." He looked up at Lena. "They are both dead. There was a lot of coverage on it in the papers."

"Oh, God," she said. "That's awful."

"I can explain how Bobby was an abusive husband, but I can't explain why my dad had an affair."

"Becker probably doesn't think it's a coincidence that your dad disappeared near the anniversary of her death," O'Neill said.

"He thinks we're all kooks," Cooper said. "And he thinks it knocked Dad over the edge. But it doesn't make sense to me. Dad's affair was a huge deal, but I don't think he blames himself for Amy's death. I think he blames Bobby Senior. I wouldn't think that would trigger him to do something stupid like running away."

"You mention the dead couple's kids. Are they still around?"

"Oh, yes. Marcie and Bobby Junior are still around. They live a mile or so away."

"How did they feel about your father?"

"Seamus," Lena interrupted, "I do have to get to work."

"I'll make it quick," Cooper said. He turned toward O'Neill. "Marcie and Bobby Ring absolutely hate my father. I brought them up yesterday with Deputy Peterson. I also talked with Becker about them this morning when he interviewed me and my sisters. But Becker says they couldn't have been involved in Dad's disappearance. Bobby Junior drives a truck, and he was making runs with gravel. He was in line at the quarry at the exact time you called 911. Marcie started work at Hardee's just a few minutes later. Becker says they couldn't have done it. He even wrote up a timeline for me to illustrate it."

A sense of disappointment poured over O'Neill.

"The murder-suicide was obviously tough on the Ring children," Cooper said, "but it was tough on me and my sisters as well. When school started that fall, I was a freshman in high school. My sisters were at school too, as were Bobby Junior and Marcie. The whole thing was weird. We were Verona Area High School's principal topic of conversation."

"That's awful," Lena said in a quiet voice.

"But it's a dead end. They had nothing to do with Dad's disappearance. They couldn't have."

"Anyone else you can think of that didn't like your dad or would have benefited from him disappearing?" O'Neill asked.

His head shook. "No. Then again, I did not know about my dad having an affair until shortly before Bobby Ring killed his wife and himself. You might be better off talking to my uncle, Roman. He's my dad's older brother, and while they had somewhat of a spat recently, they are close. If there's anyone who Dad would talk to about personal things, it is Uncle Roman. The only other person I can think of is Father Brennan. If my dad gets down, he talks with him. They became close after my mom's death."

"What was the spat between your dad and uncle about?"

"Oh, nothing important. I think it was about a piece of equipment that Dad said he would pick up for him. Roman came by to pick it up, but Dad couldn't find it or forgot to buy it. Roman told him off. It was the sort of thing that happens between them. A few times a year, Roman gets ticked off; then after a few weeks, they act as if nothing happened."

"Sounds like brothers."

Cooper nodded and provided contact information for his family and the priest. Both sisters were living at home and one was inside the house, but Lena needed to get to work, so O'Neill noted the contact information on the back of Detective Becker's business card.

"Thanks for talking about things," Cooper said as they exited the shed. "I know you're not doing this for money, but if you have any ideas or anything, please let me know. Talk to Roman or to my sisters. I'll let them know you might call. Hopefully, Becker is right and Dad just ran away. But I'm glad you're looking into it. It would be good for someone to consider that something else might have happened."

O'Neill asked if he could borrow the timeline that Becker had written up. The farmer went inside the house as Lena started the Dane County Parks truck. O'Neill sat in the passenger seat with the door hanging open. Cooper returned and handed him an envelope. He shut the door, and they yelled goodbyes as Bernie ran along the driveway.

"Randy seems like a nice guy," Lena said. "I can't imagine him being involved in his father's disappearance."

"Yeah, he seems like a good guy." The pickup stopped at the edge of the driveway. "But that doesn't mean he's not pissed at his dad for having an affair. And it doesn't mean he wouldn't help his dad disappear."

"Oh. I hadn't thought about that. Is that what you think? Do you think the guy ran away and his son is covering for him? It sounds like the need to escape might run in the family. The anniversary might explain why it happened when it did."

"It's possible he ran away, but I doubt it." O'Neill swallowed as the truck pulled onto the highway. "I think Vernon Cooper is dead."

"Dead?" She stopped chewing her gum. "Are you sure?"

"No, I'm not sure. But I can't get over the thermos without fingerprints. Becker is bothered by it too, which is why he wanted to determine what you touched in the cab. It also explains why he wanted to understand whether Randy Cooper had touched anything."

"Couldn't the dad have wiped the thermos off himself? Or maybe he wore gloves. I know it was warm, but farmers wear gloves for reasons other than warmth. Maybe he wore a pair and Randy didn't notice."

"Sure, it's possible. Yet there were no prints at all. There's no reason for Randy or Vernon to wipe their own prints off the thing. But if someone else was there, they might not want theirs to be found." He adjusted the chair, pushed his sunglasses tight to his nose, and shut his eyes. "What is more important is that the thermos was outside the tractor cab."

"How do you know that?"

O'Neill chuckled. "There were fingerprints in the cab and no evidence that someone wiped prints off the steering wheel or the gears or anything. Why get inside with gloves on, then take them off and get a drink?"

"Okay," Lena said. "I guess that makes sense."

His eyes opened. "I think Vernon either got out of the tractor and took the thermos with him, or he handed it to someone else."

"Why? And if so, why did they put it back in the cupholder?"

His eyes closed. "That's what I aim to find out."

Chapter 14

Lena shook her brother's shoulder as the pickup idled in front of his apartment. O'Neill opened his eyes and slid out of the truck. As he thanked her, she turned the engine off and stepped out. She locked the vehicle and reached into the back, pulling out part of his new bedframe. He grabbed the wooden headboard. Its weight surprised him, and he struggled as he entered the building and carried it up the staircase. Lena set the frame on the steps and held doors as he carried the headboard into his apartment.

After repeating the process with the rest of the frame, O'Neill gave his sister a hug, and she hurried to work. Inside, he gulped a beer as he ate a potato and a handful of Cheez Whiz-covered saltine crackers. The outer door buzzed, so he finished his drink.

"Yeah?" he said into the security system.

"Yo, O'Neill, you up?" a voice said through the intercom.

"Johnson? Just a second." O'Neill hit the buzzer, then opened his apartment door and waited for The Johnson to walk up the steps. "You're early," he said. "It's not even five thirty."

The Johnson and O'Neill had been friends for years, and they both played in O'Neill's current band, Schumacher's Flour Mill. He wore a Motorhead T-shirt and a faded jean jacket that was cut off at the shoulders, revealing two eagle tattoos. Both eagles looked backwards, watching his back. "I had to pick up Mika, and the traffic wasn't bad. Besides, I wanted to talk."

O'Neill waved his friend into the apartment. He switched out his bottle of vodka for his backup flask. It was nearly empty, so he took whiskey from the cupboard, filled the container, and pulled out another beer from the refrigerator.

The Johnson rested against the door. "Did you just open a beer?"

"Been busy, and I want a drink."

"Remember, Mika's parents don't want drinking at practice. She's out in the car."

Mika was the band's fiddler and The Johnson's brother-in-law's ten-year-old niece. "That's why I'm slamming one before I go," O'Neill said.

The Johnson shook his head and rolled his eyes. "Have you heard of a band named Bang Shoot?"

"No. They sound redundant." O'Neill left the bottle on the kitchen counter. "Who are they? Not local?"

"They're from Austin, Texas. I was flipping through CDs at B-Side Records and I was looking at theirs. The track listing is on the back. Do you remember that 'Spring Coat on a Winter's Day' song of yours?"

"Sure. That was on the second Theoretically Trashed CD. Haven't played it for years."

The Johnson reached into a pocket and pulled out a compact disc case. The cover showed four young white men standing underneath a bridge. "Your song is track four on Bang Shoot's newest album. Mika and I listened to it on the way over."

"You're kidding? Am I credited?"

The Johnson nodded. "It says 'S. O'Neill.'"

O'Neill took the case, opened it, and pulled out the liner notes. Even though he had three bands that released six CDs, seeing his name in the notes still gave him a charge. Not only was this the first time another artist had recorded a song of his, it was also his first on a national label. He wondered how they knew about the tune and why they chose it. Seeing the song's name was like seeing an old friend.

The Johnson grabbed the CD. "They should pay royalties to the composer, so I did a little research. Fallen Records owns the marketing and distribution of anything that came out of Theoretically Trashed's old label. Fallen Records keeps half of any composition royalties and you get half. Things are set, so it's not like there's a contract to negotiate or anything."

"Then why haven't they paid me?"

"BMI is the licensing company that collects your royalties, but they don't have contact information for you. I called them, saying I was your agent. They're sitting on about a hundred and sixty dollars of your royalties. You might as well call them. If you want me to do it as your agent, that's fine, but you'll have to pay me ten percent or whatever the industry standard is for an agent. That would be a whole sixteen bucks."

O'Neill gulped his beer. "I would feel better if you did it. What information will they need from me?"

"BMI will have to verify you're the right person, so they'll need your social security number. To get paid, they'll need banking information, or at least an address to send the check. I may have to sign up for some sort of online account since they'll probably pay out regularly. I'm assuming it's okay if I do that."

"Sure." Lifting his mattress, he pulled out his checkbook. He had only written ten checks since opening his first-ever checking account at age thirty-three. Until this week, all the checks were to his landlord or to Madison Gas & Electric. He voided a check and handed it to The Johnson. "Wait. Let me add my social security. I'll write it backwards."

"This is cool," The Johnson said. "I wish someone would record one of *my* songs."

"You said you already listened to it. How does it sound?"

"It's okay. You want me to play it on the drive over?"

"Course." O'Neill took another drink. "By the way, I only had two drinks yesterday. That's what I'm doing now on Tuesdays."

"Good. You should cut down."

O'Neill finished his beer, and the bottle banged on the countertop. "Yeah, but I get to spring loose today."

"Make it after practice. Remember, Mika's parents..."

"I know," he said as The Johnson stepped out of the apartment. "They don't want drinking at practice." O'Neill locked the door, and they walked down the stairs, each carrying a musical instrument.

"Hey, O'Neill!" yelled a girl's voice. The Fiddler was sitting on the hood of The Johnson's silver Chevrolet. She wore white shorts, sandals, and a *Toy Story 2* T-shirt. She looked younger than her ten years.

"You ready to ride in back?" he replied.

"I already called shotgun." The Fiddler slid off the car and put her hand on the passenger door handle.

"No," O'Neill said. "We talked about this last time. You got the front seat three times in a row. Today is my turn."

The Johnson unlocked the trunk and placed the guitar and banjo inside. "You agreed," he said, shutting the trunk. "Let O'Neill sit in front this one time. You can be in front on the way back."

"Aw, okay." The Fiddler moved from the front to the back door, dragging a hand along the vehicle.

The Johnson opened the driver-side door and flipped the automatic door lock. The Fiddler was seated before O'Neill opened his door and, as the car started, music filled the air.

"Bang Shoot is poppier than I expected," The Johnson said. "One review on Amazon said they were like the Real McKenzies with flutes, whistles, and harmonicas instead of bagpipes. I don't really hear that."

"Not sure I want to hear that," O'Neill said.

"What are you guys talking about?" she asked.

"The band I was telling you about who recorded one of O'Neill's songs. It's the CD we played on the way over."

"Did you like it?" O'Neill asked.

"It's okay, I guess," she said.

The Johnson turned down the volume. "The band's got a drummer, a guitar, an acoustic bass, and another guy who plays the electric guitar on some songs, but he also plays flute, fiddle, harmonica, and piano. Closest thing I can come up with is The Violent Femmes, with a more straightforward lead singer and more eclectic instrumentation."

"The fiddling is boring basic stuff," The Fiddler said.

O'Neill shut his eyes and listened to Bang Shoot. He didn't know what song it was, but it wasn't his. As he listened, he tried to ignore The Fiddler, who was rubbing something against the back of his head. Finally, she brushed along his ear and he reflexively opened his eyes and jerked forward.

"Mika, quit bothering him," The Johnson said.

"Yeah, and remember, I can do the same thing to you on the way back. And you've got a lot more hair to mess up."

"You want to hear your song?" The Johnson asked. O'Neill nodded, and the CD player went back to track four. No one spoke as the music began.

The song was about getting through a Wisconsin winter without a winter coat.

"What do you think?" The Johnson said as they pulled into a parking spot.

"Sounds okay, I guess," O'Neill said. "I don't remember the Theoretically Trashed version that well, though I think it rocked more. Don't think I ever played the song live after the Trashed broke up."

O'Neill and The Johnson's current band, Schumacher's Flour Mill, had been together for less than a month. The group was originally a tool to immerse O'Neill in a case that the Ryder Detective Agency was investigating. He told The Johnson that it wasn't a real band and they would only play one or two times. But the case was closed, and they were still practicing. They had a show in a week at a Monroe Street coffee shop and were signed to appear at a festival on Atwood Avenue in August.

For O'Neill, the band meant something. It showed he had not given up on music. He wanted his life to move forward, but he couldn't imagine a world without music. Music had kept him alive for most of his life and he couldn't move forward without it, even if it was no longer the center of everything.

"Let's go," The Fiddler said before slamming the door.

The Johnson took the CD from the car's player and stuck it inside the case. O'Neill stepped out and waited for The Johnson to open the trunk.

The three musicians continued to Topper's apartment, which was above his pipe shop. Topper was the band's banjo player. The Johnson played guitar while O'Neill played a mix of guitar and tin whistle. They entered through the pipe paraphernalia store, where Topper's girlfriend, Mandy, was closing the shop for the day. She unlocked a door, allowing them into the back room. Topper came down a circular metal staircase, moving better than he had since being injured several weeks earlier. His skin was pale as always and his sandy blonde hair was in a ponytail.

O'Neill tuned the banjo as Topper went to a nearby refrigerator, pulling out bottles of Coke and Diet Coke. Once The Fiddler's instrument was in tune, they started on their twenty song set list. The songs were covers or traditional tunes and included six instrumentals. O'Neill and Topper slipped into the bathroom several times to spike their drinks. It was nearly eight PM when they finished.

"You want me to drop you home?" The Johnson asked O'Neill.

"Nah, I'm leaving the banjo here so he can practice. I can walk the guitar to my place, so you can take The Fiddler home." O'Neill's glance hopped between the two men. "Either of you want to do something? I could go for a few beers and some music."

"Sorry," The Johnson said, "but after I drop Mika, Kate and I are meeting Tooth McGregor and Kate's sister at the Crystal Corner Bar. It's a double date and there's some band Tooth wants to see."

Topper pointed at O'Neill. "Looks like it's just us two. I doubt if there's too much music on a Wednesday night, though there's a blues band at The Annex and apparently at the Crystal Corner. Either that or Mandy's going down to the Angelic to meet her friends. We could tag along."

"Can I pick up my guitar later this week?" O'Neill asked Topper. "There are two black cloth cases behind it. The finger picks are already inside one case, so that one is for the banjo."

The lanky banjo player nodded and put a bottle of Cutty Sark on the table. Mandy followed with three glasses. He poured, and O'Neill snagged the closest glass and took a sip. The Scotch tasted fabulous.

"I'm leaving in a minute," she said, itching at her nose ring. "You coming along?"

"I'm up for it," O'Neill said. He turned toward Topper. "A bitter sounds good, and I want to ask you a few questions about running a small business."

"I'm the guy," Topper said. "What type of business?"

"Farming."

"I'm not the guy."

"Well, you're all I've got."

Chapter 15

O'Neill, Topper, and Mandy walked to the Angelic Brewing Company, pausing along the way when a teenager pulled Topper aside and again when Mandy recognized an old boyfriend. When they arrived at the brewpub, a group of friends greeted Mandy. O'Neill ordered a bitter before joining the women at a table near the entrance, far from the bar counter. A John Lee Hooker song played in the background, and a spattering of customers sat at nearby tables drinking beer and eating dinner.

Topper sat at O'Neill's right, a painting of fairies in a clearing decorating the wall behind him. The women headed to the counter, leaving the men alone at the table.

"Why are you asking me about farming?" A match flared, and the flame hung in front of Topper's face.

"Trying to figure out the motive for what may have been a murder. Thought you might know something since your grandpa farmed."

"Yeah, but my dad didn't inherit the place, so he ended up as a bus driver. Guess I know a bit about the business side of farming just from hearing my uncle and cousins talking and complaining." His cheeks sucked in and the flame widened then faded. "I'm assuming this relates to your detective job."

"Yeah. Keep it quiet."

"I know. We've been through this before. What's the story?"

"This forty-four-year-old farmer disappeared near Verona, and I think he's dead. His wife died a few years ago from cancer. The son seems like a nice kid. He's about twenty and there are two sisters that are a few years older. Anyway, the son gives me the impression that him and his sisters got along fine with their old man, but that could be bullshit. I'm trying to figure out how much the kids benefit financially from their father's disappearance."

"Probably not a lot from a disappearance," Topper said. "Someone has to be declared dead before an estate goes through probate. Does the guy have a will?"

"Don't know. If there's one, I'd be stunned if the money didn't go to the kids. He also has a brother."

"Is the brother a suspect?"

"Don't know, but it strikes me as odd that he's the older brother, but he didn't inherit the family farm. Reminds me of a story about the same family from a few generations earlier."

"You think the brother is pissed about not getting the farm? My dad wasn't the oldest, so he never expected to get his dad's place. He got a share which my uncle eventually bought out. But if my uncle hadn't gotten to run the home place, he would have been pissed."

"Yeah. Hard to imagine the brother getting stiffed like that without being ticked. How much is a farm worth nowadays?"

Topper laughed and blew smoke out of his nostrils. "Why ask me?"

"Don't know any farmers, and you're the only person I know with business savvy. Ryder owns a business, but I don't see him as insightful, and he knows even less about farming than you."

"Okay, I'll give it a shot," Topper said. "What size of farm are we talking about?"

"Two hundred and forty acres. They have forty acres of hay and the rest is a mix of soybeans and corn, though mostly soybeans."

"Do they milk?"

"They used to, so I'm assuming they have a milking parlor or whatever it is you'd need to milk. My guess is they stopped milking after the mother died."

"Do they have steer or pigs or anything?"

"Don't think so. At least, I didn't see any."

"Is the land near the city? Any chance developers are looking to buy the place so they can build houses or a strip mall or whatever?"

O'Neill rubbed his eyes. "The farm is a few miles outside Verona. I mean, eventually it will probably get bought up after Madison and Verona smash together, but that's a long way off."

"We're probably just talking about the value of the land and equipment for farming, plus the farmhouse. It's not potential development land and there's no oil, minerals or anything valuable underground. If it's that simple, I'm guessing everything is worth somewhere between being in the red and eight hundred thousand. The house, land, and equipment might be worth a million bucks, but how much debt they have is key. Farming is a weird business; even I know that. It's not only capital intensive, but farmers need to buy seed and everything in the spring and don't get paid for the finished product until the fall. Even then, things are dicey since prices fluctuate and they're often screwed over by the weather. My grandpa was never satisfied, saying it was too wet or too dry. But take all this with a grain of salt. Like I said, I'm no expert. I'll send my cousin an email. I'll let you know if he thinks I'm way off."

A brunette slightly taller than O'Neill returned with their drinks. After the men thanked her she turned around, heading back to the counter. He set a beer in front of Topper. They clicked their glasses together and drank.

O'Neill licked the foam from his lips. "The son told me that his sister does the books for the farm. Does that change anything?"

"Not unless she's been stealing from her dad and killed him to cover it up. Murdering him might delay people figuring out what she did, but that's about it." He smelled his beer, then took a gulp. "Are the missing guy's kids and his brother the only suspects?"

"No. There's this brother and sister from another family who hate the guy who is missing, though they have alibis. Otherwise, this guy's a well-respected salt of the earth farmer. Course, there might be someone I don't yet know about. What if the guy's dead and there's no will? Who inherits?"

"Wisconsin probate law would have the guy's estate go equally to any kids, since he's an unmarried widower. The brother won't get anything unless there's a will and he is a listed beneficiary. Though the most valuable thing is the land. The deed to land can be payable on death to someone, and that happens outside a will. Also, make sure you check if the farm is incorporated."

"Like it's a business?"

"Yeah. A farm is a small business, so why not be organized like one? My uncle's farm is incorporated. I think that's common nowadays. The will might say that all the money goes to the kids, but if the corporation owns all the farm equipment, the corporate charter or whatever it is might define what happens to shares of the corporation upon someone's death."

"Sounds more complicated than I expected."

"It's probably not complicated. The deeds probably either don't have payable on death language or, if they do, they go to the kids. And if there is a corporation, it's probably wholly owned by the dad. I forget whether the corporation's stock just flows through to an estate or whether it can list a beneficiary."

Mandy and her group joined them at the table. She sat across from O'Neill next to Topper. A brunette was on O'Neill's left, and a quartet of blondes completed the group. A server ambled over, interrupting a spattering of talk.

"Are we getting something to eat?" Mandy asked Topper. She rested a hand on his arm. "Maybe nachos and curds?"

"Sure." He shrugged his shoulders and looked at O'Neill. "You want something?"

O'Neill couldn't think of the last thing he'd eaten. "Get whatever you like," he told her. "I'll have a little of whatever you order."

She nodded, then turned toward the server. "We'd like two orders of cheese curds, one of nachos, and..." Mandy looked at her friends.

"Do you have anything healthy?" asked one blonde.

"We have a vegetable platter," the server replied. She placed a menu on the table. "It's got carrots, broccoli, and greens and comes with our homemade ranch dressing."

"One of those too," she said.

The server bowed her head and was gone.

"What are you talking about?" Mandy asked the men.

"Farming," Topper said.

"Oh." She turned away and started a conversation with the woman on her right.

O'Neill fanned the smoke away from the table and poked Topper's shoulder. "I'm going to talk to their priest, too. The family is close to the one in Verona."

"A priest? Why talk to him?"

"People talk to priests. Some of them know a lot of what's going on in the community."

"I'm not Catholic," Topper said, "but I don't think priests can talk about people's secrets. It's against their credo or whatever."

"He won't tell me something he learned in the confessional. I'm just figuring I'll ask about how the family is handling the disappearance. His reaction might tell me something. It might tell me he knows nothing about it, or he might say the family is pulling together. Either way, it might give me a sense of what he thinks about them."

"Sounds like you're fishing."

"Course I am. Don't know what else to do."

"Tell your fat ass boss that it's his problem and not yours."

O'Neill laughed then polished off his beer. "I got involved in this case myself. I want to figure it out because it's bothering me. Plus, I was there when it happened, so I feel responsible for figuring it out. Feel sorry for the family, I guess."

"But the family are suspects?"

"Sure they are."

Topper's head was shaking. "Did this investigation come from that woman you like? The cop you say is tall."

"No, it didn't come through her."

"You still trying to make the moves on her?" Topper asked.

"Yeah."

"You really think that will work?"

"Don't know. People probably tell her I'm below her, but I think she likes me. And I worked with her on an earlier case, so I think she sees me as more of a normal person. Though I suppose she's keeping me at a distance, thinking I want to sleep with her and disappear."

"Don't be too hopeful." Smoke blew out of his nose. "A police detective is part of that solid middle class. She'll be looking for someone with better long-term prospects than you, and someone who drinks less."

"Suppose you're right," O'Neill said. "But I do know she doesn't like feeling vulnerable, and I think it's put her on a lonely path. I think we could be good for each other."

Topper motioned toward Mandy's lone brunette friend. "Is your girl taller than Cindy? She might be six foot."

"Oh, yeah," O'Neill said. "No doubt."

"Wow. How old is she?"

"Thirty-one."

"Wow again." Topper looked at the women at their table, all of which looked to be in their early twenties. "Throw out everything you've learned about women so far in your life. A cop in her thirties? You said she's never been married, right? You might as well be dealing with someone from another country. Your drinking doesn't bother her?"

"Don't know," O'Neill replied. "She knows I like a drink, but I try not to overdo it when she's around."

"Well, good luck. And don't tell me you're trying to solve this farmer's murder just to impress her."

"No, that's not it at all. But the guy's officially only disappeared. No one has found his body. Another weird thing about it is that the missing guy had a great-great-uncle who vanished in the same field a hundred years earlier. May be a coincidence, or maybe it's pointing at something."

"Like what?" Topper asked.

"The cops think the guy had a mental breakdown and ran away. It's a little more complicated than that, but they're probably considering the stories and assuming the family has issues up here." He touched his head. "The guy's son told me that his great-grandpa was eccentric and, as he got older, he would run away. The last time he went off, they found his body in a ditch along the highway."

"People want to blame genetics for everything, which is bullshit." Topper finished his beer. "Your dad was out on a bender and ended up dead. Doesn't mean the same thing will happen to you."

"Let's hope that's not how things end for me," O'Neill said.

"So you don't think this guy ran away? Not the guy from a hundred years ago or the great-grandpa, but the guy who just vanished."

"I don't think he ran away, but I don't want to ignore the possibility. My focus is on who might have a motive to kill him, so I want to figure out how strong of a motive the farmer's kids and brother have." O'Neill looked at his empty glass, then got to his feet. "Who paid for the first round?"

"I did. Mandy started a tab with my card."

"I'll buy this next one." O'Neill stood and meandered to the counter. He had been to the brewpub before and neither the counter nor the building was of interest, so he focused on the taps. He ordered two more bitters. As he waited, Mandy's friend Cindy strode up beside him.

"Would you mind getting one for me too?" she said. Her eyes were brown, and her hair on one side was pulled behind an ear, revealing a line of earrings.

"Sure. What you drinking?"

"Whatever you're drinking is fine." She smiled, and her tongue slid along her top lip. "Mandy says you used to be in Sea City Chaos. I saw you play a few years ago at the Annex. It was probably the first show I got into after turning twenty-one. I'm Cindy, by the way."

They shook hands. She was slightly taller than him, but he didn't think she was six feet, as Topper had said. He turned back to the bartender and held up three fingers. "Make it three bitters." He was tempted to mention Topper's tab, but added a ten-dollar bill to the two fives on the counter.

O'Neill drank several more bitters, putting most of them on Topper's tab. He sat at the counter with Cindy, answering questions about what it was like playing rock & roll in front of a live audience. She sat next to him again at Topper's table. At some point, Topper announced he was leaving, so O'Neill went outside with him. They shook hands and parted. Then he walked home alone through the drizzle on the warm June night.

Chapter 16

The alarm clock buzzed. O'Neill rolled off his mattress and hit snooze. Minutes later, the process repeated, though he didn't need to roll off the mattress since he was already on the floor. He floated back to sleep, but his eyes fluttered open as he realized someone was knocking on the door.

"Seamus, wake up!" a female voice yelled.

"What ya want?"

"It's me, Lena. American TV & Furniture called yesterday, and they're delivering your bed this morning. Dawson's with me. Sorry, I didn't notice the message until this morning. I called you about ten times, but you didn't answer."

"Second," O'Neill said. He was in boxer shorts. Most of the clothing he had worn the night before was still damp and lying near the front door. Pulling himself to his feet, he stumbled to the closet and grabbed a T-shirt. There was one more knock before he undid the dead bolt and opened the door. Four-year-old Dawson rushed past the wet clothes and jumped onto the mattress. The boy's brown hair was lighter and longer than when O'Neill had last seen him.

"Morning," Lena said, handing him a bottle of sparkling water. She kicked his clothes to the side and closed the door.

"What's this for?" O'Neill asked, holding up the water.

"I figured you would need it."

"How'd you get through the outer door?"

"The people downstairs were leaving the building, and they let me in. Suppose Dawson makes me look like a good risk."

"Where's banjo?" Dawson said in a loud voice. He twisted off the bed and skipped to the guitar stand. Normally, the stand held two acoustic guitars and a banjo.

"Surprised he remembers it," O'Neill said to his sister. Then he turned toward the child. "I lent the banjo to a friend. He also borrowed one of my guitars."

Dawson crouched next to the remaining guitar, and a finger plucked at the string.

"You want Uncle Seamus to play a song?" Lena asked.

He nodded while pulling at the strings.

"Let me go to the bathroom and put on pants first. Be right back." O'Neill closed the bathroom door before relieving himself and brushing his teeth. His mind was fuzzy as he opened the door.

"I've got the pictures for your wall," Lena said as she set a box on the floor. "Is it okay if I put them up where I think they work best?"

"Go for it." He gulped the water, and the plastic bottle made a crinkling sound. He pulled on the damp pants and walked toward Dawson. "Should we sing a song?"

"Barney, Barney," Dawson said. Then he sang, "I love you! You love me!"

"Great. The Barney theme song. Well. Okay. It's just 'This Old Man,' or 'Nick Nack Paddy Whack,' or whatever, though I don't know the words." He took the guitar from its stand, and, without a pick, started into "This Old Man."

Dawson nodded fervently, so O'Neill kept going, humming rather than singing. Dawson sang a smattering of the lyrics. The four-year-old yelled "Again!" as the song finished. They launched into another rendition, but this time the child sang more of the words as his mom banged nails into the wall.

Lena snuck outside while O'Neill played, returning with the brown chair they had bought at St. Vincent de Paul. O'Neill thought it impressive that she got the chair up the stairs on her own, yet he knew that, despite her diminutive size, she was fit and strong. And she was used to doing things on her own.

When they finished the song, O'Neill transitioned into "Baby Beluga." The boy sang along and O'Neill thought they sounded good. She returned with an end table, setting the oak furniture next to his thirteen-inch television. As they started "Yellow Submarine," she opened the box and hung the three framed drawings.

"Dawson," she said after the song. "Let Uncle Seamus come over and help me. I need him to make sure this one is straight."

"I like that," Dawson said, pointing at the largest drawing. It was a skyline of Madison which highlighted the Wisconsin State Capitol, Lake Monona, and the Monona Terrace Convention Center.

"That one is generic," she said. "The sort of thing I try to sell to tourists. The smallest is out-of-date, but I thought you might appreciate it."

The drawing showed a guitar, a fiddle, and two tin whistles lying on a wood table. O'Neill knew instantly that the instruments represented him and Lena. It was out-of-date since she no longer played fiddle or the tin whistle. She no longer played anything.

"I like it. I like all of them."

"Does the landscape look straight? I used two existing nail holes, but I think they were even, and they probably used them for one picture."

"Yeah, that's fine."

"What do you think?" Lena asked her son.

Dawson shrugged his shoulders.

"I like the look." O'Neill finished the bottle of water then walked into the kitchen and tossed it into the bin underneath the sink. "Appreciate this. It's kind of weird. We've seen each other three or four times over the last year, and suddenly I've seen you three days in a row."

She stopped chewing. "The three of us are the only family we've got. We should do things together more often. It's good for us; it's good for Dawson."

"Yeah. Course."

She embraced him in a tight hug, holding it longer than he expected. After releasing him, she wiped her eyes. "There are a few other things we're going to need that I hadn't thought of before. Your project is already at budget. Is it okay if we spend a little more?"

"How much you talking about?"

"Not much. The bathroom rug is a joke. You need a new one and a broom, so another ten bucks for them. Finally, the toilet is another story.

You need toilet bowl cleaning stuff and a plunger that isn't torn. I'll pick things up over the next week and drop them off sometime. You can pay me back then."

"Sure. I got Ryder's check deposited, so I should be able to handle ten or twenty more bucks. What time is the bed supposed to arrive?"

Lena looked at her watch. "They gave us a window between ten and twelve. It's almost ten thirty. Like I said, I tried to call, but you didn't answer. I thought I better come over, so they didn't surprise you. I'm late because I borrowed the truck from work to bring the chair over. Just make sure the movers take this disgusting mattress. And you might as well throw away those sheets. They won't fit the new bed and they're super thin."

Lena opened the window and explained that she had to return the truck. She and Dawson gave O'Neill a hug, and they were gone. He took his laptop and sat on his new used chair. Once Windows loaded, he opened his email and found a note from Ryder about another website problem.

A ring from the outer door interrupted him. O'Neill buzzed the person in and stepped out of his apartment, leaving the door open. Two men stood in the outer foyer, one tall and wiry, and the other short and stocky.

"We have a full-sized bed for delivery," the stocky one said. He spoke with an accent that O'Neill couldn't place. "American TV."

"Great. I got an old twin mattress to get rid of."

The two men discussed the situation and then the wiry one climbed the stairs two steps at a time while the stocky one cranked the outer door open.

O'Neill led the wiry man into his apartment. He took the sheet off and the man grabbed a handle on the mattress's side and dragged it out of the room. The stout guy waited for his partner to pass before carrying a single mattress up the staircase. Then the pair carried the bottom mattress together.

"You want us to leave bed on frame?" The stout one asked.

"Yeah. That would be a big help." O'Neill picked up part of the frame. "How's this work, anyway?"

The two men exchanged glances. "Here," the stout guy said. He took the metal from O'Neill and the men quickly put the frame together and set the bottom mattress on top of it. "You need help with the headboard?"

"Yes. I don't even have a screwdriver. Guess I could borrow one."

"No problem. We take care of it. No problem." The two spoke briefly in a language O'Neill couldn't identify, and the wiry one rushed down the steps, returning with a toolbox. It only took a minute before they had the board attached to the frame. "That is it," said the stout one. "Okay?"

O'Neill nodded and pulled a ten-dollar bill from his wallet. He was low on cash, but felt they deserved something. The wiry one waved him off, but he followed the pair down the stairs and the stout one finally took the money, nodding as he walked out.

Back in his room, he took his new sheets out of the closet and made the bed. There were two pillows still in plastic bags. He slid them out and wrapped them in brand new pillowcases.

With his back leaning against the door, he took the room in. The bed looked huge, but it was a massive improvement, and the pictures on the wall made it look like an actual home. He adjusted the chair and considered how to use his new end table. He thought about getting rid of the milk crate, but decided the television looked too small when it sat on the floor.

As he gazed in satisfaction at his bachelor pad, he thought of his sister and a pang of guilt overcame him. She had been more helpful than he had hoped, yet he thought she seemed lonely. He knew he had to find time to spend with her and Dawson. And then his thoughts turned to Vernon Cooper and his brother, Roman. He shut down the computer, showered, and got ready for work. He was eager to talk to Roman and hear the older brother's view of Vernon Cooper's disappearance.

Chapter 17

O'Neill bought two loaves of day-old bread at Sam's Subs and entered the Ryder Detective Agency shortly before noon. Ryder was at his desk, rummaging through a brown accordion file of what appeared to be vendor invoices. O'Neill muttered a good morning, slid behind his desk, and booted up his computer.

Ryder's lips moved as if he had a question but nothing came out, so O'Neill pulled up the current online edition of the *Wisconsin State Journal*. There was nothing on the website's front page, but the local section included an article that was accompanied by a photo of Vernon Cooper on a tractor. The farmer had darker hair than his son and a thick mustache and wore a green hat with no logo. It listed Vernon at two hundred and twenty pounds, which was heavier than what was stated in the earlier article.

The story focused on Vernon's disappearance and quoted Detective Martin Becker and Vernon's daughter, Annie. There was no mention of Stephen Cooper or his century-old disappearance. The story concluded by asking anyone with information to contact the Dane County Sheriff's Office.

O'Neill checked his cell phone and listened to a voice message from Randy Cooper that had come in at eight in the morning. The message said Cooper had concluded, based on a conversation with his neighbor, that the tractor would have been going two and a half miles per hour. O'Neill opened Microsoft Excel and verified his estimate that, if the tractor started at the curve along Cooper's Chance, it would have driven between nine and ten minutes before crashing.

While he was not supposed to be investigating anything, he rationalized that he was a witness and not an investigator, so he wasn't afraid to make a phone call. Roman picked up after one ring. O'Neill introduced himself, and Roman's gruff voice lightened. He asked for a moment, saying he wanted to step outside away from his kids. They spent several minutes talking about the disappearance.

"It's frustrating," Roman said. "People conflate things. My great-grandfather's brother disappeared a hundred years ago and my grandpa ran away a few times. Vernon disappears, and it's just another one gone. Everyone thinks all us Coopers are nuts."

O'Neill asked about the hundred-year-old vanishing of Stephen Cooper, but Roman suggested he talk to his aunt Mabel Purcell for more information. He said she was the unofficial family historian, and she had done research on the disappearance. O'Neill took her contact information, though he wasn't sure that talking to an old lady about the disappearance would accomplish anything.

When O'Neill turned the conversation to Marcie and Bobby Ring, Roman cut him off.

"The Rings were the first people I thought of," Roman said. "They blame Vernon for the death of their parents, so I told Detective Becker about them. He dug into it and talked with each of them. He came back yesterday and went through a timeline with me. It definitely shows that both the Rings were at work when Vernon disappeared."

"Randy told me that Bobby Ring was at some quarry when your brother disappeared and his sister was working at Hardee's."

"That's the gist of it. He was at Roger's Stone, which is southeast of Verona. I don't know the address."

"Roger's Stone, huh." O'Neill wrote it down. "Bobby was picking up a load, right? Where was he going?"

"There is a road project west of Verona. Becker said Bobby ran his dump truck all day between those two spots."

"How long to the quarry from the spot where your brother disappeared?"

"Maybe six miles. Driving time would be maybe ten minutes. Detective Becker told me that Bobby was in line at the quarry for ten minutes before

Vernon disappeared. The stone company logs in the trucks as they come in and logs them out as they depart. That's how he figured out that he wasn't involved. One of my buddies works at Roger's Stone, so he asked around for me. He spoke to the guy who checked Bobby in. This guy apparently knows Bobby by sight and swears it was him. They also check in the plate, and it matched the one assigned to him."

"What about his sister?" O'Neill asked as Ryder's phone rang. "If I remember correctly, her alibi wasn't as airtight as her brother's."

"She works at Hardee's in Verona. Detective Becker said she clocked in a minute after the 911 call came in. My daughter, Melanie, is sixteen. She works there too and saw Marcie show up. Becker could give you the exact information. My daughter says it's a mechanical clock, so that's probably why they're confident of the time. The Ring place is close to ten minutes from her work. There ain't no way someone could kidnap or hurt someone and get from where Vernon went missing to Hardee's that quickly, even if it took a few minutes to call 911."

"Yes, Randy shared a timeline with me, so I think I know what you mean. Did Becker talk to you about your activities?" O'Neill asked.

"Yes, he asked," Roman said with a chuckle.

"Did he treat you like a suspect?"

There was a pause. "I told them I was working in the shop with Greg. He's my hired man. I left for about twenty minutes when I ran to the hardware store for a filter. I don't know the exact time I left, but I think it was around three."

"You get a receipt? At the hardware store, I mean. Just thinking that might have the time on it."

"Sure. I gave it to Deputy Franklin, though I took a photo of it. Just a second while I find my camera." The phone went quiet for a few moments. "Okay. Just a sec. Here. It says I made the purchase at three fourteen that afternoon. Don't tell me you think I'm a suspect, too?"

"Can't ignore anyone or anything," O'Neill said. "Randy wants me to look at this from the angle that your brother didn't run away. When I think about you, I can't help but think about you being the older brother."

"And?"

"It makes me think of Stephen Cooper. He was the oldest son, but he didn't inherit the farm, which spurred his move to Wisconsin. Guess it seems like a similar situation."

"Look." Roman cleared his throat. "I may be the older brother, but back when my dad died, Vernon was the mature, responsible one. I was riding around on my Harley-Davidson while he was home milking cows. When my dad wrote up the will, he was right to leave the farm to Vernon. But he didn't leave me out of the will or anything. My mom was still alive, so it didn't seem to be that big of a deal. In essence, Vernon just continued doing the same thing he'd been doing. He continued to be the head hired man while I helped part time. I got money when my dad died and more when my mom died, so they didn't leave me empty-handed. Yes, it was not nearly the value of what Vernon got, but he deserved it. He was the one my father trusted and relied on."

"You're not bitter?"

"How can I be? Though I do wish my dad had lived longer. If he'd made it another five or ten years, he would have seen me mature. I think he would have given the farm to both of us, though that doesn't really matter, does it?"

"Suppose not," O'Neill said.

"I assume you'll ask about Patty. Becker did, though I don't think he knows anything."

"Course." Though O'Neill couldn't even think of who Patty was. "I was about to ask."

"She was in Randy's class," Roman said, "but we started dating when I was a junior and she was a freshman. It only went on for eight months. I may have been two years older than her, but I was the one who was immature. She dumped me because I had something on the side with Gina Klein and she found out. But I got over her. I was happy that Vernon and Patty got together."

O'Neill's eyes widened as he realized Patty was Roman's deceased sister-in-law. "So, your relationship with Patty ended before your brother married her? Correct?"

"Way before," Roman said. "Listen. I thought Vernon and Patty would be a good couple. I even tricked Vernon into asking her out." He chuckled.

"I called her and when she answered, I handed him the phone and set a piece of paper in front of him with a script. He would have never had the guts to ask her out if I hadn't tricked him into it, and the idiot wouldn't have known what to say if I hadn't written it out for him."

The line went silent. O'Neill's thoughts raced as he tried to think of another question. "It must've surprised you," he finally said, "when Vernon hooked up with Amy Ring. Did it disappoint you? I mean, you put in this effort to put them together and he ends up fooling around on her."

"Good Lord, yes!" Roman said. "I was stunned. And yes, he disappointed me, but so what? I'd disappointed him most of my life. I couldn't be self-righteous. Either way, Amy was the instigator. Vernon was too nervous and...passive to seduce anyone. She probably hit on him and he was too much of a wuss to tell her to stick it."

He fumbled for another follow-up, but Roman turned the topic to other potential enemies and relationships. The farmer soon announced that he had to go. O'Neill hung up the phone, realizing he hadn't asked about the argument the brothers had recently had. He glanced at Ryder, who was talking on another line.

Setting the notepad on his desk, he pulled out the timeline that Randy Cooper had collected from Detective Becker. He spent a few minutes rewriting it and adding his own information.

- 2:00 pm (approximately per Randy Cooper) — Vernon and Randy start in the field

- ? pm — Bobby Ring Jr. leaves work site west of Verona

- ? pm — Roman leaves home

- 3:14 pm (per unverified receipt) — Roman at hardware store

- 3:20 pm (per Wisconsin Quarry) — Bobby Ring Jr. checks in at quarry

- 3:24 pm (estimate) — Tractor starts on road

- 3:34 pm (estimate) — Tractor crashes

- ? pm — Roman gets home

- 3:37 pm (per Dane County 911 Center) — 911 call

- ? pm — Marcie Ring leaves for Hardee's

- 3:38 pm (per payroll records) — Marcie Ring clocks in at Hardee's

- 3:42 pm (estimate) — Randy Cooper at scene

- 3:45 pm (per Dane County Sheriff's office) — Deputy Leon Franklin on scene

- 3:50 pm (per Wisconsin Quarry) — Bobby Ring Jr. leaves quarry

- 3:52 pm (per Verona Fire Department) — Fire department on scene

As he reviewed the timeline, he heard Ryder's phone slam down followed by footsteps.

"Seamus, what in God's name are you working on?" The balding detective's paw planted on the edge of O'Neill's desk. "And I'm assuming you haven't read the draft report I sent you."

O'Neill was so deep in the details that it took him a moment to process the question. "Course not. Didn't even see it."

"What are you doing?"

"Just curious about this accident I was at, so I was asking a few questions and I made a timeline."

"I'm sorry you saw a car accident, but you will not investigate it. The sheriff's office is equipped to investigate car accidents or tractor accidents or whatever."

"This isn't just a tractor accident, it's a disappearance." O'Neill looked about the office, trying to find their copy of the *Wisconsin State Journal*. "Didn't you see the article in today's paper?"

"Yeah, I read it." Ryder sat in the chair opposite O'Neill and lifted his black shoes onto the desk. "Sounds like some guy was about to lose his farm and had a nervous breakdown. Straightforward."

"It's straightforward, but it's a murder rather than a disappearance."

Ryder laughed in his high-pitched squeal. "Where's that coming from?" The detective shot to his feet and slapped a hand on O'Neill's desk. "It's a guy running away from debts and a crappy life. What makes you think it's murder?"

O'Neill went through an explanation of the accident and Vernon's disappearance. He mentioned the thermos without fingerprints.

"I admit it's odd," Ryder said. "But who would want to kill some random farmer?"

"I've got six people who either hated Vernon Cooper or might benefit from his death," O'Neill said. "First, there are these two siblings, Bobby and Marcie Ring, who blame Vernon for their mother's death. He had an affair with their mother, leading to their father killing her five years ago. The kids blame Vernon. Then there's Cooper's brother, Roman, who got passed over in his parents' will. I don't really know if Roman would have wanted his brother dead, but I get the sense there was a conflict between them. Finally, there are Vernon's three kids. They would inherit the house and the land. Farms are worth some money, you know?"

"Seamus, I'm not stupid. I know farms are worth money. But how many farmers get killed by their kids so they can inherit the place? As for the others, it sounds like they have longstanding issues with the guy who disappeared. I mean, this affair was five years ago, and the brother got stiffed on an inheritance even earlier. Why would they wait all this time and kill him now?"

"Don't know yet," O'Neill said. "That's why I want to look into it. I also need to figure out who had the opportunity to commit the crime."

"Even if this was a murder, why limit the investigation to these people? If Vernon had an affair with one woman, why couldn't he have had an affair with another? Going with your argument that this is murder, it could mean a jealous husband, or a discarded lover. Though even that is speculation, since you don't even know if a crime has been committed."

O'Neill knew there was legwork to be done, but that didn't change anything. "The other part of this is the tractor. Why was it left in gear?"

"How the hell should I know? I'm a detective, not a farmer."

"The farmers don't know either. There is only one reason the tractor was left in gear on the road with no one behind the wheel."

"And why is that?" Ryder said, his voice rising.

"To cause a crash."

"Why would someone want a tractor to crash?"

"To set a time for the disappearance," O'Neill said. "And to establish an alibi."

Ryder opened his mouth as if he was going to shout out a reply. But nothing came out.

Chapter 18

Ryder asked O'Neill to go through the details of the accident and the disappearance once more, making notes as he listened. He appeared to be interested and agreed that the incident was perplexing, but he argued that many things in life were confusing. That didn't mean a crime had occurred.

"What do Becker and the sheriff's department think?" Ryder said.

O'Neill slid to the chair's edge. "Becker seems to assume Vernon left on his own. He probably thinks Randy helped his dad disappear or was aware of it. He likely views the tractor crash as a mistake or a diversion, and he thinks Vernon was having a breakdown because of crippling debt. It was also near the anniversary of Bobby Ring Senior killing his wife and himself, so Becker thinks the anniversary kicked Vernon over the edge. Also, there's a history of mental issues in the Cooper family. Vernon's grandpa was a boozer who would sometimes wander off when he got old. The last time he wandered off, they found him dead in a ditch. And then there's this one from a hundred years ago." He flipped through his notebook. "Stephen Cooper, who settled on the land, also disappeared."

"A family with a history of odd behavior," Ryder said as he returned to his desk. "No wonder Becker thinks that's the solution." He grunted as he fell into his chair. "Could be there's something in the Cooper genes that leaves them open to nervous breakdowns? Or it could be something else. Maybe he's having another affair with a married woman or something. She picks him up so they can go to another state to start a new life free from debt, annoying spouses, and whatever troubles they have."

"Randy doubts his dad would run away, as does his brother, Roman. The family may have some issues, but he doesn't sound like someone who would have a breakdown. Randy says the dad was solid as a rock."

"Seamus, kids don't see a complete picture of their parents." Ryder walked behind his desk and turned on the computer. "I'm siding with the sheriff's department on this one. The guy probably ran off. Odds are, he'll show up somewhere or come back home."

"What about the thermos?" He explained how there were no fingerprints on the thermos even though it was mostly empty and Randy Cooper claimed he touched it. "Someone wiped Randy and Vernon's fingerprints off the thing? Why?"

Ryder put a hand against his jaw. Then he shook his head. "I don't have an answer other than the random odd actions that we all take. Maybe Vernon took a swig just before leaving the tractor and wiped it off with a handkerchief or something."

"For no reason?"

"We all do odd things sometimes."

"Especially you." O'Neill got out of his chair and walked across the room, stopping in front of Ryder's desk. "There are six people with a motive to kill Vernon Cooper. Can't we dig into their alibis? If nothing breaks, then maybe you're right. But my guess is there will be a hole in one of them, and the tractor left in gear could be the key to identifying it. Can we work on this for a couple of days? That's all it should take to dig into them. We already know a lot about the Rings' alibis and some about the brother's. We'd just need to analyze them closer and get information on the kids."

"You were just talking to the brother, right? You said he got passed over in his parents' will?"

"When his dad died, he gave the farm to Vernon even though Roman was the older brother. Not sure about all the details, as the mother was still alive, but that's the gist of it."

"Is there a story behind why Roman didn't get at least a share of the farm?"

"Roman said he was a wild one when he was young and he still has a temper. Vernon was younger, but did the work to help his dad keep the farm running. The father didn't trust Roman, so he gave the farm to the one he trusted. It's the same thing that happened to Stephen Cooper a hundred years earlier."

"When did Vernon and Roman's father die?" Ryder asked.

"Early or mid-80s, I think. So fifteen years ago or more. He had heart issues and died of a heart attack in his early forties."

"Why would Roman kill his brother now?"

"Don't know. Though I wonder if the anniversary of Bobby and Amy Ring's murder suicide might have played into it. If you remember, Amy was having an affair with Vernon Cooper."

"Yeah. What's that have to do with Roman?"

"Roman once dated Vernon's wife."

Ryder laughed. "So what?"

"I'm just saying there was potentially bad blood between these brothers. It's worth looking into."

"Okay, I agree it's messy," Ryder said. "But even if he blamed his brother for his ex-girlfriend's death, why wait five years to act on it? That doesn't make any more sense than waiting fifteen years after being passed over in a will."

O'Neill scooted the chair closer to Ryder's desk. "It's the five-year anniversary of the Rings' death. Maybe Roman thought people would assume Vernon ran away, but if they thought there was something more, he may have assumed they'd look at the Rings first. Remember, that's exactly what happened. Both Randy and Roman mentioned them to the sheriff's department."

"But the Rings have an alibi." Ryder turned and looked out the window.

"Roman wouldn't have known that."

"Okay, I surrender," Ryder said after a pause. "Ten hours. I'll give you up to ten hours of my time pro bono. If it goes a minute over, you will pay. And if I go to Verona more than once, you'll pay the mileage."

O'Neill lifted a fist into the air.

Ryder was, however, concerned that it would look like O'Neill was investigating a case for the agency or on his own, so he called his contact with the state and summarized the situation. His concern was that if anyone notified the Wisconsin Department of Regulation and Licensing, it could impact his license application. He explained the accident and Vernon Cooper's disappearance and said that O'Neill wanted the Ryder Detective Agency to investigate the incident.

The state official said the agency could investigate the case with O'Neill as a client. Yet it would have to be Ryder who interviewed police officials, witnesses, and persons of interest and did surveillance or field work. O'Neill might take part as a witness or a client, but he could not perform investigative functions.

After hanging up the phone, the big detective reclined in his chair and tightened his tie. "Up to ten hours from me provided you toe the line. I am the one investigating, and I'll decide what steps to take. Do you agree?"

O'Neill nodded. "Course."

"And you'd better follow through since this really pisses me off. We've got clients waiting to pay, but I'm working pro bono." The burly detective tossed a pen against the wall. His eyes widened then seemed to relax. "I'm only doing this because I agree it shouldn't take long to verify alibis for the suspects you're talking about. And besides, I know you too well. You'll be worthless if you don't get your fix. If I don't do it, you'll investigate it yourself and do something stupid."

"I appreciate this. Especially you working for free."

"So are you, since I'm not paying you for any time you spend on it. If you want to accompany me on a visit to the sheriff's office or something, that's fine, but it will be on your time and not mine. And, for once, you can leave your stupid looking earring in and wear your sunglasses. People will think you're a wannabe rock star rather than a detective."

"Got it. This should be straightforward."

Ryder squealed out a laugh as he shook his head. "A gang banger shooting another gang banger is straightforward. A man disappearing on a tractor with no sign of the body or even of a crime is not straightforward."

"What I mean is that we've got an obvious motive and clear suspects. We just got to figure out whether one or more of them did it and exactly how. And if they didn't, we got to figure out who else might be involved."

"Wow. When you put it that way, it sounds like all we need to do is *fucking everything*. Like I said, we'll look into their alibis. If they all stand up, we're done, even if I haven't spent ten hours on it. Agreed?"

"Agreed."

Chapter 19

Ryder decided they should talk to the Cooper sisters. The older sister, Jenny, answered the phone after one ring, and they soon had a three o'clock meeting set at the Cooper farm. Annie Cooper's phone rang to voicemail, so Ryder left a message.

They had several hours before the meeting, so they stopped for lunch at Rocky Rococo. As they waited for their pizza, O'Neill filled a wax paper cup with water and grabbed a window booth while Ryder filled up on Coca-Cola.

The restaurant was in a small strip mall on Regent Street. O'Neill watched through the window as a vintage baby blue Mustang convertible pulled into the lot. The blonde-haired driver hopped out and made his way to the neighboring bakery. As Ryder sat down, a group of college-age women passed by and one pointed at the sports car.

The detective sat opposite O'Neill, carrying a tray. He dropped a box in front of O'Neill and flipped open the other. After taking a bite of his pizza, he announced that, after eating, they would go back to the office for an hour before heading to Verona.

O'Neill cut into his pizza. "Since we got time to kill, would you mind if I contacted that Purcell woman?"

Ryder pointed across the table with his fork. "Who the hell is *that Purcell woman?*"

"She's an aunt of the missing guy and the family historian. Roman told me she researched the vanishing of Stephen Cooper. He's the one who disappeared in the early 1900s."

"Sure, so long as you're not on the clock. I can't see anyone having an issue with you talking to some old windbag about someone who disappeared a century ago. Does this relate to Vernon Cooper's disappearance?"

"Probably not." O'Neill watched as the blonde guy tossed a white bag in the back seat of his Mustang and jumped inside without opening the door. "The cops are making assumptions about Vernon based on what his grandpa and his great uncle, or whatever he would be, did. I'm thinking this is a murder, but I shouldn't ignore the family history. I'd like to learn more."

"Are you hoping she'll meet with you right now?" Ryder laughed. "She might not even answer her phone."

"Roman gave me the impression that she'd love to talk about her research on Stephen Cooper, and I'm assuming she's retired, so she might be home." O'Neill pulled out his phone and found Mabel Purcell's contact information. "She lives on Kendall, which is within walking distance. Though you might need to pick me up on the way to our meeting with Jenny Cooper."

After six rings, an answering machine picked up. The automated male voice said the Purcells were not available. After the beep, O'Neill explained his interest in the research Mrs. Purcell had done on Stephen Cooper. Before he finished, a woman's voice came on the line.

"Hello," she said over the automated voice. "Just a minute. This darn thing. There." The automated voice stopped. "This is Mabel. Roman told you about my research?"

O'Neill could tell that she was smiling when she mentioned her research. "Yes," he said. "Roman suggested I talk to you. Would you have half an hour? I could stop over, or, if you prefer, we could talk on the phone."

"History is more interesting when you can look at it. You should come here since I have photos, maps, and historical documents. When would you like to talk?"

"Would half an hour from now work? Maybe one forty-five?"

"Um, let me see," Mabel said. "I need to find a few things and I have some files to organize, but I should be ready in half an hour. Did Roman give you my address?"

"Yes. You're on Kendall?"

"Yes. What was your name again?"

"Seamus. Seamus O'Neill."

"Interesting name. Okay, Mr. O'Neill. I'll be ready. When you arrive, knock at the front door, but be patient; I'm not too spry anymore."

"I will. Thank you. Excited to see what you have. Goodbye."

"You better get moving." Ryder gestured at O'Neill's slice. "That's a long walk and you've only got twenty-five minutes to get there." O'Neill cut off the crust with a fork and stuck it in his mouth. He motioned to Ryder, who grabbed the slice's cardboard box and slid it onto his tray.

"Have fun with your history lesson, but it's hot out, so make sure you're hydrated."

"Yes, Mom."

"At least I don't have to tell you to take your earring out."

O'Neill touched his ear, surprised the earring was not there. "What the?" He patted his pocket and found the ring safely inside. "Don't remember taking it out." He shook his head as he rose to his feet. "This in and out shit is messing with my head."

"Wait and put it in after meeting with the old lady. Old people don't trust guys who wear earrings."

"Right, Boss. Your wisdom is invaluable."

An ambulance maneuvered through lunchtime traffic as O'Neill walked to Mabel Purcell's house. Sunglasses and ice water teamed with a wispy cloud to protect him from the June sun. As he passed another pizza place, a group of men in suits and hard hats walked around the perimeter of the University of Wisconsin Field House's sandstone façade.

By the time he was halfway to his destination, his water was empty and sweat puddled on the rim of his sunglasses. He pulled his shades off and shook away the moisture. Then he peeled off his blue Mad City T-shirt and used it to fan his skin.

Ten minutes later, he spotted Mabel's house. It was small and white with a reddish roof interrupted by a skylight. The Purcell yard was well manicured and showcased a variety of flowers.

It was exactly one forty-five, but he stopped underneath a tree, fanning sweat from his head and torso. After a minute, he pulled the shirt over his sticky body and walked up the steps to the residence. After knocking twice, the door opened, revealing a short, thin, white-haired woman.

"Mr. O'Neill?" the woman said. He nodded, and she opened the door. "Don't tell me you walked here." She opened the screen door and held it until he took hold. "Where did you start from?"

"Rocky's on Regent Street."

"That's quite a way in this heat." She turned her back to him, and his gaze settled on the bend in her aged spine. "Let me get you some water and bring you a towel. In case you didn't put it together, I'm Mabel."

The room was dark, so he took off his glasses and waited, standing on a circular rug. He could hear a portable air conditioner running, but the room was warm. Two chairs, one leather and the other velvety red, sat in the room facing a console television. The wainscot-lined walls were peppered with photos. O'Neill's gaze moved along the color and black and white portraits.

The woman waddled back into the room holding a red hand towel. "You can use this to wipe your forehead and whatever else you need to wipe."

"Thank you very much," he said. He lifted the towel to his face, and a droplet fell from his nose, landing safely on the cloth. "I didn't realize how hot it was today."

Mabel turned her back to him again. "Let's go to the kitchen table. That's where I have my research. It's cooler in there anyhow."

He slipped off his sneakers and followed her down a short hallway. "So, Roman's your nephew?"

"You wouldn't think so, would you? All the Coopers are big and burly, except me." She looked back at him and smiled. "I'm the family runt."

A chuckle escaped O'Neill's lips. "That's okay. I come from a family of runts."

She glanced over her shoulder and smiled. "Yes. You are a runt, aren't you?"

Two neat stacks of materials sat on the kitchen table. Mabel negotiated her way around a chair and twisted into another. She let out a sigh as she sat, which evolved into a gentle laugh. She motioned toward the wooden chair across from her, so he took a seat.

"What, Mr. O'Neill, got you interested in the disappearance of Stephen Cooper?"

"I spoke with Randy and Roman. What happened to Vernon led to them mentioning it, but it struck me as an interesting puzzle, and I like puzzles. Then Roman said you had tried to solve it, so I was curious."

"Yes. I did research, but the mystery remains."

"You grew up at Cooper's Chance, right?"

"No." Mabel held up a finger. "There were two Cooper brothers that settled in the area. Stephen's property was Cooper's Chance, and it lay on the south side of what is now Chance Road. Solomon Cooper, my grandfather, built his place on what became County Highway M. The land of the two farms connected, but at the time, they were separate operations." She shuffled through several sheets before pulling out a map and sliding it in front of O'Neill. "You'll see this is a 1904 plat map of the Town of Verona. You can see plots for both properties, though it isn't very helpful because they listed both as 'S. Cooper.' One is for my grandfather, Solomon, and the other is for Stephen."

"Okay. That makes sense. When did this disappearance happen?"

"Stephen vanished on the eighteenth of May in 1904. He was plowing the field near the house. His nine-year-old daughter, Belle, brought him lunch at eleven-fifteen. He stopped working to eat, but he asked her to bring a pail of water for his horse, so she went to the well behind the house. The girl came back and the horse and plow remained, but Stephen was gone."

"How long would it have taken her to get the water?"

Mabel smiled as if she liked the question. "In the late 1950s, I tracked Belle down. She lived on a farm near Sun Prairie and was in her sixties, but she remembered the day her father disappeared as if it was yesterday. Belle said she was gone less than five minutes, which is why people assumed something was amiss." She slid a piece of paper from one of the two piles and spun it toward O'Neill. "This was the first article that was printed. It was in the *Wisconsin State Journal*."

The article was a faded yellow, but was taped onto white typing paper. At the top of the sheet, someone had written in blue ink, "Friday, May 20, 1904."

Stephen Cooper Suddenly Disappears from Verona Farm

The disappearance of Stephen Cooper, a Verona farmer, causes alarm and grief from his relatives. Cooper was plowing a field on his farm near Verona, shortly before noon on Wednesday. His daughter brought him lunch, but was sent back for a pail of water. When the daughter returned, Cooper was nowhere to be found. He has not been heard of since. His wife, three daughters, and other relatives and friends are at a loss to account for his disappearance.

O'Neill pulled the article close. "I would have been concerned that he disappeared after telling the girl to bring a pail of water. That sets a very short timeframe for when something occurred. It implies that something happened to him and he didn't just wander off. And if he ran off on his own, why ask his daughter to come back and risk her seeing him leaving? Were there follow-up articles?"

"There was one more article published two weeks later," she said as she put another sheet in front of him, "but it doesn't add new information."

"So they never found him?"

"Correct." She pushed her wire-rimmed glasses to the base of her nose. "However, Belle told me two things that were interesting. First, when she came back, Stephen's food was gone, and second, she said it was good that she went back to get the bucket since it was an unusually warm May day. The horse gulped down the water. That made me wonder. Maybe he didn't want to leave the horse hooked to the plow after working in the sun with nothing to drink."

He wiped his forehead as he looked at the map. Mabel apparently realized she had forgotten to offer him a drink of water. She apologized profusely and lifted herself out of the chair. She gave him a red tinted glass filled with water and three ice cubes.

"Where was I?" she said as she sat down. "Oh, yes. Stephen Cooper. Yes, well, two years later, the house caught fire and burned down. They declared Stephen dead, so his wife remarried, sold the land to my grandfather, and moved away. Grandpa knocked the barn down a few years after that. There were rumors and innuendo. As a child, I heard the story of Stephen's disappearance many times. It was like a ghost story. People said the land was haunted. Others said it was cursed or that it had been an Indian burial ground or there was a curse on the Coopers. My grandpa did not rebuild the barn or the house, though they used a shed that was on the property for many years. It was in the sixties when my brother knocked it down. There's nothing left of Stephen's place now except an old cistern and part of the windmill."

"What do you think happened? Do you think he ran away? Or was it something else?"

"I don't really know, but my grandpa once told me he got a letter from Stephen several years after he disappeared. He told me his brother was living out west under a different name. He said Stephen lived in Walla Walla. I remember that because it was a funny name for a city. But there was never any proof."

They talked for a few more minutes. She gave him a four-page writeup on Stephen Cooper and the Cooper family. The document included a copy of his photo and a family tree.

O'Neill's phone rang, and he glanced at a clock on the wall. He could hardly believe how long he'd been sitting in Mabel's kitchen.

"I hope you enjoyed our talk," she said. "I certainly have. Now let's pray we hear good news about my nephew Vernon. I doubt if he'll resurface in Walla Walla, but maybe the stories he heard inspired him. Maybe he planned to run away, or perhaps he saw his chance and went with it. Perhaps Stephen gave him hope to start his life anew."

"Perhaps."

"Where are you off to now?"

"I'm going to meet with Vernon's daughter, Jenny. Guess she does the farm books and such."

"Oh, poor Jenny," she said as they walked to the front door. "She is such a darling, and she's so bright. She took her mother's death so hard."

"And now she's got to deal with her dad's disappearance." O'Neill shook his head.

"Yes, it's hard." Her mouth hung open. "Make sure you send her my love. My husband and I enjoyed her staying with us. She's the closest thing we have to a daughter."

He glanced at the photos on the wall. "Jenny stayed with you?"

"Oh, yes," Mabel said. "Vernon and Patty had some...problems. Jenny fell out with her dad and refused to stay at home. Her grandparents died when she was young, so we always gave attention to her and her siblings. When things got difficult, she asked to stay with us, and I couldn't turn her down. Patty and Vernon agreed it was for the best."

"How long did Jenny live here?"

"The first time, it was only a few months."

"The first time?'

She nodded. "She was a junior in high school."

"And the second time?"

"It was during her senior year. She just showed up on our doorstep. The poor thing blamed her father for the problems with their parents' marriage. She stayed with us all the way until she started at the university. She spent a few summers here as well. This summer is the first one since her mother died that she's lived at home. We still have a bedroom set aside for her."

"So she didn't get along with her father?"

"No." She leaned forward as if she was going to whisper. "I think she blames him for her mother's illness."

"She took it all pretty hard."

Mabel nodded her head. "That, she did."

Chapter 20

R yder said he would pick O'Neill up in the parking lot next to a nearby bar. It was a short distance from Mabel Purcell's house, but staying on the sidewalk would triple the length of his walk. So O'Neill cut through an apartment building's grounds, hopped a fence, and was in the lot which the bar shared with a neighboring apartment building. Resting against the building's brownish-yellow façade, he took a sip of bourbon from his flask. As he stuck the flask back into his pocket, Ryder's black Chevy S-10 pulled in.

"How was your visit with the old lady?" Ryder said after O'Neill hopped inside.

"Fruitful."

"Fruitful?" He laughed. "Did she give you a piece of apple pie or something?"

Shaking his head, he shared Mabel's information about Jenny Cooper and her relationship with her father. The big detective nodded as he listened.

"We'll have to ask Jenny about it," Ryder said. "And about her alibi."

"Mabel also talked about Vernon Cooper. She thinks he may have used his great uncle as inspiration. She thinks Vernon ran away." He put his earring in, then rested his head against the window. "If she is right, I don't think it was a spur-of-the-moment thing. I think Vernon planned it. I'll look into things he did over the last few months. If he planned to run away, maybe there's something he did that would tip off where he went. Maybe there's some sort of pattern."

Ryder seemed to ignore the comment. "Do you have the address for the Cooper farm?"

"No, but it's on Highway M, and I got their home phone number and cells for Randy and Jenny. If we get lost, we'll call." He shut his eyes.

As they entered Verona, Ryder woke O'Neill, complaining there were quicker routes than going through town. They stopped at only one stoplight and soon they were in the countryside.

"There it is," O'Neill said, pointing at the farm. "Pull into their driveway. The one with the blue Harvester."

"All Harvesters are blue," the big detective said as he slowed the truck and turned onto the gravel driveway. They parked past the house at the edge of a circular path.

Before exiting the car, O'Neill heard barking. This time, Bernie ran to him. He crouched down, much as his sister had, and the black dog tried to lick his face. The door to the house opened and a young woman called to the dog. The dog rushed to her, allowing them to approach the house.

"Hello, I'm Jenny Cooper," the woman said. She was of average height and built as solidly as her brother. Light brown hair hung over wire-rim glasses. They shook hands as she tried to control Bernie. Opening the screen door, she ushered the detectives inside while keeping the dog outside.

"I appreciate you meeting with us on short notice," Ryder said, looking around the entry area. "I can't imagine the stress you and your family have been under these past few days."

"You're the ones helping us, so it's no problem." She brushed her hair back and stepped backward. "I've been working on the books and insurance issues and getting some cleaning done." She smiled, implying it wasn't as bad as it sounded. "Why don't we sit down and talk?"

The entry had a washer and dryer, several cabinets, and a small desk that appeared to be used for storage. She nodded toward the adjoining kitchen, and they followed her into the room, sitting at the wooden kitchen table. She brought Ryder coffee in a John Deere mug and O'Neill a can of Diet Coke. The sound of traffic through the open window was nearly constant.

"As you may know," Ryder said, "Seamus was at the scene of the accident when it happened. He works for me in an administrative role, but I asked him to come along since he knows details about the event."

She nodded, and O'Neill pulled out his pen and notepad, deciding he should look like he was doing something administrative.

"To start, I want to get a sense of your father," Ryder said. "I want to understand the type of person he is and the things he is interested in."

Jenny nodded her head slowly. "I don't know; he's just my dad. Like a lot of farmers I know, he works hard and has been working hard for his whole life. Farming is a way of life, you know. It is how he grew up. He enjoys working crops and seeing things grow. It is what he knows and loves."

"How is your relationship with him?" Ryder glanced at O'Neill, then back at Jenny. "Are you close?"

Her nodding sped up. "I wouldn't say we are close. I was closer to my mother, though Dad and I are more alike than I like to admit. We're both kind of introverted and we kind of hold things inside. When I was younger, there were times when we clashed. But since I got older, I think we get along better. I love him, even though it's not something I would necessarily say to him."

"Sounds complicated," Ryder said.

"I wouldn't say that. It was just that we all went through a very difficult time. You see, my mother got very sick when I was in high school. It was cancer. She passed away when I was a sophomore in college."

Ryder touched her shoulder, though only briefly. "I'm so sorry. And now your father is missing. This must be a difficult time."

"It is." Her head nodding slowed. "When mom got sick, everything changed. First, we stopped milking. Milking is a drag on time and is constant, so it wasn't easy to do without Mom. We had a hired man then, but we would have been in trouble if he left, as it would have been Randy and Annie as the only help since I was away at school. That wouldn't work since Randy and Annie were involved in sports and stuff at school. My dad still occasionally keeps steers, but that's all. After this last thing, we moved the steers to my uncle's place."

"Did your dad ever consider giving up the farm?" Ryder asked.

"No. Never."

"He enjoys farming?"

The nodding stopped as she laughed at the question. "Yeah. I guess so."

"What are his other interests?"

"He follows the Packers, the Brewers, and the Badgers. And the Bucks."

"Sounds like someone I know," O'Neill said, nodding to Ryder. "Does he fish?"

"He used to when he was young. He also played softball, but he stopped about five or six years ago. Occasionally, my parents bowled, but they quit when my mom got sick. Dad always said he would take it back up, but he never did." She dabbed her eyes with a Kleenex. "Or rather, he hasn't yet picked it back up."

"Bowling, huh," Ryder said. "Does he have close friends or people he socializes with?"

She sipped her coffee before answering, and the nodding returned in full force. "People he went to high school with still live in the area and there is his brother Roman. Since my mom died, Dad mostly just goes to family and community events like weddings and funerals. He also goes to Hometown Days, which is Verona's annual festival. That's about it. Farming is everything. It's his life."

"How about women? Has he dated anyone since your mother's passing?"

"Twice since Mom died. At least, that's all I know of. They're both local women. I'll write their names down if that's helpful." Her eyes bounced between O'Neill and Ryder. "You probably heard about...Amy Ring."

Ryder sipped his coffee before responding. "Your brother told us that your father had an affair with Amy a few years before they diagnosed your mother with cancer. That must have been upsetting."

"It was, though having an affair was out of character for my dad." She licked her lips. "I couldn't believe it happened, but it did. I know it did since he admitted it. It led to a lot of problems between us, so I'm not one to make excuses for him, but he had known Amy since high school. He said it started with him trying to help her since he knew her husband abused her." Jenny's eyes widened, yet her head's slow nodding continued. "Mr. Ring was scary when he drank. I think Dad got too close to Amy, and it turned into something it should not have."

"How did your mom handle the affair?"

She rubbed her cheeks with both hands. "About how you would think she would. She felt betrayed, completely betrayed. But she eventually forgave him. I think her faith helped. Father Brennan, the pastor at Verona's Catholic Church, helped a great deal. He convinced her to forgive Dad. He convinced her it was the Christian thing to do."

O'Neill wrote the name in his notepad.

"How did you and your siblings handle it? It must have been upsetting to your whole family."

"Without a doubt. I couldn't believe Dad would do that to her." Her nodding switched from up and down to side-by-side. "But Mom wanted us to forgive him. She expected it. She told us he needed and deserved our forgiveness."

Ryder set the coffee cup on its saucer. "And you did?"

She nodded a few times before answering. "Eventually. Forgiving was easiest for Randy. It took a few years before Annie and I forgave him. It was only after our mother had passed."

"How about your uncle?"

Her nodding slowed, and her forehead scrunched together. "You're asking whether Roman was upset about my dad having an affair?"

"Yes."

"I don't know; I never talked to him about it."

Ryder and O'Neill exchanged glances. Then the big detective cleared his throat. "I recognize this might be an insensitive question, but we are trying to determine if anyone had a reason to hurt or threaten your father. Someone besides the Ring siblings."

"If you're going to ask whether Dad had other affairs, the answer is no," Jenny said. A smile slid onto her face. "He swore that there hadn't been anyone else and that there wouldn't be anyone else. That's what he told me and that's what he told my mother. That was your question, wasn't it?"

"Yes, it was," Ryder said. "How about after your mother's passing? You said he had two dates, correct?"

"Yes. A blind date sort of thing, and a date with a local woman who was recently divorced. Keep in mind that I have been living on or near campus in Madison for the past four years, so I wouldn't know everything. Annie has lived here the past few years and Randy has all his life. I asked both, and they said there hasn't been anyone special."

O'Neill leaned closer to Ryder and whispered, "Ask about Roman."

Ryder nodded, then looked at Jenny. "How is your dad's relationship with Roman? I understand that they sometimes don't get along."

"Roman?" Her nodding slowed. "Sure, they argue. That's what brothers do. They're very different people, but they love and care for each other. When I had problems with my dad, I usually went to Roman for help and advice. Him and Aunt Mabel. She's actually my dad's aunt, but I am very close to her."

"Aunt Mabel, hmm," Ryder said, as if he had never heard the name before. "Okay. Let's switch gears. Tell me about the business-end of the farm."

"Yes, of course." For the first time, her head stopped nodding. "I helped my mom with the books even before she got sick, and I've managed them since she passed, even when I didn't live here. There are, however, a few things, such as taxes, that I work with an accounting service on, and Annie helped with some day-to-day things when I wasn't onsite. Now I do almost everything. Doing the books got me interested in accounting. I'll graduate in December and will be eligible to sit for my CPA exam."

"Speaking of the books," Ryder said, "I got the sense from your brother and the sheriff's office that the farm is struggling. The implication is that your father might even lose the farm. I also had the impression that the sheriff's office thinks these business struggles weighed heavily on your father. What's your read on how the business is doing?"

"Dad is a worrywart and can be Mr. Doomsday." Nodding again, her gaze bounced between the men. "He is always worrying, and Randy hears him and ignores me. But fretting is what farmers do. It doesn't mean that the farm is being run into the ground. The biggest concern my dad had was about our move away from dairy and its impact on cash flow. Milk prices vary a ton, but not nearly as much as the weather. And my dad struggles with the time lag between planting and harvesting crops. Everything is going gangbusters, then there's flooding or drought and it goes to the birds. That's farming."

"Sounds worse than running a detective agency," Ryder said.

"I wouldn't know about that," she said with a nervous laugh.

"So your view is that the farm is struggling, but not going under?"

"We've lost money three of the last four years, but most of that is because of our abrupt departure from dairy. We had contracts and equipment that we had to get out of or to sell at a loss. But our farm revenue is still over three hundred thousand, and our expenses have balanced out. My dad is not only a hard worker, but he is methodical. He planned for the long-term and has the discipline to stick to plans. Dad doesn't do anything fancy or plant experimental crops. He takes the safe, consistent route, manages what crops he plants, and focuses on the viability of the land. It pays off. I expect we'll be in the black this fiscal year, assuming he returns or Roman helps enough."

"Are there businesses or people that you owe a ton of money to? Or is there someone looking for you to go under so they can acquire the land? Once again, I'm trying to determine if anyone benefits from your father's death or departure."

"The farm is worth a good deal of money because it is good farmland, but we're far enough outside Verona that developers are not interested in the property, even if they could get it re-zoned. I can't imagine anyone wanting us to go bankrupt so they could buy the land." She shook her head side to side, then stopped. "As to loans, we certainly owe to the bank and the co-op. That's the nature of farming. You don't rely on cash flow to buy crops in the spring and you don't have the cash to buy a new combine. Our situation is far from ideal, but it's nothing unusual or extreme. Running a family farm is always a struggle."

"Who gets the farm if something happens to your father?" Ryder asked. "Does your dad have a will?"

"Yes. My parents worked with a lawyer in town after Mom got sick. It's a little complicated because it gives Randy the option to keep the farm running. Yet all three of us would have an equal share. We'll split everything evenly."

"Were you here on that day?" Ryder asked. "Were you here when your father disappeared?"

"No. I was at a WICPA symposium. That is the Wisconsin Institute of Certified Public Accountants. They had a symposium on small business accounting in downtown Madison, and I helped. The last session ended at three and I was home at maybe four fifteen. When I pulled in, Randy was inside with that woman deputy — Deputy Patterson or maybe Peterson."

"Was your sister home yet?"

"No, she usually works at church until five, but Randy had called her at work. She wasn't there. Eventually she called and got home shortly before five."

Ryder and O'Neill exchanged a few words, but after a moment of silence, Ryder went with his own questions. "Before we wrap up, could you tell me what you think happened to your father?"

Jenny nodded her head again as she stared straight ahead before answering. "I don't know. I can't imagine him having a mental breakdown, as the sheriff thinks. First, I don't think he dwelt on the anniversary of Amy Ring's death. As for Dad's worries about the farm, I don't think they understand him. I tell them he's methodical, and they infer he's a control freak. I tell them he's a worrier, and they decide he's depressed. The sheriff's office wants to think the worst, since it supports their theory that he had a breakdown. But I must admit that I don't have an explanation, since I don't know of anyone who would want to hurt him."

"Including the Rings?"

"Oh, no. Bobby and Marcie hate him more than anyone could hate anyone. If there's anyone that would want to hurt Dad, it's the Rings."

Chapter 21

The sound of beeping interrupted the discussion. Jenny stood and walked through the kitchen and into the entry area, which she called the porch. Ryder mouthed something, but O'Neill didn't understand him. Then Ryder touched his own shirt and O'Neill realized Jenny was doing the laundry.

"Sorry about that," she said after a brief wait. "Randy and Dad go through so many clothes. It's like we're doing laundry all day." She returned to the table. "Where were we again?"

"You were telling us that the Rings didn't like your dad," Ryder said, "but they have alibis. Do you think one of them might hire someone to hurt your father?"

Her nodding returned, then turned to a shake. "If Marcie wanted to hurt Dad, she'd do it herself."

"Sounds like she's quite the prize," O'Neill muttered.

Ryder gave him a dirty look. "I understand why they would be angry with him, but that level of hatred is uncommon."

"Bobby Senior convinced his kids that my dad seduced their mom. Which is funny, since even my mom said he wouldn't be able to seduce anyone." Jenny snorted and looked out the window as a green tractor drove past. "Mom even joked about it. She told me he would need to write up a seduction plan outline and refer to which step he was on. I think that's one reason she forgave him. He isn't a passionate person; he is methodical, quiet, and awkward." She smiled, and the nodding slowed. "He talks to himself more than to anyone else. When the affair happened, she was sure Amy was more to blame than he was. But Bobby Junior and Marcie believed their dad, even though he was the one that killed their mom. He controlled them and continues to control them from the grave. Crazy."

"Yeah, crazy," O'Neill said.

"If Bobby Junior and Marcie wanted to harm your father, who would lead the charge? Is one of them the leader?"

"Marcie, without a doubt." The speed of her nodding increased. "She's not only older, but she's a puppet master. She was in my class in high school. Before her mom died, she was the leader of what I would call the *in* clique at school. She was on prom court and was the popular, pretty girl that the guys wanted to date and the girls either wanted to be like or were afraid of. The only thing she lacked was money."

"This was before her parents died?"

"Yes. It was senior year when they died, and Marcie melted down. All she wanted to do was to make life hell for my sister and me. She did all sorts of mean things to us."

"Such as?" Ryder said.

Jenny looked down and rubbed her thumbnails together. "A few of her friends convinced me that Pete Meadows liked me and wanted me to ask him to this one dance where the girls ask the boys. She convinced Pete to record me asking and him...torching me." She rubbed her eyes again, but switched to a smile. "Marcie played it to everyone."

"Like I said, she sounds like a real prize," O'Neill said. "And this Pete Meadows guy sounds like a dick as well."

"Yeah, I hated her, and I blamed my dad a bit. But I can't help feeling a little sorry for Marcie. It all burned through her." She looked up at Ryder. "Marcie is smart, you know, and was accepted by the UW before me. She was going to study accounting, just like me, but she failed out after a semester. She also got fired from her part-time job at the UW Veterinary School after getting caught stealing drugs. Now she works at Hardee's making minimum wage. Nothing wrong with that, but she could do more. Her father ruined her. She was mean before, but she wasn't what she is now."

"How about Bobby Junior?"

"He's a jerk, but at least he doesn't give me the finger when I see him drive by. Randy knows him better than I do, so he might think differently, but Bobby at least has a decent job. He probably makes twice as much as she does. He's the one that keeps their household afloat."

"Bobby and Marcie live together?"

"They got the farm after their parents died, but they auctioned off everything except the second house, which their parents had used for the hired man. That house is where they live."

"Do you have their address?" Ryder asked.

"It's about three quarters of a mile from here as the crow flies." Pointing away from the highway, Jenny reached across to a small table beneath the phone and grabbed the phone book. She flipped through pages. "Here it is," she said, setting a page in front of Ryder that included a basic map. "I'll look up the address for you and write it down."

O'Neill took a last drink from his Diet Coke as a pickup truck drove past the house and turned left onto the highway. "Is that Randy leaving?"

She nodded. "There's a part he has to get in town."

"Is Annie home?" O'Neill asked. "We haven't met her."

"Annie's at work. She works part-time as a secretary for the City of Verona and part-time for the church. She'll be home shortly after five."

Ryder thanked Jenny for her time and she led her guests outside, allowing them to get to the truck without interference from Bernie. "Can I leave Seamus here for a few minutes?" Ryder asked as he stood beside the pickup. "I want to stop at the Rings' place. Maybe I'll be lucky and one of them is home. If so, Seamus probably shouldn't be at a suspect interview. I'll be back to pick him up, okay?"

"Sure, that's fine," she said, holding Bernie in her arms.

"I'll be back soon." Ryder got into the truck.

"Just a sec." O'Neill opened the door and jumped into the passenger seat. "What are you doing? Why can't I go?"

He started the engine. "I'm thinking we should have dug further into the head-bobbing Jenny Cooper. I want you to talk to her some more."

"Thought I wasn't allowed to interview people?"

"Don't interview her," he said as he glanced into the rearview mirror. "Just let her talk a bit about her dad and everything. See if she opens up."

O'Neill felt exhausted and needed a drink. The last thing he wanted to do was to sit inside and talk with Jenny. But he realized his boss had a point. "Why don't we both stay and interview her longer?"

"I couldn't handle more of her perpetual nodding. It was driving me crazy. But as we got to the truck, I realized we should have stayed longer."

"I would have asked questions, but I figured you would have yelled at me. At least it allowed me to listen to your 'speaking of the books' lead-in. That was smooth."

"Screw you," Ryder said. "Just figure out whether she's an open book or a master bullshitter. It's one of the two. We know her father's affair put her through a lot and she wasn't exactly forthcoming about the clashes she had with him. I'll be back after meeting with their lovely neighbors, the Rings."

"What if they aren't home?"

"Then I'll call them later today or tomorrow." Ryder slipped the vehicle into drive. "One thing for sure is that this is the only time I plan on coming out here. Hopefully, I will catch them in person. If there's dirt on the Coopers, they'll give it to us. They may even point their fingers at Roman or the Cooper kids." He paused as he looked into his rearview mirror. "Our suspect is waiting for you."

O'Neill got out of the pickup and looked toward Jenny, who waved him over. He looked back at Ryder and heard Bernie approaching. He wanted to give his boss the finger, but he just slammed the truck door shut and crouched down to prepare for the dog galloping toward him.

Chapter 22

The dog ran circles around O'Neill as the truck pulled onto the highway. Jenny slipped into the house, and a breeze blew dirt into the air. He looked up at a group of low-lying clouds and wondered whether they would dump rain onto the fields.

As he got to the porch, Jenny stepped outside. Throwing a dog treat onto the grass, she waved O'Neill inside.

"He's keyed-up," she said, as the screen door slammed behind her. "I figured it was best to distract him so you could get inside." She closed the main door and O'Neill heard the dog run onto the stoop. "Do you want another soda or a beer or something?"

"I could use a beer," he said, suddenly glad he hadn't gone to the Ring residence. "Been a long day."

She opened the refrigerator and, after a search, pulled out a Natural Light. A light beer was not his preference, but it was better than nothing. "Do you want a glass or is the can okay?"

"Can's fine." He popped the lid and gulped down half the contents. "Thanks. Tastes good for a light beer. Helps that I was ready for one."

"Anything else I can get you while you wait?"

He meandered to the kitchen table and spotted a host of newspapers and magazines on one chair. "Mind if I read your paper?"

"Please do. I'm going to get back to work. If you want another, you're welcome to grab one from the fridge."

"Appreciate it."

Jenny walked into the next room. He heard a computer beep and he imagined her at a desk, staring at a spreadsheet. As he paged through an agricultural newspaper, he tried to think of questions, but his thoughts wandered to the farm records she was working on.

Once the can was empty, he set it on the counter and opened the refrigerator. The shelves were full, and a slice of watermelon inside a plastic bag fell out, landing on his knee. He balanced the fruit atop a jar of pickles and opened a drawer before finding two light beers. Flipping the tab on one, he took a sip, and called out Jenny's name.

"Could I ask you a question about the farm's records?" he said. It wasn't the type of question Ryder wanted him to ask, but he thought it might lead somewhere.

Jenny appeared at the kitchen entryway. "Sure. What do you want to know?"

"How does your dad spend money? I don't mean to sound stupid, but does the farm pay for everything? Or does your dad pay for personal stuff out of his own money and farm stuff out of farm money? I'm trying to determine whether his recent spending might cast light on his frame of mind, but I don't even know where to look."

"You have it right. Dad has a personal checking account and a credit card for non-farm expenses and separate accounts for the farm. The personal accounts are not part of the records I manage, though I have online access to his bank and credit card accounts." She waved him into the next room and sat in front of a desktop computer. He leaned over as she navigated to a credit card website and logged in.

She pointed at the screen. "As you can see, there has been no activity on his credit card since Monday."

"Makes sense."

"As for the farm, we keep the books on an accounting program." She closed out the website and logged into another system. "All the business transactions flow into this. I import them from the farm bank and credit accounts and create journal entries for other things." She looked up at him. "Does that make sense?"

It didn't, but he nodded.

"The Sheriff's Office asked for copies of the farm's books, his personal credit card, and checking account. Do you want me to email the same files to you? It will have everything. I do, however, want you to delete the files when you're done with them."

He nodded, so she sent him an email with the files as he stood behind her. He assumed it wouldn't lead anywhere, but if Vernon Cooper had planned his escape, some information must hint at it.

"Another question about the farm," O'Neill said. "How is it run? Is it a partnership or a company or something?"

"My parents incorporated the farm years ago. It's called VEPA, Inc. That's for the first two letters in each of their names."

"Okay," he muttered. "What does that mean if your dad passes? Who owns the company?"

She swiveled the chair, turning away from the computer. "After Mom died, Dad became the sole owner of VEPA. When Dad dies, the three of us kids will inherit the corporation's stock."

"So this is all one big company, huh?" O'Neill muttered, looking around the room.

"Not quite. VEPA owns the farm equipment, extends futures contracts, and owes for loans. But it doesn't own the land. Dad owns the land and the real property attached to it. That would mean the house, the barn, and the sheds."

This time it was O'Neill who nodded. He tried to remember what Topper had told him about inheriting land. "Does the deed to the land define who gets the farm? Can't the deeds pay someone on death regardless of what the will says?"

She looked surprised by the question. "Yes, of course. Transfer on death is common for property and investments."

"What's your farm's deed say?"

"I assume it will be transferable on death to the three of us, as I'm assuming they updated the deeds when they redid the will. I know where Mom kept them. Let me go see."

She walked into another room and O'Neill looked about the desk and the nearby filing cabinet. It was tempting to open a drawer, but he resisted the urge. When she returned, she was holding a manilla folder.

"Find 'em?" O'Neill said. Jenny stared straight ahead and her head was not nodding. She stepped closer to him and held out a folder.

"Three parcels go to me, Annie, and Randy." She swallowed hard, and her eyes locked onto his. "The other three go to Roman."

"Roman gets the land? What the hell?"

The nodding started again. "My thoughts exactly."

"Your dad did this? Why?"

She teetered slightly, as if she might lose her balance. He reached out, guiding her to the chair.

Fifteen or twenty seconds passed before she spoke. "I wonder if Roman knows?" After taking several large breaths, the nodding stopped. "Can you do me a favor?"

"Course."

"Don't tell anyone about this. Not yet." Her eyes locked onto O'Neill's. "Let me talk to Roman first. I doubt he knows. What will the police think?"

"They'll think he might have something to do with your dad's disappearance."

"Let me talk to him first." She grabbed his hand. "Please. Let me tell him. I think he'll be stunned and, if something happened to Dad, he might even write the deeds over to us."

"What are we talking about, money-wise? Are those the most valuable plots or something?"

"No." She released his hand. "They are the sections that were part of Cooper's Chance. They're valuable farmland, but they don't include the house. It's maybe forty percent of the real property, but it would be debt free. Randy, Annie, and I get all the loans and the corporation, but only half the land. That would be difficult." She looked at the ceiling and around the room. "Very difficult."

A vehicle coming up the driveway interrupted them. O'Neill returned to the kitchen and spotted Ryder's truck. "Looks like it's my boss. That was quick."

She followed him into the kitchen. "It's okay if Mr. Ryder knows, but don't tell the sheriff or anyone else. Not yet. I'll tell Roman tonight. Then he can go to the sheriff's office tomorrow. They'll certainly think better of him if he tells them about it, won't they?"

"Can't hurt," he said.

"Promise?"

"Just until tomorrow. But make sure Roman knows that Ryder and I know about it. Don't let him think that you're the only person who knows about the deeds." The last thing he wanted was for Jenny to disappear.

"Oh, thank you!" She grabbed his hand again and, for a moment, he thought she was going to kiss his fingers. Then she released him and walked to the porch.

He returned to the office area, paging through the deeds again and making sure he saw Roman Cooper's name on a document. Hearing the door open, he polished off the remains of his beer and left the empty can on the counter. As he stepped outside, Bernie ran from Ryder's truck to Jenny's outstretched arms. A cloud of dirt and dust hung in the air.

"Someone was at the Ring home," Ryder said as he got out of the pickup, "but he or she wouldn't answer the door."

"It's probably Marcie, since Bobby probably isn't home from work yet." Jenny's head nodded and there was a tremor in her hand. "She probably thought you're a salesman or a bill collector."

"Is that what you would think if I came to your door?" Ryder asked.

She nodded. "Especially if you came to the front door."

"I tried to call them as well," he said to O'Neill. "I could hear the phone ringing, but no one picked up and there was no answering machine."

O'Neill leaned against the pickup. "Maybe we can come back when Bobby's around."

Ryder laughed. "If that's how you want to use up your pro bono hours, that's fine, so long as you pay for my mileage. It's too bad. I think she'd want to talk with us if she knew what information we were trying to get at. I'll try a call tomorrow."

Jenny sat on the grass alongside the gravel driveway. She looked exhausted. "Do you really think Marcie or Bobby would talk to you?" Her lips quivered when she spoke.

"This might sound bad," Ryder said, "but I want to give them an opportunity to criticize your dad. I was going to tell them I wanted to hear about your dad's bad side. If they are the haters they seem to be, they'll talk about him. And if someone besides the Rings doesn't like your dad, they won't be afraid to tell us. That could be the lead we need."

"That's actually a good idea." She pointed at O'Neill. "Send him to their house. If Marcie's there, she won't think he's a salesman."

Ryder laughed. "You're right there. But would she open the door to him? Wouldn't she think he was lost or something?"

She bit her lip. "If he took out the earring and changed his shirt, he might pass as one of Bobby's friends."

O'Neill looked down at his blue Mad City T-shirt. "Suppose no one in Verona would wear this."

"Let me go grab one of Randy's shirts." She got to her feet and went inside. Bernie tried to join her, but she closed the screen door quickly, leaving the dog on the concrete stoop.

O'Neill found a stick underneath a nearby tree and threw it across the driveway. Bernie obligingly ran after it, returning in only a few seconds. He tossed it again, but Bernie stayed beside him, as if out of energy.

"Okay," Ryder said. "If she's right and Marcie's at the Ring house, tell her you're there to let her know I want to talk to her about Vernon Cooper's dark side. Ideally, she'd let me come over. If not, she can call me, or we can arrange a time."

"Course," O'Neill said, though he intended to ask the questions himself.

Jenny came outside carrying an orange Menard's T-shirt. She handed it to O'Neill. He held up the shirt. It said, "Race to Savings" on the front and included a picture of a stock car. It was at least two sizes too big, but it would do.

He pulled off his T-shirt and replaced it with the Menard's shirt. Jenny looked away, as if not wanting to intrude on his privacy. He took out his earring and stuck it in a pocket. "How do I get there?" he asked as he tossed his own shirt into the truck.

"Oh, yeah," Ryder said to her. "We have another problem; Seamus can't drive."

"DWI?" Jenny mouthed.

"No. Seamus has never driven before. That's just as well as it's prevented him from having a chance to drink and drive."

She turned toward O'Neill, and her eyes squinted. "Can you drive a four-wheeler?"

Ryder stepped between them and pointed at O'Neill. "Don't let *him* on your four-wheeler. Maybe I can take him to the corner and he can walk, though I don't want Marcie to see me dropping him off."

Jenny was no longer shaking, and her usual slow nod had returned. "He can borrow my old bicycle. It will just take him a few minutes to bike there." She walked back inside the house and opened the garage door. They followed her to the garage, where she pulled out a Schwinn bicycle. It looked like they built it for an off-road biking middle-schooler.

Both tires were semi-flat, so Jenny pulled out a hand pump and blew them up. When she was done, O'Neill sat on the bike. His legs churned and his knees hit the handlebars. "Suppose this will do."

"Do you know where you're going?" Ryder said.

He gestured in the same direction that Jenny had. "That way."

Chapter 23

The two men lifted the bike over the tailgate. Ryder said he would bring O'Neill to Chance Road. This would allow him to avoid biking on the highway and minimized the chance of him getting lost. Jenny waved as the truck turned onto the highway.

"I wonder what Marcie will think if she spots you biking up her driveway," Ryder said. "Maybe she'll run you off her property."

"Long as there's not a dog."

"When you're done, head back and call me. I'll pick you up at the same spot I leave you. All you need to do is to take a right onto a gravel road and then a left on the first blacktop road. The Ring house is the first one on the left. You can't miss it."

As they drove, O'Neill noticed that the field Cooper had tedded two days earlier was clear of hay. The truck stopped at the intersection, and Ryder pointed at a red tractor in the other hayfield. A bailer was connected to the vehicle, and a full trailer followed. They had seen Randy Cooper leaving the farm in his truck, so O'Neill assumed Roman was behind the wheel, though it could have been anyone they hired to rake and bale the hay. If it was Roman in the tractor, he wondered whether the farmer realized he was going to inherit the land he was currently working on.

The truck stopped, and O'Neill got out. He hopped onto the back step of the pickup and vaulted into the cab. Lifting the bike over the truck's tailgate, he set it on the pavement. The Schwinn bounced lightly before falling to its side. He stood the bike up and sat on its saddle.

Once the bicycle started moving, he stood, putting his weight on one pedal at a time. Unlike city roads, there was no parking or bicycle lane, so he rode near the edge of the blacktop. He looked sideways at the clump of bushes on Cooper's Chance and continued forward. At regular intervals, he glanced backward, worried he would see an approaching vehicle. As he came to a stop sign, he rode up a slight incline and stopped at the intersection. Then he heard a distant rumbling. Looking back, he saw a semi approaching. Rather than staying on the pavement, he pulled the Schwinn into a mix of weeds and gravel and stood waiting for the truck to pass. It was a Peterbilt with no trailer. He waved as the vehicle eased up the hill and the driver waved back.

The semi went straight, so O'Neill waited for the dust to clear before turning right onto the gravel road. The bike bounced on the uneven ground and when he braked, the bicycle slid sideways. He navigated the hill, bouncing until arriving at another stop sign. A light blue house to his left caught his attention. He was sure it was Marcie and Bobby Ring's, and his legs pumped as he turned onto a blacktop road and then onto the dirt driveway.

The house had black shutters and white shades. A garage with two black doors sat on one side of the driveway. Gliding behind the house, he saw a silver Ford Taurus parked on the grass. Dents were in the front and back bumpers.

Tilting the bicycle against a pole, he spit road dust into the dirt and noted the thick imprint of tire tracks on the ground. The tracks were large enough that he assumed they were from either a tractor or a large truck. Leaving his sunglasses on, he took a nip of bourbon from his flask and knocked on the door. Through the curtains, he could see movement and he heard the faint sound of a woman's voice.

The inner door opened. A woman in her early twenties with highlighted hair and wide brown eyes gave him a brief look. She pushed the screen open and O'Neill stepped inside while she held a cell phone to her ear.

The entryway was six feet deep. Two pairs of boots and a pair of tennis shoes sat on one side, and yellowish gloves and two hats sat on a small bench. The woman turned away from him, so he followed her into the kitchen.

She was in a blue shirt and cutoff jean shorts and was barefoot. Bracelets hung on both wrists and a silver anklet circled one ankle. Her legs were tan and smooth. He admired the view as she bent down and opened a filing cabinet. She slammed a drawer shut.

"There's one payment for two hundred from Bobby on May the twenty-first," she said into the phone as she walked toward O'Neill, "and then one on my credit card for a hundred and fourteen twenty-six on June the fourth. I've got the receipts and the credit card statements right here. We're good. Right?" She looked at O'Neill and rolled her eyes, implying the person on the other line was an idiot. "Okay then. Send me a revised statement. Right." She hung up the phone and looked at him. "Fucking septic assholes. Shit. They claimed we hadn't paid them in full when we had. One more thing and I'll be with you. Okay?"

"No problem," he replied.

She dialed a number and started another conversation. "Yeah, this is Marcie Ring. Yeah. Bobby said he wants it tomorrow at the latest. If we're not here, just have them leave it inside in the entry, okay? We only lock up at night. Right. Thanks." She hung up and turned toward O'Neill. "Sorry about that. We're waiting for a delivery. Donny, right?"

"Huh?"

"Donny?"

He realized she thought he was someone else. "Me? No. I'm Seamus, not Donny."

"What the fuck is a Seamus?"

"That's my name."

She rolled her eyes. "I thought you were someone else. What do you want?"

He pulled out a business card. "I'm from the Ryder Detective Agency."

"*You're* a fucking detective?" She spit out a laugh, then leaned against the kitchen entryway. Sunlight sparkled off her right earring. "What do you want?"

"My boss is investigating the disappearance of Vernon Cooper, and he was hoping you could help us." He spoke quickly, trying to get everything in before she could interrupt him. "We know you had nothing to do with it, but we were hoping you knew someone who might have an issue with Vernon. Someone who, unlike you and your brother, might not have an alibi."

"I had nothing to do with it and don't know anything about it, so get the fuck out of here." She turned away and stuck the file into the cabinet. "Besides, everyone knows it was just another Cooper running away." She shook her head. "Damn detectives."

"People act as though Cooper had no enemies besides you two," he said. "I can't believe that's true, and I thought you or your brother might tell me if Cooper was up to anything or if he had other enemies. I'm hoping you might tell me things that other neighbors might not."

Marcie slammed the cabinet door shut, then paused and seemed to stare at his feet. "I didn't know Vernon Cooper very well," she said. "I only know what he did to my family. And while I don't know about his enemies, I know he was seeing someone. Julie Ryan. She's divorced from Scooter Ryan. Could be he's pissed about her dating him." She looked up. "No idea, so I'm not accusing anyone of anything."

"Vernon's children never mentioned her," he said.

Marcie laughed. "They're fucking clueless. Julie and Scooter bowled with the Coopers, but I don't know when they started hooking up. Otherwise, I'd look closer to home. Talk to Kaiser. He's the only Cooper worth talking to."

"Who is Kaiser?"

"Jesus!" she yelled. "You say you're a fucking detective?" She shook her head. "I have to get ready for work. You need to leave. Now."

O'Neill backed away as Marcie closed in. He looked at her while he reached for the doorknob. "Thanks for your help." Pushing the screen door open, he retreated outside.

Marcie shut the inner door, and the screen door closed on its own. As he grabbed the bicycle, a black Chevy S-10 pulled into the driveway. He assumed it was Ryder, but a younger man wearing a yellow hat was driving.

The garage door opened and the truck stopped at the entrance, then pulled inside. He concluded it was Bobby Ring coming home from work, so he sat on the bike and waited. After a few moments, a man came out of the garage and the door closed.

The man stopped walking when he noticed O'Neill. He was as tall as Meyer and lanky. His hair was dark brown like his sister's, and a five-day beard covered his face. Dressed in jeans, boots, and a blue shirt with no sleeves, he pulled off his hat and his brow pushed down. "Who are you?"

"I was visiting Marcie. Are you her brother, Bobby?"

The man nodded, then started toward the house.

There was movement inside, and O'Neill was concerned that Marcie was coming out. Rather than face her, he pushed the bike forward and his legs churned past Bobby and down the dirt driveway.

Chapter 24

Lifting a leg over the bicycle's crossbar, O'Neill glided forward as the truck approached. The pickup stopped and O'Neill slipped off the bike and threw it inside the cargo bed. Ryder turned the vehicle around and drove slowly as they watched the tractor in the hayfield. Ryder opened the window and waved. The tractor's operator returned the wave without more than a glance toward them.

"Bet that's Roman," O'Neill said. "Looks like he's about done."

Ryder laughed as the truck sped up. "You're becoming quite the expert on farming."

"It's not rocket science to see that he's just got a few rows of hay to pick up, and the trailer is full. Either way, that's good." He pointed out the driver-side window. "Look at those clouds coming in. It might rain tonight. A storm will probably cool things off, and I'm sure they want that hay out of there before it's soaked."

"Right, Farmer Seamus. So, are you going to tell me how it went? Did you talk to either of the Rings?"

"Course. Marcie told me that Vernon Cooper was dating a woman named Julie Ryan. She is recently divorced and her ex-husband's name is Scooter. That's a good name for a suspect."

"You asked her questions?" Ryder said, his voice rising. "You were just to get her to accept my phone call."

"Calm down. I gave her your card and told her you wanted to talk to her about anyone that might have issues with Vernon Cooper. She said she didn't know anything, except that Vernon was dating this Ryan woman. She also told me to talk to some guy named Kaiser. Don't know who that is. Then she threw me out. Yet I think she told us what we wanted to hear, ya know?"

"Julie Ryan is one of the two names Jenny gave me, so it's not new information," Ryder said. "I don't know who the Kaiser is. Is she going to call me?"

"I asked her to, but I wouldn't hold my breath."

Ryder shook his head and made a puffing sound. "What's she like?"

"Scary, but hot. She was wearing Daisy Dukes."

Ryder took his foot off the accelerator, and the pickup slowed. "You are kidding?"

"No. Jenny said she was good looking, so that didn't surprise me. Also, Bobby Ring Junior has an S-10 just like yours. Same color. You two must have similar taste."

"So he's got good taste."

"I thought you said he had a dump truck."

"He drives one for work. But it's not like he would drive a dump truck home or to the store or whatever."

"Where does he park it?"

"Bobby doesn't own the dump truck, you idiot." The big detective laughed as they turned onto the highway. "Roger's Stone Company owns their vehicles. He probably parks at the headquarters or the quarry."

"Got it. I just didn't know how that stuff worked. Not like I know lots of dump truck drivers."

When they pulled into the Cooper driveway, Ryder gestured forward. The garage door was open and Randy Cooper was walking toward the house. He stopped as Ryder hopped out and introduced himself. He explained their visit.

Cooper smiled as he hauled the bicycle out of the pickup's bed. "It's funny you took Jenny's," he said. "I have a full-size bike somewhere in the shed."

"Hey Randy," O'Neill said, leaning toward Ryder's window. "Who's Kaiser? Marcie said we should talk to him."

He pulled off his hat and furrowed his brow. "That's Roman's nickname. I don't know why she wants you to talk to him."

"Okay." He glanced at his boss, then turned back to Cooper. "One other thing. I saw tracks in the Ring's driveway from a big truck. Wondering if Bobby sometimes parks the dump truck at home. Or do the Rings own a tractor?"

Cooper laughed before responding. "The Rings don't own any farmland, so they don't have a reason to own a tractor, though both drove tractor when their dad was alive. He needed them, since he could never keep a hired man. Nowadays, they, like everyone, have a four-wheeler, but nothing bigger. As for the dump truck, I've seen it drive past a few times. Think I saw it parked at their place once last week. He probably stops home for lunch sometimes."

O'Neill nodded. "Makes sense."

"We're heading back to Madison," Ryder said to Cooper. "We'll touch base again soon."

"Sure. I appreciate your help with this. We still haven't heard anything from my dad or the sheriff's office. I'm getting more and more concerned."

Jenny came out, so O'Neill changed shirts in the truck and apologized while handing it over. Ryder turned the vehicle around and they waved as they drove off.

O'Neill gave a brief rundown of his discussion with Jenny and about Roman being the beneficiary of Cooper's Chance. Ryder agreed to wait until the next day to talk to Becker about Roman's alibi. O'Neill also told him about the files Jenny sent him.

"We've obviously got to look closer at Roman," Ryder said. "I don't want to make too much of Marcie's comment about him, but he certainly has issues with his brother, and he benefits from Vernon's death. We need to meet him. Do you want me to look at the files Jenny sent you? I'm already through two of your free hours."

"No. I'll look. I want to see if there's a pattern in his spending that might imply he ran away."

"If not?"

"Then I'd like to see data on our prime suspects. If they were planning a murder, is there anything they would have done or bought in the weeks or months before?"

"Don't know, but I must admit that Roman, the Rings, and at least Jenny Cooper have motive," Ryder said.

"Lust, greed, spite, and revenge. Can't beat that."

"But it doesn't mean any of them did it. Shit." He pointed at a road sign. "I should have started back the other way and gotten onto Fish Hatchery Road."

O'Neill jerked forward. "You going back the way we came? Through Verona?"

"Yeah. I came the way you took me. It would have been easier if I had taken a right, which would have taken me into Madison through Fitchburg."

"Since we're driving through Verona, maybe we should stop at some bar and see what we can find out about Roman? Strike the iron while it's hot and all that. Maybe he's got financial trouble."

Ryder shook his head. "Without your disguise, we would stick out and farmers probably wouldn't be forthcoming. There are obviously non-farmers in Verona, but they won't know jack squat about Roman or Vernon Cooper."

"Okay then. Do you know where Verona's Catholic church is?"

Ryder looked at O'Neill, then back at the road. "Now what? Does Seamus want to go to mass?"

"Course not. But I wanna talk to the priest." He put his earring back in, then pulled out a notepad. "Father Brennan is one non-farmer who might know something about the Coopers. Remember, Jenny mentioned a priest who gave her mom spiritual guidance or whatever?"

"Yeah. So what?"

"Randy brought up Brennan as well, and the other sister works part time at the church. The priest may have the inside story and might know where the other sister was when Vernon disappeared. He's also got to know Roman."

"Sure, but keep in mind that priests can't share anything they hear in confession."

"I know that. Went to Catholic school for two years. I know a little about dealing with priests."

"Didn't they boot you from Catholic school?"

"Doesn't mean I don't know how to deal with them."

"If we stay on this road, we'll go past the church." Ryder slowed the car as they approached a red light. "I still don't see how this gets us anywhere. You're not going to pretend to be religious, are you?"

"Course not. I'll just tell the truth about being at the accident. Hopefully I'll get a sense of whether Roman and Vernon were on the outs. I'll also get a sense about whether he thinks there's something amiss with the Cooper kids and, if it comes up, I'll ask about the one sister's alibi."

"He won't know anything about the Rings, will he?"

"Nah. Can't see them coming close to a church."

Ryder shook his head. "We'll stop there, but keep in mind that I'm on the clock, so you're using up more of your free time. Also, make sure you act like you're there as a concerned friend. Don't act like you're investigating the disappearance. What do I do while you shake down the priest?"

"I don't know. Go to Hardee's and find out what co-workers have to say about Marcie Ring or Roman's daughter. Remember, she works there too."

"No way. If Marcie is there, she might recognize me. She'll probably throw a rock through my windshield or spit on my hamburger."

"Okay. You go for a walk while I commune with the priest."

Chapter 25

As they drove through Verona, Ryder gestured toward St. Andrew's Catholic Church and pulled onto a side street. "I'll wait in the truck. You go on in. If the priest is not there, which is just as likely, come out and we'll head back to the office."

"Odds are, he lives in an adjoining building or nearby. I'll see if they have any offices open. If so, maybe I'll find the other Cooper sister."

A long, straight path led to the church, while a shorter one went to what appeared to be a single story administrative building. He paused, then decided on the shorter walk. He tugged on the brown metal door, but it was locked. After glancing at Ryder's truck, he took two steps back before the door flung open. A man in a blue striped shirt and thick glasses stepped out.

"Sorry, we are closed."

He assumed the man was a janitor. "I was looking for Father Brennan. Hoping to talk to him about one of his parishioners."

"Go around back," the man said, motioning with his head. "The father is having a smoke."

O'Neill thanked him and walked around the building. As he passed a large bush that seemed to guard the corner, the priest came into view. "Father Brennan?"

"Yes." The priest was short and had light brown hair and a matching beard. One foot and a shoulder were leaning against the building's brick wall. He took a puff of his cigarette.

"My name is Seamus O'Neill. I'm a friend of Randy Cooper."

"Oh, Randy. Sad situation with Vernon missing. That family has been through several ordeals." The priest nodded slowly. "How do you know him? I don't recall seeing you before. I would remember the cross earring and the name."

O'Neill chuckled and unconsciously touched his ear. "I don't think we've met before. My sister and I were at the accident on Tuesday that involved Vernon's tractor. I was the one who called 911. And I've talked to Randy a bit about his father and his family. I'm sort of worried about him and his family."

"His sister, Annie, works for me. She and I have talked as well." The priest pushed himself away from the wall. "Would you like me to pray for him? Or are you looking for guidance yourself?"

"Randy mentioned that Annie worked for you. I'm curious. I just..." He wanted to pull out his flask, but he held off and the urge passed.

"Yes?" Smoke blew out of the priest's nostrils.

"I heard Annie was at work when the disappearance happened. Jenny told me she called and Annie came home early."

"Yes. Annie was upset when she left. She would have gone home earlier, but she and I were driving back from a meeting in La Crosse. We hurried back. We had to drop Father Leist off first, but she got home as soon as she could."

That would mean that Annie couldn't have been directly involved in her father's disappearance. O'Neill cleared his throat and tried to think of another line of questioning. "Randy told me about his mother's death a few years ago from cancer. The same thing happened to my mother, though I was younger." The urge to drink pulled at him again, and his mind went blank. He touched his ear, and a different thought surfaced. "The cross on my earring," he said, "was from my mother's rosary. She was holding it when she died."

Father Brennan tilted closer. "The Lord was obviously in her thoughts when she passed."

"Anyway, I don't mean to make this about me. Just wanted you to know why I am concerned about Randy and his family. He's a very different person than I am, but I know what it's like to lose a mother when you're young, and now he may lose his father. My father died a few years after my mom, so I understand that as well. How do you think Randy and his sisters will manage if they lose their father? Will they be okay?"

"I think so. They are good people. They'll navigate this with God's help. And I will be available to them."

"Okay. Good. Randy told me that his mother's death was tough on Jenny."

"Yes. Both Jenny and Annie were close to their mother. Jenny even went to live with a relative in Madison for a while. She harbored some anger toward her father. Fortunately, she's worked through her emotions."

"How about Vernon's brother, Roman? Do you know him?"

"Oh, yes. Everyone knows Kaiser."

"I heard that was his nickname," O'Neil said. "It's unusual. How did it come about?"

The priest chuckled. "It's just his friends who call him Kaiser. Someone told me they originally called him Caesar as a twist on his first name, but that didn't have enough of a ring to it."

"Kaiser makes him sound somewhat *infamous*."

"Oh, there was a time, but he's matured. He's a bigger personality than all the other Coopers combined. But he has taken a journey in life." The priest pulled out his cigarette pack. "When he was young, he was what you might call a troublemaker. A rabble rouser."

O'Neill gave him a sheepish smile. "I know something about that. But I take it *Kaiser* is now on the straight and narrow?"

"Yes. Roman grew up, you might say. He's got his own family and his own farm. Both his kids are in high school. And while he's not a churchgoer, he's matured into a good man and a hard worker. He's still got a temper, but he controls it." The priest dropped the cigarette at the building's edge, where it joined a half-dozen other butts.

"Randy mentioned that Roman and his dad had a falling out recently, though it sounds like that happened often."

"This one was a little different," the priest said. "This one was about the Rings."

"The Rings? I thought it was about a part Vernon was supposed to buy or something silly."

"It was something silly," Father Brennan said, "but it wasn't about a part. It was about Roman being friendly with Bobby Ring Junior."

"Really. I hadn't heard that."

"Vernon saw his brother talking with Bobby at the hardware store. He told Roman that he shouldn't talk to either of the Rings. According to Vernon, Roman told him he could talk to whoever he wanted. There wasn't really anything more to it than that. I told Vernon that I thought Roman was right and he should apologize to his brother."

"Did he?"

"I think he did, but I'm not sure. Anything else I can do for you?"

"Actually, there is." O'Neill touched his ear again. "If you've got a minute. Would you mind...blessing my cross?" The welling in his eyes surprised him, so he looked away. "Always meant to have it done, but never got around to it."

The priest smiled and nodded. "Let's go inside the church. Come along."

He followed Father Brennan around the building. They cut across the grass, finally crossing onto the long entryway he had seen from the road.

"You can either leave it on or take it off for the blessing. My suggestion is to leave it on since that's how you live with it."

Father Brennan opened the church door and O'Neill inched inside. The priest dipped his fingers into a holy water container near the entrance. Pulling out a rosary, he recited a brief prayer. O'Neill closed his eyes and droplets of cold water slapped against cheek, neck, and ear.

The priest did the sign of the cross, then reached up with his wet hand and touched the earring. He smiled. "That's it."

They walked the path to the road and discussed the potential for rain. When they parted, the Father walked toward his office while O'Neill jogged across the street.

"It's about time," Ryder said as O'Neill got into the truck. "Did you get anything on Roman or the one woman's alibi? Or was this just another silly Seamus exercise?"

"The fight between Vernon and Roman wasn't about an engine part; it was about Roman speaking to Bobby Ring Junior. Vernon said he shouldn't talk to him, and his brother told him to mind his own business."

"So Randy and Jenny lied?"

"Or that's what their dad told them."

"Anything else?"

"On the afternoon of the disappearance, Annie Cooper was driving back from La Crosse with two priests. She couldn't have been directly involved unless the priests lied." The truck started, and he rested his head against the passenger-side window. "We're down to five suspects."

"Great," Ryder said. "Our most unlikely suspect is in the clear. We'll pretend that's progress."

O'Neill wanted to respond, but he knew Ryder was right. The only progress they made was to exclude a second-level suspect and to show that there had been conflict between Vernon and members of his family. They still didn't know if a crime had been committed.

They were nowhere.

Chapter 26

Their next step would have been to talk with Detective Becker of the Dane County Sheriff's Department about the Coopers and their alibis. But Ryder didn't want to speak to Becker unless he could talk about motive, including the property Roman would inherit. The only thing for O'Neill to do was to dig into the CSV files Jenny had sent him. He hoped that, if Vernon Cooper had planned to run away, prior spending might provide clues to where he had gone or why. O'Neill felt it was a necessary step.

When they pulled up to O'Neill's apartment, the June sun was still above the horizon. As he climbed the stairs, he tried to remember how many beers he had at home. Inside, he opened the refrigerator door and a lonely bottle of pale ale stared back at him. He yelled an explicative and, after visiting the bathroom, started the walk to the liquor store.

The Irish Pub was on the way, so he stopped for a single tap beer before proceeding to the liquor store. With two six packs of Berghoff's Famous Red Ale and a two-liter of Diet Mountain Dew in hand, he headed home.

O'Neill spent most of the evening playing with the files Jenny Cooper had emailed to him. It took him a few minutes to conclude that he would need to analyze the files in Microsoft Excel. He used Excel regularly, but was far from proficient. After getting the data into a spreadsheet, he spent hours slicing, dicing, and summarizing the information. But none of it led to any firm conclusion, so he shut down the computer and pulled out his guitar, falling asleep with it on his lap.

He woke at eleven in the morning. After returning the instrument to its stand, he showered and shaved. Low on food and time, he microwaved a potato and gnawed on it as he walked to the office. When he arrived, he was greeted by the "Will Return Soon" sign. Unlocking the door, he flipped on the lights. Ryder's screen saver was on, so he had at least been in the office sometime that morning. O'Neill booted up his own computer and took a soda from the office refrigerator.

He found a few emails from Ryder, including one saying he would be back in the office by three o'clock. The memo said he was working on a case that actually paid.

After finishing several routine tasks, O'Neill called up the Excel file he had sent to himself the prior night. A knock at the door interrupted him. He got to his feet and, as he reached for the handle, the door cracked open.

"Hello," a gruff male voice said. The door pushed further open and the man's head ducked into the office. He was solidly built with wavy blonde hair that puffed out of a pristine trucker's hat. His mustache was trimmed, and he wore a patterned shirt, jeans, and cowboy boots. He looked like a farmer about to go to an interview with his banker. "You..." The man squinted. "Are you Mr. O'Neill?"

"Yeah, that's me."

"My name is Roman Cooper. We talked on the phone yesterday."

A jolt of energy shot through O'Neill. "Yeah, Roman. I remember." He retreated toward the desks and motioned for the farmer to come inside. "My boss, Mr. Ryder, should be back any minute. Come on in, but watch your step."

Roman moved cautiously, his muscular frame crouching slightly as he stepped forward. O'Neill glanced at the visitor and sat behind his desk. "Let me give Ryder a call so he knows you're here. He'll want to join us." He pulled out his cell phone.

"Don't bother," Roman said. "I'm fine with talking to you; it won't take long."

O'Neill didn't know if that was good or not. He felt uncomfortable being alone with a prime suspect, but he needed information, and he didn't know when he would have another opportunity to speak with him. He set the phone down and pointed at the empty chair that waited in front of his desk.

"My niece Jenny stopped by to talk to me yesterday," Roman said, as he settled into the chair. He looked side-to-side as he spoke, as if expecting someone to sneak up on him. "She brought over deeds for her dad's properties. I think you know this already, but three of them list me as the guy who gets the property if her dad dies."

"Yeah, I saw them. So did Ryder."

"I'm on my way to meet with a deputy about them. I tried to get in earlier, but the detective is off today and the guy who helps him was out until noon. Don't know what I'm going to tell them, but I want them to know that I didn't know anything about the deeds." He paused, and for the first time, seemed to relax. "Vernon must have done that, and probably after Patty's death. I don't think she would have stood for it."

O'Neill leaned back and plucked off the sunglasses that sat atop his head while trying to think of a response. "Why did he do that? Why are you going to receive half of the farm?"

Roman let out a huff and shook his head. "Guilt. That's probably what made him do it."

"Guilt about what?"

"About the farm. About Patty." He paused and stared into O'Neill's eyes. "I was the oldest son, but my dad gave him the farm. He got almost everything. Vernon probably knew it wasn't fair. He knew it wasn't right."

"It wasn't, huh?"

"Oh, don't say it like that. It wasn't fair, but that doesn't mean I was mad at Vernon about it. I didn't even know that my brother put me on the deeds and, even if I did, I wouldn't want something bad to happen to my little brother."

"You're right to tell the cops about this. And, if the cops aren't aware of it, you're best off telling them about Patty as well." He looked down at his phone. "They'll find out one way or another, so better it comes from you. That's assuming they don't already know."

Roman's eyes widened, and he leaned forward. "Did you tell them?"

"Me?" O'Neill chuckled. "No. I avoid cops."

Roman looked at the ceiling and then out the window. "All I can say is that I had nothing to do with my brother disappearing and all. I love my brother. He may be a geek and an idiot, but I love him. And me and Patty? That was ancient history."

"I hear you and Vernon had a fight recently. That true?"

Roman shook his head, as if disgusted. "I was just pissed about something stupid. About a week earlier, I ran into Bobby Ring at the hardware store. We were talking about a road project he's been working on when Vernon came in. Vernon told me he wanted a minute, so we went outside and he lectured me about who I should and shouldn't talk to."

"Bobby was on the shouldn't talk to list?"

"Yes. He was being a stupid shit, blaming Bobby for what his dad did. I told him to stick it and he left in a huff. Unfortunately, it was the last time I spoke to him."

"Tell the cops about it. Unless your brother turns up, they'll look at you as a prime suspect, so they'll find out everything. They'll also dig deeper into your activities on the day Vernon disappeared. When we talked on the phone, you mentioned you went to town and had a receipt for something."

He nodded. "I bought a filter. After lunch, I was mostly in the shop with Greg — he's my hired man. My son was with us on and off, too. We were working on a tractor, as ironic as that might sound, and doing a few odd jobs. I went to town at roughly three in the afternoon. I remember we had ESPN on and were going to listen to a College World Series game at two, but it got rained out. They did SportsCenter instead. It was within that hour that I left."

"How long were you gone?"

"I told the deputy who interviewed me that it was twenty minutes. Thinking back, it was probably more like half an hour."

"Greg and your son will back you up?"

"You bet, though my son was in and out. He might not have been in the shop when I left for town, but Greg and my wife probably saw me leave."

"Did they go anywhere during the afternoon? Or were they home?"

"My wife and son?"

"Yeah."

"My daughter took the car to work, so my wife and son were at the house or in the shop. It's doubtful they will remember how long I was gone."

"Where'd you go again?"

"Hardware store. It's probably eight to ten minutes from my place."

"Where is your place? How far are you from your brother's farm?"

"I'm west of him maybe six miles. It's maybe an eight-minute drive to Vernon's." He jumped to his feet. "Shit. I would never do anything to Vernon, even though he does stupid things like giving me half his farm. The idiot."

"When you talk to the cops, don't call your brother an idiot."

Roman looked down at him, then chuckled and returned to his seat. "He's my little brother, you know? We've called each other a lot worse, and neither of us say it in a mean way. Truth is, he is a bit of a geek. People make him nervous while I'm more out there, fun loving and easygoing."

"Did you use a credit card when you went to the hardware store?" O'Neill asked after a long silence. "Just trying to establish whether the cops will think you could have done anything to Vernon."

"I was only buying a filter, so I used cash. Like I told you, I gave the deputy my receipt." He reached into a pocket and pulled out a folded piece of paper. "I took a picture and printed it out," he said. "Lip should remember me stopping in. Lip Hermanson was working the counter that day, like most days."

O'Neill looked over the receipt, then wrote the name and information on his notepad. "Okay. Let's move to something else. Can you tell me about Jenny and Annie's relationship with their dad? I've heard they blamed their dad for what happened to their mother."

"Are you saying Jenny and Annie did something to Vernon?" His head shook as he let out a puff of air. "They may have gone through a period where they were mad at Vernon, but it was nothing like that. Those are church-going girls. They wouldn't do anything to their dad. Nothing."

O'Neill leaned forward. "Then who? It seems the Ring kids were Vernon's only enemies, and the cops say they have a perfect alibi. Anyone else who didn't like him? Anyone else who would benefit from his disappearing or his death?"

Roman rubbed at his brow, and for the first time, he took off his hat. "Naw." His head was shaking. "No one hates Vernon. I can't see anyone other than the Rings wanting to harm him, but I can't see him running away like people are saying. And even the Rings wouldn't go that far. It had to be something random. Maybe someone coming down the road who walked up to him and robbed him or something. Nothing else makes sense."

O'Neill nodded.

"Do you have other suggestions for when I meet with the sheriff?" Roman asked, as he put his hat on. "Jenny thought you or your partner would be the people to ask."

"Just be honest. If this guy at the hardware store backs you up and the time of the receipt is correct, I'm struggling to understand how you, by yourself, would have had the time to get to that field, done something to your brother, and started that tractor down the road."

"Yes. You're right."

"It's almost the same alibi that Marcie has. Neither of you had enough time to do it by yourself. But if there is someone else you're close to, let the cops talk to them. And let them talk to your Greg guy without you being there. Don't let the cops think he's lying for you."

"One last thing," Roman said. He paused and stared at the floor. "If Vernon is dead, I won't take the land. I'll sign it over to his kids. I have two of my own, but Vernon's kids are almost like mine. And while I have my own money issues, there's no way Randy could successfully run that farm with the debt they have and only a hundred and twenty acres. No way." The farmer looked at his watch. "Oh, shit. I got to go to meet with that deputy sheriff. Should I tell the cops that I won't take the land? Or does that seem like I'm just saying it to divert suspicion?"

"I wouldn't offer it up, but tell them if they ask."

He nodded slowly, then reached over O'Neill's computer. They shook hands. "Thank you for taking the time. I appreciate the advice."

A knock on the door interrupted them. Roman released his grip as the door opened. They both waited as Detective Erin Meyer stepped inside.

Chapter 27

O'Neill assumed Meyer was there to cancel their upcoming date. She stepped in, her eyes down and a nervous smile on her face. She had her hair pulled into a ponytail and wore a dark blue blazer and pants with a white shirt and necklace. Very business-like.

She looked at Roman Cooper and her jaw dropped. "Oh, sorry. I didn't mean to interrupt a meeting. I'll come back."

"That's okay, ma'am." Roman slid off his hat. "I was just leaving." He nodded at O'Neill and started toward the door. Meyer eased to the side of the entryway. He looked at her with a puzzled expression before pushing the door open with his backside.

She waited until the door closed. Then she looked at O'Neill. "I'm sorry to bother you."

"No problem. Come in, but watch your step." He stood and moved toward her as she navigated the entryway. "People trip on that extra step. Have a seat." He backed up and sat on the corner of his desk. "This is my spot." He slapped the desk with his hand. "Ryder's is the big one over there."

"I want to talk to you about Saturday."

His heart sank.

"I was thinking. Maybe it's not a good idea." Staring at the floor, she stopped about six feet in front of him. "I don't think we should turn our friendship into something more."

He was confused. They met early in the month when their paths crossed on a case they both worked on. During the case, they shared a passionate kiss. While they were friendly, he didn't know her well enough to call her a friend. Besides, he was interested in more than friendship, and he thought she felt the same way.

"You're a nice guy, but we're from different worlds." She looked up and forced a smile. "It wouldn't work."

"Okay. If that's how you feel."

She dropped her gaze again. "Yes, I do."

"Before you go. Can I ask what you mean by *different worlds*? Do you mean class stuff? Like you're middle class and I'm, like, not?"

"No, no." Her eyes widened. "I mean, there's nothing wrong with dating someone from a different social status. What I mean more is lifestyle. And values. You have this rock & roll lifestyle. You drink a lot, party a lot, and date a lot. That's not me. And I wouldn't be good in that world."

"I used to drink and party a ton, and I had girlfriends," he said. "But I'm not twenty anymore, and I'm no longer in a rock & roll band. I still drink more than I should, but I've cut down. As for women, I'm trying to find someone special, like everyone else. Music is always going to be an important part of my life, but I'm trying to leave the rock & roll lifestyle in the past. Guess you could say I'm trying to grow up."

There was a long silence.

"One of our detectives saw you out a few days ago with a woman," she said, her voice cracking. "He told everyone at work about it since he knows we're...friendly. He said you were with this dark-haired tattooed woman. She was sitting on your lap. That's why I was thinking you still date and carouse and all that."

It took him a moment to process what she said. "Someone at your work was talking about me? How do they even know who I am?"

"Seamus, most of the uniforms know you for being in a band and for being a sort of downtown mainstay." She looked around the room. "And the detectives know you through your work here with Ryder."

It surprised him to learn that he was a topic of conversation at the City of Madison Police Department. "I'm not sure who this tattoo woman is that you mentioned." He tried to remember the last few days and his thoughts came to a couple of nights before, when he was out with Topper. He remembered having seven or eight pints at the Angelic Brewing Company and he bought a drink for Mandy's friend Cindy, who had been sitting next to him and was interested in his music. They talked a bit, but for the past several weeks, his thoughts had focused on Meyer. He was sure he wouldn't have even flirted with Cindy. The only thing he could think of was that some cop had been at Angelic, saw him with the woman, and made assumptions. His mind spun as he tried to remember the night. "I don't know what this person is talking about." He couldn't even remember if Cindy had tattoos. "What can you tell me about this woman?"

"Does it really matter?"

"It must. You brought it up."

She licked her lips. "Morris said tattoos covered one of her arms and, this is mean, so I wouldn't normally repeat it, but he said she looked like Joan Jett after three weeks on a deserted island. That was what he told people. Penny already thought our date was a bad idea, but when this came up, it made me realize she was right." He knew Meyer was referring to Penny Jefferson, her coworker and closest friend. "You weren't doing anything wrong. I mean, you can date whoever you want. But it illustrated to me that we come from different worlds, and it's safer if I stay in mine."

"Where did this Morris see me with this woman?"

She glanced up. "He said you were at American TV."

A feeling of relief shot through him. "American TV? That was my sister helping me with shopping. She sat on my lap as a joke in the store because I fell asleep in a recliner. We were just kidding around. No idea why this dickwad thought we were a couple."

There was a long silence as her gaze jumped between him and the floor. "I-I'm sorry. Morris said it was a girlfriend. I don't think he even thought about her being your sister. I didn't even know you had a sister." Tears welled in her eyes. "Maybe it is good I talked to you, so I know."

O'Neill struggled to find something to say. Meyer's friends and coworkers obviously thought she shouldn't date him, and he understood why. "Who is this Morris guy, anyway?"

She turned away as a tear slid down her cheek. "He thinks you and I are dating, though we really haven't done anything but gone running and stuff. He was teasing me, being a jerk."

"Tell this Morris dickwad that my sister better not hear the Joan Jett desert island comment or she'll punch him in the nuts. And don't think I'm joking."

"Okay. Sorry."

"Does this mean we can still go out on Saturday? Or are you still sure I'm from another world?"

She turned back toward him. "I'm up for it if you still want to," she said in a quiet voice. "I'm not saying it's a good idea. Maybe we really are from different worlds. But it's only one date and if you're still interested...?"

"Course I am." He stood and eased closer, his gaze raising to hers. "Your friends think I'm sketchy. I get that. But despite what people think and despite this Morris dickwad, I think we can have fun and I think we can be good for each other." He reached up, setting a hand on the back of her neck. She felt warm. "Besides, you're the only woman I think about." She closed her eyes and crouched down, so he pulled her close and their lips met.

She lurched forward, whispering his name while a teardrop rushed down her cheek. He backed into his desk, but she held onto him and her left leg slid above his waist. Something hard, which he assumed was a holster, pushed against his ribs. His hand ran along the upstretched leg, and his tongue glided up her neck. Glancing backward, he made sure he didn't knock his laptop onto the floor.

"How much time do we have?" he asked, as his hand ran down her back.

"An hour," she said. Then she stopped and pulled away. "Seamus, no. No. I did not stop by for...I'm not ready for...that. I just got...carried away."

O'Neill let go. This time, he was the one looking at the floor. "Sorry."

"No, I'm sorry. I got ahead of myself for a moment. I'm not very good at this."

He took a large breath. "Either way, I'm glad you came by."

She smiled, and there was a long silence.

"You said you have an hour?"

Her head tilted to the side. "The Captain stopped at my desk and told me to take off for an hour or so." She smiled, and a chuckle came out. "Penny said something to him; I don't know what exactly, but she convinced him that I needed to get out of the office."

"Did you drive here?"

She nodded.

"Then you've got enough time to give me a ride to Verona and back."

"Verona?"

"Yeah. I left something at the house of this one woman."

"What woman?"

"It relates to this case I'm working on. It's the disappearance of Vernon Cooper. The sheriff's office thinks he disappeared to start a new life, but I think he was murdered and I'm down to four or five suspects. One of them is the guy you just met."

"The blonde guy who was just here?" Her eyebrows raised. "He's one of your suspects?"

"Yeah. There's him, his niece, and then these two siblings. And maybe his nephew. I'm trying to figure out which one or ones are the killer or killers. Wanna look at the financial records to see if any show a pattern or purchase or something that might imply that they were planning something. If you take me out to Verona, I can check out the siblings."

"Even I would need a search warrant to access their financial records."

"I know," O'Neill said. He got off the desk and stood in front of her. "But the last time I was at this house where the siblings live, I saw where they keep their financial stuff. It's a brother and sister named Marcie and Bobby Ring. Bobby's a dump truck driver. She works at a fast food place. Must admit, she's attractive in a dangerous killer sort of way."

Her chin dropped, and her head tilted. "Dangerous killer sort of way?"

"Yeah. Let's say I accidentally left Ryder's digital camera in her house." He walked to Ryder's desk, held the camera in the air, then stuffed it in his pocket. "Just want to pick up the camera so Ryder doesn't get mad at me for losing it."

"What were you doing at her house?"

"She invited me in. Kind of a long story."

"I'm sure."

"I'll just knock. If she answers, I'll ask if she found a camera. If not, I know she leaves the house unlocked during the day, so I'll step in, grab it, and we're off. Just so you know, I won't take a quick look at her files while I'm there." He winked at her. "That would be illegal and us private detectives don't do illegal things."

"I thought you just worked for a private detective."

"Oh, yeah," he said. "Either way, I wouldn't ask you to take me there if I was going to *get caught* doing something illegal."

"Yes, I couldn't take you if I knew you were going to do something illegal."

"That's what I figured."

"You know this attractive woman leaves her house open? Should I be jealous?"

"Nah," he said. "I don't like killers."

"You think she's a killer?"

"Maybe. But if she is, you've got a gun."

Chapter 28

O'Neill sent Ryder an email saying he was taking off for a few hours and would be back later that afternoon. After flipping the sign and locking the door, he followed Meyer down the steps. She led him to a black Lincoln Continental, asking him about the case as they walked.

He was worried that she would spend the trip trying to talk him out of entering the Ring house without permission, so he was relieved that their conversation focused on family. They spent several minutes talking about Lena and her son Dawson. He mentioned that both of his parents were dead, but she didn't push for details. He then steered the conversation to her family. She talked about her overly protective parents, a younger sister, and an older brother. As they drove into Verona, he closed his eyes and warned her of his tendency to fall asleep on car rides. She laughed, but didn't comment.

"Seamus," she said, a few minutes later, tapping his shoulder. "We're coming to the road you told me they live on."

O'Neill's eyes popped open. "Where are we now?" He focused on the approaching road sign.

"We're on Gifford Road."

He didn't remember the directions he had told her, but he said to turn left. After passing the next intersection, the Ring house soon came into view and he pointed at it.

"You don't see too many one-story farmhouses," she said.

"Suppose not. Think it was where the farm helper lived."

They pulled into the dirt and gravel driveway, and O'Neill was relieved to see that Marcie's car was nowhere to be seen. The garage door, however, was down, so either her car or Bobby's truck could be inside. Meyer glanced at her watch, so he hopped out of the vehicle. Finding the garage's side window, he cupped his hands together and looked inside.

It was empty, so he gave Meyer a thumbs up.

The car window rolled down. "I'll turn around and wait beside the house," she said. "It should be obvious if someone shows up. Got it?"

That would give him a warning system. If Bobby or Marcie returned, they wouldn't be able to park until she moved her car. While he assumed the house was empty, he still knocked on the door and waited while Meyer turned the vehicle around.

After a second knock, he counted to twenty, stuffed a hand inside his T-shirt, and opened the screen door. Pushing it back, he slid between the doors. With his hand inside his shirt, he tried the knob and it rotated. Relieved, he pushed the door open.

"Hello?" he yelled.

There was no answer, so he hurried inside, leaving the inner door open. The filing cabinet was against the wall next to the kitchen table. He opened the same drawer that Marcie had on the previous day. At least twenty hanging file folders were inside, each with a white label. The first label read "AT&T." For a moment, he thought of rifling through phone records, but he decided that would be impractical.

He noticed a tab for the Bank of Verona. Pulling out the folder, he placed it on the table. Counting five statements, all from 2000, he went through page-by-page, taking photos. Once done, he returned the file and continued looking until he found one labeled, "GM Card." He took nearly twenty photos before returning the statements and repeating the process for a file marked "Visa."

He wanted to go through three folders labeled "Miscellaneous," but decided it would take too much time. Instead, he opened the next drawer. It was full and appeared to contain records from the prior two years. The other two shelves were filled with legal and financial records and a thick file labeled "Mom & Dad." Paging through, he found death certificates and numerous newspaper articles about their death. A honk from Meyer interrupted him. He closed the drawer, wiped the cabinets with his shirt, and slipped outside without touching the handle. There was no sign of Marcie or Bobby, so he opened the passenger door and sat inside.

Once the car door closed, Meyer put her foot on the gas and turned left onto the road. "Geez, Seamus," she said. "That took an awful long time. Did you find what you were looking for? The camera, I mean?"

"Hopefully." He was struggling to locate his seat belt. "I won't really know until I get back to the office and do some data analysis."

"Data analysis?" She chuckled. "That doesn't sound like a rock & roller's line."

"See?"

She rolled her eyes and sped down the road.

O'Neill watched a tractor in the distance and his thoughts went back to the Linda E, which was sitting somewhere at the bottom of Lake Michigan. According to news reports, the US Coast Guard was searching for the boat. He wondered whether they had found it or whether they had given up. Then he remembered something Randy Cooper had said the last time they talked. An idea floated around him, but like some tunes, he couldn't grab it. He closed his eyes, hoping it would come closer.

O'Neill woke when Meyer stopped the car a block from the Ryder Detective Agency. He yawned then patted the camera in his pocket.

"I need to get to work," she said. "My hour is more than up."

"Thanks for the ride." He leaned toward her and they kissed. "See you tomorrow night. I'm looking forward to it." The car door opened, scratching against the concrete sidewalk. She gave him a disapproving look. He stepped out and the door lifted slightly, allowing him to slam it shut.

It was one in the afternoon and the only thing he'd eaten all day was a potato. Yet he walked past Sal's Subs and rushed up the stairs to his office. The Will Return sign was still there, so he unlocked the door and went inside.

After checking his email, he connected the camera to his computer and downloaded the pictures. His idea was to enter every transaction on the bank and credit card statements into an Excel spreadsheet. It would be a laborious but necessary task, which he hoped would expose some sort of pattern.

Entering the bank statement's transactions went reasonably fast since he only entered date and amount. The credit card statements, however, included the same information plus the vendor and the vendor's location. Once the data entry was done, he rewarded himself with a beer from the office refrigerator.

Summarizing the information revealed little other than that Marcie and Bobby spent most of their money on car payments, utilities, groceries, and gasoline. There were also multiple payments to Menards and the local hardware store. But there were no significant deviations or suspicious purchases, though there were many that he would have liked to have known more details about.

He did, however, notice something about the location of credit card transactions. On a Tuesday evening in May, one of them made a $19.00 purchase at a Citgo in Belleville, Wisconsin, which was about a dozen miles south of their home. They also made a $27.21 purchase on the following Tuesday at the same gasoline station. Finally, there was a $1.26 transaction on a Saturday night at a Dayton, Wisconsin, gas station. The last credit card statement ended on the fifth of June. He wished he could see more recent detail, but this would have to do. These were the only gas station purchases outside of Madison and Verona.

While he knew where Belleville was, he was unsure of Dayton. A Dane County Map was inside his desk, but he didn't find Dayton on it. He searched Ryder's desk, but couldn't locate a state map. Eventually, he went to the computer and found a map on the Wisconsin Department of Transportation's website. He determined that Dayton was an unincorporated community south of Belleville.

After saving the spreadsheet, he grabbed the remaining beer from the refrigerator. Walking back to his desk, he looked out the window and the thought that had come to him earlier returned. His eyes closed, and he saw a farmer driving a tractor on Cooper's Chance and a boat sitting at the bottom of Lake Michigan.

His eyes opened, and he nodded in satisfaction. He was smiling when Ryder stepped into the office.

Chapter 29

O'Neill claimed he thought better with a beer in his hand. So when he told Ryder he had a theory, the big detective agreed to talk it through at a bar. O'Neill assumed they'd walk to one of the nearby watering holes. Instead, they got into Ryder's truck. Ten minutes later, they stopped in a parking lot on Madison's west side.

The pair meandered through the lot, approaching a single story stand-alone building. A Copps Grocery Store and a TJ Maxx stood nearby. Ryder held the door open and O'Neill stepped inside.

A half dozen silver kettles and vessels were to their left, and O'Neill realized they were at a brewpub. A rectangular bar counter gave the place a central focus. Steins hung from the ceiling, and black and white caricature drawings lined the walls. He started to walk toward the brewing equipment before a woman behind the host station got his attention.

"Do you need a table, sir?" the host asked. She looked too young to drink, but her shirt said, "Beer, proof that God loves us. - *Benjamin Franklin.*"

O'Neill paused and joined Ryder in front of the host station. He motioned toward the counter. "Can we sit at the bar by the taps?"

"No," Ryder said before the host could respond. He turned to the host. "Set us at a table so we can talk business." He gestured at the tables that surrounded the counter. "Maybe a booth near the bar?"

She took two menus and motioned for them to follow her.

O'Neill stared at the counter as they slid into a nearby booth. It did not look like an antique or salvaged bar, but the wood looked solid, and it wrapped around a central counter that housed lines of liquor bottles. "How old is this place?" he asked as he looked at the dropped ceiling, which had white tiles interspersed with some that looked as if they were cut out from an old tin ceiling.

"The building?" The host's eyes widened. "No idea. J.T. Whitney's has been here for as long as I remember. Your waitress will be around shortly. Thank you."

"This has got to be late sixties or early seventies construction, wouldn't you think?" O'Neill said after the host had left.

"Who cares? Either way, our child host doesn't have a lot of perspective. This place has been a brewpub for maybe five years. Back in the seventies and eighties, it was a breakfast place. It was a few other things before becoming a brewpub."

Their server arrived carrying glasses of ice water. She was short and stout and old enough to be the host's grandmother. O'Neill grabbed the beer menu and quickly chose an Irish ale. His boss did the same, and the server nodded and walked toward the counter.

"Are you gonna tell me about your theory?"

"Course. Soon as the drinks arrive. As you know, I think better with a beer in my hand."

"You're going to drive me to the grave, you know?" The big detective's head shook as he picked up a menu. "Think I'll probably end up with the raspberry ribs."

O'Neill sipped from his water glass and the drinks soon arrived. A hint of froth dripped down the side of the mug as he took a drink. He smiled and set the glass on the table. Ryder put in his food order as O'Neill looked at his menu for the first time, quickly settling on a grilled chicken sandwich and ugly potatoes.

"No more excuses," Ryder said as the server stomped away. "Who did it?"

"Don't know for sure."

"Oh, my God. You are paying for this meal for sure. You said you had a theory that solved everything."

"I know how he was killed and I know who *could have* done it." O'Neill leaned back in his chair.

"What led to this revelation?"

"A few things. First, I was thinking about that boat they're searching for on Lake Michigan and about how it's hard to tell one sunken boat from another. Then, when I was biking on Chance Road, I saw someone out baling hay. I'm assuming it was Roman, but that was just a guess. And finally, when we talked to Randy, he mentioned that Marcie Ring used to drive tractor for her dad."

"Yeah. So what?"

O'Neill took a large gulp and set the mug on the table, staring into it as he spoke. "The cops inferred a time of disappearance based on when the crash happened, adjusted for the time it took for the thing to travel down the road. That gave Roman Cooper, Bobby Ring Junior, and Marcie Ring alibis. I'm not sure whether it gave Jenny one."

"Yeah, you already told me this." Ryder took a drink from his glass.

"But what if Vernon was killed, say, thirty minutes earlier than we thought?"

"He couldn't have been."

"Why not?" O'Neill said.

"You said it was only eight or ten minutes that Vernon was out of Randy's sights."

"Yes, Randy saw Vernon's tractor about nine minutes before Lena and I nearly crashed into it. But when Randy saw it, how did he know his father was driving?" O'Neill sipped his beer. "Suppose someone killed Vernon then got into the tractor and continued tedding the field. Suppose that person is dressed like Vernon. There's twenty-acres of soybeans between the two tractors. That's more than the length of two football fields."

"Okay." Ryder ran his fingers along his chin. "That hadn't occurred to me. You're suggesting that, at that distance, Randy wouldn't be able to tell who was driving his father's tractor."

"Exactly."

Ryder's face seemed to widen as his cheeks pushed out. "Who was driving it?"

"Don't know for sure, but I think Marcie. I think she killed him and Bobby disposed of the body."

"Marcie? How would she get him out of the tractor? How did she kill him?"

"My guess is Marcie parked her four-wheeler or maybe a bike in the culvert on the road. When Randy was driving the other direction, she came out and either got Vernon's attention or else she lay down in the field in Cooper's Chance. I think it was the latter. Though she'd have to make sure she was visible so she wouldn't get run over." He let out a chuckle, then took another sip of beer. "When Vernon saw a woman lying in the cut field, he did what many of us would do. He hit his horn, then when the woman didn't move, he got out of the tractor thinking she was dead or needed help."

"Wouldn't he be suspicious seeing Marcie lying in his field? He knows she hates him."

"Would he be able to tell that it's Marcie? She could lie face down. He wouldn't see anything but a woman's body. But there was one thing he did, which she didn't expect. Vernon grabbed his thermos, probably thinking the woman might be passed out in the field and needing water."

"So Vernon gets out of the tractor and walks toward Marcie while holding his thermos."

"I'm not sure what happened next, but unless she's a karate expert or something, I'd guess she shot him. Maybe she used a silencer since Randy was only a quarter mile away and didn't hear a gunshot. Or maybe she had something else that would incapacitate him without him getting close to her. Marcie looks fit, and she's no shrinking violet. But Vernon was forty-four and active. I can't see her stabbing or overpowering him."

"A gun works, but keep in mind that a gun with a silencer still makes noise. Particularly a handgun."

"Oh, really." O'Neill swished beer around in his glass before lifting it to his lips. "I thought silencers just made a *too, too* sound."

"That's on TV. A silencer reduces the sound, but not as much as they imply on TV. But Randy was in his tractor, which makes a bit of noise itself. It might work, particularly if it was on a rifle. It's counter-intuitive, but a silenced rifle might be quieter than a silenced handgun. Let's go with the assumption that Marcie used a silencer. What do you think happened next?"

"She makes sure no vehicles are coming down the road. If she has enough time before Randy's tractor turns toward her, she drags the body to the side of the road by the culvert. If not, she just makes sure the body is in an uncut portion of the field. She moves it to the culvert when Randy is driving away from her. She already has a hat and a shirt that matches Vernon's, or maybe she put his clothes on. So, dressed like him, she gets into the tractor and calmly goes about tedding the field, destroying the crime scene as she goes."

"Okay." Ryder licked his lips. "And the thermos?"

"When she shoots him, he drops the thermos in the field. She can't just leave it there, so she picks it up. Maybe she does that before she put gloves on, or maybe she was wiping off the spilled water."

"How do you know she wore gloves?"

O'Neill put a finger in the air and took a last gulp of his beer. "Vernon's prints were everywhere in the cab. They were on the gears, the steering wheel, and the door handle. Everywhere except the thermos. Even Randy's prints were inside the cab. So when Marcie drove the tractor, she avoided touching the spots on the steering wheel that Vernon regularly touched. Her wearing gloves and not touching obvious spots is the likely solution. She didn't want to smear or destroy Vernon's fingerprints, as that would imply that someone wearing gloves got into the cab after him. Maybe she held the spokes of the steering wheel and didn't touch the top of the gearshift when changing gears. She would have known that the ball of the gearshift would be what Vernon regularly touched."

"Okay. I'm with you with the argument that, if this happened, she wore gloves when she drove the tractor. And I can buy the possibility that she wasn't wearing them when she shot him, and I can buy that she might have touched the thermos and had to clean it off."

"Either that or the water had spilled when he dropped it and she was wiping it off with her gloves. That's a natural thing to do."

Ryder nodded his head slowly.

"Everyone assumed Vernon was driving the tractor the whole time," O'Neill said. "The Rings relied on the police making that assumption. It seemed logical since only Vernon, Randy, and Lena's prints were inside the cab and no one besides Vernon and Randy were seen in the area. And Randy was the ideal witness, saying he saw his dad in the tractor until the tractor disappeared. Perhaps most importantly, the Rings took advantage of Cooper family lore which was a history of disappearing, including a family member who vanished from the same field for no apparent reason. Marcie even alluded to it when I talked to her. She wanted people to assume that Vernon was another unstable Cooper. She wanted everyone to think he made a run for it."

"How long do you think Marcie drove the tractor?"

"We can't know for sure, but Randy said he heard a horn about half an hour before noticing that the tractor was missing. If we assume Vernon honked when he saw Marcie in the field, it means she drove the tractor for almost half an hour. After she started tedding the field, her brother came along in his dump truck. Bobby may have stopped the dump truck on the road, hopped out, threw the body into the truck, then continued along his way and dumped the body somewhere or else took it to his house. If it was me, I'd be worried about stopping a monster like that in the middle of a country road. If someone else drove by, they would remember it. Plus, Bobby would have to stop the truck again to get rid of the body."

"Did anyone report seeing a dump truck in the area?"

"Not that I know of. While no one would think twice of seeing a truck or semi driving along those roads, they would notice if a dump truck was parked. Certainly, if Randy had seen a parked dump truck, he would have mentioned that even if it was half an hour earlier than when he thought his dad had disappeared."

"What did the Rings do next?" Ryder waved to the server, pointing out that both of their mugs were empty. "Do you think he brought the dump truck home and took another vehicle back to get the body?"

"Yeah. As you mentioned earlier, Bobby parks his personal truck at the quarry when he's at work and drives it home at day's end. My guess is he parked the dump truck at home and took Marcie's car to the culvert. That's why I saw the large tire tracks in their driveway. He popped the trunk, grabbed the body which was lying near the culvert and threw it into her car's trunk and drove home."

"Holy shit. There could be forensic evidence in Marcie's trunk."

"Could be," O'Neill said. "But the Rings planned this thing out. My guess is they lined the trunk with a tarp or with something to encase his body. They would have done what they could to eliminate blood or traces of Vernon Cooper's DNA from showing up in their trunk. Meanwhile,

Marcie waited for an ideal time when her tractor was close to the road and Randy's tractor was turning away from her. She folded up the tedder thingy and got the tractor onto the road. She then put the thing in low gear, jumped out, and tore off in her four-wheeler or bike or whatever."

"Okay. What did they do with the corpse?"

Chapter 30

They ordered another round as Ryder pulled out a notepad. The bartender filled a mug, and O'Neill stared at the full beers waiting on the counter.

"I'm doubtful he would have left Vernon inside the trunk for long," O'Neill said as his partner wrote notes. "The Rings had to know that the police would want to talk to them, so they would not want Marcie driving to and working all day at Hardee's with a dead body in her trunk. My guess is Bobby took the body from the trunk and left it on their property before heading to the quarry. He got home from work around five o'clock. I'm thinking he either put Vernon in his truck and dumped him somewhere or they waited for darkness to dump it."

Ryder set his pencil down and looked up. "They also had to dispose of the murder weapon. I would not dump them in the same place. I'd drop the weapon into a lake or river; same with the silencer if there is one. I wouldn't do anything nearby. The corpse is more difficult. Dumping it in a lake could work if it's properly weighed down and everything, but I'm doubtful that amateurs like the Rings would want to risk it. Like you said, they're not idiots. If I'm them, I throw the gun in a river and bury the body in a remote wooded area."

"Any place around here that fits that bill?" O'Neill asked.

"Sure, though I'd prefer to not do anything nearby where someone might recognize me. I mean, if someone saw Bobby's truck parked off a road in the woods on the day of the disappearance, it would tell the cops where to look for the body. If I'm him, I leave the Verona area." Ryder nodded as he stared into his empty glass. "It's a nice theory, yet it might be hard to prove. And why couldn't it have been Jenny, Annie, or Roman Cooper? Couldn't any of them have done what you're suggesting?"

"Annie is out; she was driving back from La Crosse with Father Brennan and some other priest. Jenny isn't in the clear, but I can't see how she would pull it off by herself, and she doesn't know how to drive a tractor. Yet we still need to verify her alibi."

"Maybe Randy helped her," Ryder suggested.

"But he hired us. Sure, it wasn't official, but he may as well have hired us. Why do that if you committed the crime? Most importantly, why did he point out the thermos with no fingerprints? That's what made me think this was a murder. Unless he's got some grand plan I haven't figured out, he's not involved."

"And Roman?"

"The tractor started down the road ten minutes after he left the Verona hardware store. That's near Marcie's work. It would take him maybe eight to ten minutes to get from the store to where his brother was in the field. That wouldn't have been enough time to kill his brother, get the body in a trunk or something, fold the tedder, pull the tractor onto the blacktop, and start it down the road. And remember, he would have to make sure that Randy's tractor was driving away from him. Otherwise, Randy would have seen something. It would only work if he was damn lucky or had someone working with him. I can't figure out who that could be. And I can't see Roman and Jenny working together. Sure, he talked to Bobby at the hardware store or wherever, but that doesn't mean they were involved in a plot together. Nah. If Roman killed someone, it would be a spur-of-the-moment thing. He's not the planning type."

"Okay. We have a theory which points to Marcie and Bobby. But unless we find DNA or other evidence in her trunk or at their place, we can't prove anything."

"Actually, I have an idea," O'Neill said. "Earlier today, I took a look at Bobby and Marcie's credit card statements. I noticed that over the last month, they gassed up in Belleville on two Tuesday nights. On another day, one of them bought something at a gas station near Dayton, which is south of Belleville."

"How did you gain access to their credit card charges?" Ryder's body went limp. "You didn't convince Meyer to access something for you?"

"Course not. But when I visited their place, I saw where she kept the monthly statements. I just slipped in and took pictures of them."

"You broke in?" Ryder yelled.

The bartender and two men sitting at the counter glanced toward them.

"Take it easy," O'Neill said. "I already deleted the photos, and I didn't leave prints."

"I swear, you are going to drive me to the grave." He closed his eyes and took a few measured breaths. Their second round arrived, so he sipped the ale and waited for the server to drift away. "There's a good chance the weapon got thrown into a river. I mean, the police don't have any reason to suspect a shooting, so they do something that's easy, yet effective. And if they went down through Belleville on Tuesday nights, they may have been doing dry runs. Going down that way makes the Sugar River an obvious choice unless they went further or went east toward the Rock River. But that would be a hike."

"How do we find a gun in a river?"

"There are guys who search bodies of water, though they're more scuba divers and they are expensive. Too expensive for my current client — meaning you."

"Scuba divers for the Sugar River? Isn't that overkill? I mean, we're not talking about the Mississippi or even the Wisconsin River."

"Sure, you wouldn't need scuba equipment to search the Sugar River, but you'd need water skills and experience. I'm guessing most of the river is three or four feet deep, but it's high right now and I'd guess they'd aim for bridges going over wider portions. It could be five feet deep in spots."

"How about I call Lena? She or her friends know most of the rangers in the county. Most of them are outdoor types who live in the area. She could ask them where they'd dump a gun in a range of twenty miles from the Ring house going through Belleville and Dayton. If they come up with a few possibilities, she and I could search for it. Suppose we found the gun or the silencer? That would be the sort of evidence that would allow for a search warrant, wouldn't it?"

"If we connected the weapon with the Rings, it would be persuasive," Ryder said. "You said you and your sister would search the water near a few bridges. Can you even swim?"

O'Neill laughed. "Course I can swim. But Lena's the good one. She dove and swam for Ridgewood in middle school and during her one year at Edgewood. It was back before she screwed herself up. She's little, but she was good."

"We don't need someone to do a pretty dive off a bridge. We need someone to search along a riverbed for a hundred yards downstream and fifty upstream of a bridge. It's hard, dirty work."

"Figured that. Just telling you she's good in the water. Who knows, the water might not even be deep."

"You can ask her. I'm guessing there will be a dozen potential locations. If, however, Bobby and Marcie are as smart as you think, they will throw it in the river and not in some small creek, so we might be able to limit it to three or four locations. We should also consider that the Rings could have been going to Belleville for another reason. It might have nothing to do with Vernon Cooper. If they went east to Stoughton, for instance, they could have dumped it in the Yahara."

"Dayton through Belleville is the best lead we have location-wise. I'll search for free," O'Neill said, "but you'd have to pay Lena, you know?"

"If she does it, I'll pay her, though I ain't paying for her to talk with other parks geeks about Dane County's lakes and rivers. I'd pay her for water time. And my client, meaning you, would eventually have to reimburse me for all or most of the cost."

"Thanks a lot," O'Neill replied, but it didn't deter him. When their food arrived, he called his sister. He told her about their hope of finding a spot where someone could easily drop a weapon into a river or lake. They were focusing on a ten-mile area south of Belleville and going through Dayton. Lena said she'd talk to a few people and get back to him.

"I wish we could tell Becker about the Belleville and Dayton connections," Ryder said. "They'd be able to conduct a proper search. Meanwhile, it's possible that Bobby and Marcie still have the body and the weapon on their property, but I doubt it."

O'Neill took a drink and licked his lips. "Do we go to Becker and lay out our theory? Then maybe he puts the Rings under surveillance or maybe he gets a search warrant."

"Becker might buy our argument, but I doubt he'd get a search warrant for anything but phone records. Your theory breaks the Rings' alibis, but it proves nothing. And he'll know that if they killed Vernon, they likely disposed of any evidence on Tuesday night. He might not stick his neck out without a body or a weapon." Ryder squeezed ketchup on his burger. "I'd like to find something before going to Becker and the sheriff's office."

"Okay," O'Neill said. "Then let's find some evidence."

Chapter 31

O 'Neill finished his Scotch Ale as the server left the bill. Ryder slid it to O'Neill, who reluctantly pulled out his wallet. He didn't have enough cash, so, with a grumble, he took eighty dollars from the restaurant's ATM. It was more than he needed for the meal and the drinks, but he would also need cash for his date with Meyer.

The transaction weighed on him since his bi-weekly rent payment was scheduled for Tuesday, and the unplanned withdrawal meant he would be thirty-three dollars short. Unless he came up with extra cash, the rental payment would bomb. It was a problem he would have to solve, since Ryder had already transferred over all of his bonus money, and the rental company had warned him that an additional rejected withdrawal would lead to late fees.

Lena called O'Neill as they got into Ryder's truck. She told him she had spoken with her boss and a Dane County park ranger. The ranger consulted several colleagues, and they agreed that the Sugar River was the most likely option on the way to or past Dayton. They settled on two bridges as the most likely spots.

Ryder got on the phone and negotiated an agreement for her and O'Neill to search the locations identified by the rangers. He would reimburse her for mileage and pay her by the hour for time in the water. She would also receive a hundred dollar bonus if they found a gun, a silencer, or a body. While O'Neill would have to reimburse the agency for the cost, Ryder would fund any bonus.

"She's picking you up at noon tomorrow," Ryder said. "I'll drop you at your dump, then I'm going home and I'm getting some sleep. You do what you want, but keep in mind you'll be wading into a chilly river at noon tomorrow, so take it easy."

"Are you going to meet Lena and me near the search area?"

"I don't know yet. After all, I have a business to run and need to make money. I can't spend all my time working on charity cases. I will call and introduce myself to Becker, though. If he seems receptive, I'll ask whether they verified Roman and Jenny Cooper's alibis."

"Suppose we don't need you to do the search, so it's fine if Lena and I go it alone. What do we do if we find a gun or something?"

"Bring a plastic trash bag with you. If you locate a body, call the sheriff, then call me. If you find a firearm or a silencer, put it into the bag and call me. We'll take it to law enforcement, but it's a matter of whether we bring it to Becker or someone else. If you find a gun that looks like it's been in the water for a year, we'll drop it at the sheriff's office. But if it might be our murder weapon, we'll talk to Becker and have him decide what to do."

O'Neill nodded and rested his head against the passenger window.

"Seamus," Ryder said as O'Neill opened the door, "what are you going to wear when you go into the lake? You don't have a swimsuit, do you?"

"Course not. But I have running shorts. That's good enough. I'm sure Lena's got a swimsuit, though."

"That's right. She'll need something too." Ryder looked forward. "Maybe if I get a few things done, I'll try to meet you. I'll call if I'm going, so you can tell me exactly where to go."

O'Neill stepped out of the truck. "See you there."

At nine that night, O'Neill met The Johnson at the Great Dane brewpub. They planned on a few drinks, but ended up listening to a band covering Green Day songs, and he spent fifteen dollars more than he intended. Someone invited them to an after-bar party, and it was after two in the morning when he stumbled home.

At ten, his alarm went off. It had only been a few hours, and the bed was comfortable. But there were things he needed to do to be ready for his date with Meyer and his afternoon in the river. He rolled off the bed and fell to the wood floor. A sore wrist was his punishment for forgetting that he had an actual bed.

The first task was to clean up the apartment. He shook out the rugs, swept the floors, and cleaned the bathroom mirror, the window, and the countertops. He made sure he had toiletries and kitchen supplies, and he washed his two new glasses. Beer was in the refrigerator, but he had no wine. So he walked to Riley's Wines of the World, where he debated between buying two three-dollar bottles of cheap wine, or a single five-liter box. The woman at the counter told him bottles were classier, so he ended up with a white blend and a red blend. Both bottles had twist-off lids.

At a quarter to twelve, Lena called to tell him she was running late. She had taken the afternoon off, but had to finish mowing before she could leave. At about twelve-twenty, she arrived, dressed in shorts and a Ramones T-shirt. He recognized the one-piece swimsuit underneath as the same one she wore as a freshman on the Edgewood High School swim team. He had her walk through his apartment, and she made only a few comments and cleaned a few surfaces.

"The guys at my work added another spot on the Sugar River that they want us to check," she said as they got ready to leave. "It's on County Trunk Highway X, just off Highway 92. A couple of rangers from my work are meeting us at the first bridge."

"Really? What for?" O'Neill opened the apartment door and ushered his sister out.

"Don't know. They're into the outdoors. They know these places."

"Bet they just wanna check you out in a swimsuit."

"Oh, come on," she laughed as she walked down the stairs. "They do not."

"Why else are they coming?"

"They're curious and they want to help." She punched him lightly in the stomach as they stepped outside. "Besides, Seamus, not everyone is as shallow as you."

"Don't bet on it."

O'Neill's phone rang. It was Ryder, who said he would meet them at the bridge. As she started the car, Lena explained that the first spot was near

Sugar River Park, so they would leave the car at the park and walk from there. Ryder said he'd find it and be there in less than half an hour.

"Your boss is meeting us too?" Lena said after the phone call.

"Yeah. He wasn't going until it occurred to him that you'd be in a swimsuit."

"Oh, shut up."

"At least he has a reason to be there. I mean, if we find a gun, a body, or a silencer, we want him handling it. Unlike your buddies, who are coming solely to gawk."

She pulled into traffic. "Get over it, Seamus. Two of them have girlfriends and one is married. Besides," she said as she patted her chest, "it's not like I've got much to see. And looking for a gun in a river is the sort of thing they live for. They can't dive because they're working, but this is a big deal for them. They're fired up."

"You mean, these guys are on the clock?"

She ignored him, and his head was soon resting against the window. When they arrived at Sugar River Park, she nudged him. Three Dane County Parks trucks were in the parking lot, with four men meandering about and a map spread on the hood of a truck. The park's lone kickball diamond was empty. Lena parked near her colleagues, and the men approached her vehicle.

She handed her brother swimming goggles and a towel and introduced him to the rangers. It surprised him that they weren't donning the pseudo police outfits he thought park rangers wore. They shook hands and, as they asked O'Neill about his sister, Ryder's pickup pulled in. O'Neill introduced his boss as Lena swapped her sneakers for swimming shoes.

A ranger offered to join them, saying he had waders, but they decided the river was too deep for waders.

Ryder, wearing a blue business suit, stood out in the group. "Why do you think this is a likely spot?" he asked. "It's awfully close to a park and the water treatment plant." Glancing at the map, he pointed at the facility which stood across the street. "I'd be afraid someone might be in the park and see me throw something in the water."

"Trees block the view," said a ranger with a black mustache. "It's off the highway, so there is little traffic. You could dispose of a weapon without being noticed. Plus, the river is wide at that point and the current is strong. It's a decent spot, though there are better."

"What's the best location?" Ryder said.

"It depends," another ranger said. He was short and looked to be the oldest of the group.

"This is Lee Kraft," Lena said. "He grew up around here."

Lee nodded before continuing. "If I'm getting rid of a weapon, I'd throw it over at the third spot, which is a bridge on Highway X." He drew a circle on the map with his pencil. "If I also had a body to dispose of, I'd dump the gun here or at the other spot on Highway 92. Which one would depend on the amount of traffic when I arrived." He drew another circle. "Then I would park in the boat landing off Highway X, walk into the woods, and bury the body."

"Gotcha." Ryder replied. "Let's get to it then."

Crossing a road that led to the water treatment plant, they walked toward the bridge. Lee seemed familiar with the area and took the group down a thin path which led to the river. The O'Neills stripped off their street clothes at the path's entrance and set them atop their towels. O'Neill had never worn goggles, so it took him a few moments to get comfortable with them.

"Where should we look, Boss?" he asked Ryder over the sound of running water.

"This is off the highway, so it's safe to assume that, if they came this way, they turned off and were driving north. He would throw it downstream, so he would get out of the vehicle and toss it over the car and into the water. If it's a rifle, I doubt he could throw it more than fifty feet. Though he could have thrown it upstream as well, particularly if he was worried about traffic coming into view. My suggestion is we search fifty feet upstream and seventy-five feet downstream."

"I'll do the downstream part." Lena turned toward her brother. "We won't be able to see shit in there, so I think we go shore-to-shore, feeling the riverbed."

"How long ago was the weapon dumped?" a ranger asked.

"Probably on Tuesday evening," Ryder said.

"We got a few drops last night but haven't had significant rain," Lee said. "If something is in the drink, it hasn't gone far from where it went in, unless it was in a container that floated."

It was late June, but the water was still cold and O'Neill shivered as he crouched down. Lena walked under the bridge while putting her goggles on. She stuck a branch into the bank and started across the river, which ranged from thirty to fifty feet in width. O'Neill loosened his goggles, then started across. It wasn't long before his outstretched hands no longer reached the riverbed. He ducked his head underwater, but found the water to be too muddy to see anything. Closing his eyes, he ran his fingers through the mud. As he came near the riverbank, he lifted his head out of the water, crawling along and feeling for anything of interest.

Once across, he moved three feet upstream, but realized it was hard to determine exactly where he had started his last pass. Taking a cue from his sister, he marked his departure point with a stick, which he stuck into the mud near the riverbank.

After nearly half an hour, O'Neill was exhausted, but he was fifty feet from the bridge and done with his section. All he had found were two beer cans, two soda cans, and a full bottle of tabasco sauce. He stumbled up the path, fell onto the towel, and ripped off his goggles. Within a few minutes, Lena joined him and the group returned to their vehicles.

"Our other spots are actually outside Dane County," Lee said. "The first one is in Exeter Township within Green County. The township has a building near the river. I spoke with one of the Green County rangers and he's meeting us there." He turned toward his colleagues. "I'll go along, but you guys should head back. I think we might get flak if four of us are in Green County, even on a lunch break."

The rangers nodded their agreement, and only Lena and Ryder's vehicles followed Lee's truck. After five minutes, the truck pulled into a parking lot off the highway, where they met a Green County ranger who led the foursome to the river. The approach brought them along the highway and behind a guardrail. Lena and O'Neill were soon in the water again. O'Neill's hands shook as he ducked his head under. He crossed successfully, but waited a full minute before marking his entry point and starting again.

Halfway across the water, he stepped on something and yelled. Leaning down, he pulled up a broken bottle. He waved it into the air, saying it had cut into his foot. Then he continued along the riverbed. When he came to the edge, Ryder called him over and the rangers told him they wanted to see the injury. O'Neill shook as he climbed up the incline and collapsed onto his towel. Lee checked out the cut and decided he was not losing much blood and could continue. A disappointed O'Neill started another round, but a yell downstream caught his attention. Looking up, he saw Lena standing near the riverbank about twenty feet downstream, holding a rifle over her head.

Chapter 32

O'Neill was too tired to run to his sister and offer congratulations. Instead, he walked to the shore, climbed the embankment, and fell onto a towel which had been lying in a clearing. After catching his breath, he dried his chest and watched Lena arrive atop the ridge where Ryder and the rangers waited. She held the gun high with the barrel pointed skyward. It was clear she wanted to hand the weapon to Ryder, but he was putting on gloves. Finally, she passed it off and Lee gave her a hug before she stumbled to her towel, wrapping it around her shoulders but staying on her feet.

The rangers talked excitedly as Ryder held the gun close to the ground. Reaching into his pocket, he pulled out his keys and handed them to Lee, who looked at them as if they were a present.

"Go to my truck," Ryder said. "There's a box of clear plastic trash bags. Bring one to me." Lee ran off and the big detective looked over the weapon. "Looks like a Remington. A 7400, semi-automatic with a scope."

"Got a little age on it, but it's in good shape," said the Green County ranger. "It hasn't been underwater for long. Is this the weapon you were searching for?"

"I think so." Ryder's head was shaking slowly. "It's lucky we knew where to look and it's so soon after it was deposited."

"If we got a storm, it would have gotten covered in silt and mud or pushed downstream," the Green County ranger said. "Has the sheriff been looking for this?"

"No. They didn't even know a gun was involved in this crime." Ryder laughed, then glanced back at O'Neill. "We looked here based on a theory. Now we know the theory was right."

Lee returned with the plastic bag. Ryder set the rifle on it then wrapped the plastic over it, leaving the barrel pointing toward the river.

O'Neill got the energy to get to his feet. "Good one, Lena. Ryder didn't think we would find it. Otherwise, he wouldn't have offered to fund the bonus."

Lena smiled widely. "I can use it. Let's go back to the car and put clothes on. I'm freezing."

He nodded and followed her. "How'd you find it?"

"I swept my hands along the riverbed and hit something hard. The back part was stuck more in the mud, but the barrel was up at a slight angle. I sensed right away that it was a rifle. I was afraid I'd set the thing off and shoot myself."

They walked the rest of the way in silence. Lena had left the car unlocked with the keys under the seat. She pulled on her T-shirt and slipped shorts over her wet swimsuit before swapping her swim shoes for socks and sneakers. O'Neill hated getting his jeans wet, but he was cold, so he pulled them over his shorts, dried his upper body, then threw on his T-shirt. Lena gave him a light brown napkin, which he stuck inside his sock to soak up blood.

"You don't look as tired as I am," he said as they walked back to the clearing where Ryder and the rangers waited. "I'm whipped."

"I'm tired too, but I'm in shape. It helps that, unlike you, I don't drink."

Ryder and the rangers were standing on the grass far from the river, talking and nodding.

"What now?" O'Neill said as he approached his boss.

"I will call Detective Becker. I'm deciding what to tell him."

"Tell him you found the murder weapon."

"He doesn't even know he's got a murder, let alone a weapon. I'll tell him I have a theory, and this rifle we found might validate that theory." Ryder leaned toward O'Neill and put a hand on his shoulder. "When I talk to Becker, I'm going to take most of the credit for the theory. I'll gauge whether we pissed him off by getting ahead of him or if he's thankful. If he's pissed, I will minimize your involvement. I don't want him submarining your private investigator license."

"Course."

"Before I call, let's make sure we're all telling the same story." He waved the group closer. "First off, Lena, just be straight with everything. Seamus is an employee, but you're a paid subcontractor. I was paying you and your brother to search the river for a weapon or a silencer, based on a theory Seamus and I put together."

"Me searching won't get us in trouble, will it?" O'Neill asked.

"No. Detectives hire technical experts all the time as contractors and employees. Diving is not an investigative activity, and I wouldn't have been able to spend more than a few minutes in that water, so I needed you two."

O'Neill chuckled. "You in the water would have been a joy to watch."

Ryder gave him a dirty look, then motioned toward the rangers. "As for you two. What's your story? Are you going to be in trouble if your supervisors find out you were helping us?"

Lee answered first. "We'll call it cross-county cooperation. There may be some uncomfortable conversations, but we helped find a weapon used in a crime. We can't get too much shit. We're both technically on lunch break."

"Should you call your work? It will be a long lunch."

The two rangers nodded, then drifted away as they pulled out cell phones.

Ryder called Detective Martin Becker and O'Neill walked back to the vehicles, pulling out a flask when he was far enough away. The whiskey burned as it eased down his throat, and he let out a sound of relief.

Becker arrived forty minutes later, followed by deputies from Dane and Green County. A deputy interviewed Lena first and allowed her to leave so she could pick her son up from daycare.

O'Neill recognized Deputy Peterson as the person who had taken his statement after the tractor accident. Following his interview, he called Meyer to explain why he would be late for their date. After a brief discussion, Meyer offered to pick him up and take him home.

Ryder, Becker, and the others soon departed. Peterson told him she would stay until his ride arrived. "Do you want to wait in my cruiser?" she asked. "You look pretty tired."

"I'm beat, but I'm good." He sat down. "The blacktop's warm, and I have an aversion to police cars. They make me nervous."

"Police cars?"

"Yeah. They make me nervous, as do cops. No offense."

"I thought you said that the woman who's picking you up is a cop?"

He nodded and closed his eyes. "Things don't always make sense, do they?"

Chapter 33

O'Neill felt something pushing against his shoulder. His eyes creaked open and, after a brief jolt of panic, he recognized the deputy and remembered where he was.

"Your ride is here." Peterson extended a hand and lifted him to his feet. She then walked toward Meyer's car, which had pulled into the lot.

The driver's side door opened and Erin Meyer, nearly six foot four of her, stepped out. Her long black hair blew in the wind and she pulled off sunglasses. She wore jeans and a white shirt with sleeves that went to her elbows. The deputy paused, then continued toward her with a hand extended. O'Neill ambled after her.

"Hello. I take it you are Seamus' ride. I'm Deputy Anna Peterson with the Dane County Sheriff's Office. He told me you're a police officer."

Meyer nodded as they shook hands. "Detective Erin Meyer with the City of Madison Police Department."

O'Neill slid behind Meyer, brushing against her elbow as he passed. He waved to the deputy and eased against the passenger door. Peterson tilted toward Meyer and whispered something. The two women exchanged a few words and laughed before parting.

Once Meyer opened her door, O'Neill grabbed the passenger door handle, letting out a gasp as he fell into the seat. She waited until his seatbelt clasped shut before shifting into reverse.

"Sorry about being wet and about screwing up our date." He glanced behind, trying to take one last look at the river. All he saw was the bridge railing and surrounding trees.

"Tell me about what happened. Why is Ryder going back to the sheriff's office, and why were you sitting in a parking lot in Green County with a Dane County Sheriff's deputy?"

O'Neill told her about his day, focusing on the search through the cold Sugar River. He then explained his theory of how someone had brought a gun with them into the hayfield Vernon Cooper was working. After shooting him, the person left the body near the culvert and continued working the field. An accomplice then drove by, picked up the body and the weapon, disposing of the latter in the river.

"You have a potential murder weapon, but you don't have a body?" Meyer said. "Do you think that woman is the killer? Or was it the guy I saw at your office?"

"Marcie and Bobby Ring are our killers, I think. When I was at their house, I saw some credit card receipts that told me they'd made a few trips recently to the area we searched."

"Oh!" Meyer's eyes widened. "You figured they might have been planning a trip down that way? They were doing dry runs?"

"Exactly."

"And the body?"

"It's probably somewhere in Green County," O'Neill said.

"Finding the rifle changes the case." She took her eyes off the road and turned toward him. "The mistake they made was having you as a witness."

"What do you think the sheriff's office will do? Will they get a search warrant for the Ring place?"

"They'll put them under surveillance today," she said as her car merged onto the highway. "I don't know if the Rings have cell phones, but if they do, the sheriff's office should request their records. It will be interesting how often the two were calling each other on the day the farmer disappeared. If your idea about one of them driving the tractor and the other picking up the body is correct, the Rings were probably communicating since timing was important."

"That could be good evidence?"

"Yes, though circumstantial. One thing that worries me is the rangers. You said a handful of them were involved in the search for the weapon, so multiple people know about you finding it. People talk and if the Rings hear rumors that the police found a rifle in the Sugar River south of Belleville, they'll know they are being watched. If those rangers you talked to are right, and they buried the body in Green County, then they will either move it, or they'll decide that the burial place is good enough. They won't go to the body unless they're sure they are not being watched."

"My concern is that they'll pay someone else to move the body. The sheriff won't be able to prove anything, and the Rings will be under permanent suspicion but never be charged."

"What you need is the body. If, however, the rifle is owned by them, it would force the Rings to explain why they threw a gun that was recently fired into the river. Otherwise, finding the body is the chief hope."

O'Neill placed his head against the window. "There's got to be something we're missing." It seemed moments later when his eyes fluttered open and they were outside his apartment. He turned away from the afternoon sunlight. "We going for dinner, right?"

"I'm dropping you off so you can shower and get ready. I'll park in my spot and be back on foot. We can walk to a restaurant from here. It's five thirty. We'll need to go someplace besides Porta Bella, but we can still get something to eat."

He reached over, patted her leg, and got out of the car. "See you soon." He closed the door, but it didn't latch, so he grabbed it again, slamming it shut. Then he crossed in front of the car, limping toward his apartment building.

Inside, he locked the deadbolt out of habit and flipped on the kitchen faucet. Sticking his face into the sink, he drank for thirty seconds before shutting the water off and reaching into the refrigerator. He opened a Berghoff Red Ale, and took a few gulps as he walked into the bathroom and turned on the shower. He stripped, slid the curtain open, and stepped inside. The water was surprisingly warm, so he took a long shower, washing his hair and his body with a bar of soap that was nearing its end.

As he dried off, he heard the security system's familiar buzz. He hurried to the door without getting dressed. After buzzing Meyer into the building, he limped to the closet, pulled out clean boxer shorts, and slipped on his other pair of jeans. He pulled on his only short-sleeved button-down shirt as he heard a knock. Once fully buttoned, he unlocked the deadbolt and opened the door. "Sorry about that. Took longer than I should have in the shower. Give me a minute while I brush my teeth."

Meyer followed him to the bathroom. He collected the wet clothes from the floor and carried them to his closet. After emptying the hamper, he draped the wet clothes on top, then closed the sliding closet door.

"What happened to your foot?"

O'Neill realized he was limping. "I stepped on a broken beer bottle in the Sugar River." He stopped at the bathroom doorway, lifting his foot. "Doesn't hurt too much."

"We should clean it. Do you have peroxide?" Meyer kneeled and opened his bathroom cabinet. Pulling out a bottle, she examined it and slapped it onto the counter. "It expired in '98, but it will do. How about bandages?"

"I may have one or two band-aids," he mumbled as he put toothpaste on his brush. "Check below."

"There are only two little ones. I saw you limping when you walked into your apartment and suspected you might be short on medical supplies, so I brought a few things from my car, including the emergency kit." She put down the toilet lid. "Once you're done brushing, sit down. I'll clean out the cut and bandage it."

He rinsed his mouth and sat on the lid. Meyer got on the floor in front of him, so he lifted his foot in the air and she used her right leg to brace it.

"You look nice, by the way," he said. "I like the shirt and I haven't seen you in jeans before."

"Thanks, I think. Your foot doesn't look good. Something tells me you're not up for a long walk."

He felt a surge of panic. "I can walk fine. We can go. No problem."

She rested his foot on the bathroom floor. "Why don't we order a pizza and stay in? Wait while I grab the medical kit. I left it by the door."

"Staying in is fine by me," he said when she returned. Things were playing out better than he expected.

She ripped a package open and pulled out a hunk of gauze. She ran a string of tape over the bandage and across his foot. "I had a lot of nagging injuries from volleyball and got plenty of cuts and abrasions, so I'm used to gauze and tape." She patted his foot, then placed it on the ground. "All good. I suggest you put a sock on, though, to help hold it together."

O'Neill limped into the main room, hoping he had a clean pair. He opened the closet door, finding two mis-matched white socks. Sitting on the ground, he slid them on, then got to his feet. They agreed on their pizza order and Meyer pulled out her phone, sat in his new used chair, and placed the order. "It should be here within the half hour."

"You want to listen to some music or something?" he asked. "Maybe some of my stuff?"

"I would love that" She leaned back in the chair, and looked out the window as a car rumbled past. Setting a paper shopping bag on the floor, she pulled out a five hundred piece puzzle. The cover showed a picture of powdered donut holes. She said she had borrowed it from her mom and brought it inside since she thought they would stay in. She poured the contents onto the wood floor.

By the time the pizza arrived, all the pieces were face-up, half of the edging was together, and the last song on the CD finished. After setting the pizza on the counter, he opened the box, and the pizza aroma overtook the room. She was soon behind him, and he handed her a plate. She took two pieces of pepperoni and mushroom. He twisted off the lid of the red wine and poured two full glasses.

Meyer took her glass and plate and walked toward the puzzle. "Can you grab me a coaster?"

"Coaster?"

"You can't put a glass of red wine directly on a wood floor." Her head shook. Then she took a *Rolling Stone* magazine from the corner of the room and set it on the floor. "This will have to do. The last thing you want is red wine rings."

"Can't have that." O'Neill got up to change the disc, but his gaze lingered on the glass of red wine sitting on the magazine. "Hey," he said. "You're saying that if any of the wine gets onto the outside of the glass, it might get on the floor. It might also get on your hand, right?"

"Sure." She stared at him, but he didn't move. "Seamus, what is it?"

"The wine made me think about the thermos and Marcie's gloves." He set his glass next to hers. "Maybe there is something we missed."

Chapter 34

Meyer was on her side, her right hip and elbow on the wood floor. O'Neill slid in next to her, resting a hand on her waist.

"Get on with it. What's your idea?" She looked down at his hand, implying she would move it if he didn't respond. "What about a wine ring made you think you missed something?"

"Vernon Cooper's water was mixed with Red Bull. It was his caffeine fix." He hesitated, struggling to transition his thoughts to words. "That afternoon, Randy filled his father's thermos with water, mixed it with Red Bull, and put it in the tractor. Randy claims he wasn't wearing gloves and neither was his dad. The police found it with a small amount of watered-down Red Bull inside, but there were no prints on the thermos."

"Like you said, Marcie probably wiped it clean."

"Yeah. I think Marcie shot Vernon and he dropped the thermos. She picked it up and had to wipe it. That implies she didn't have gloves on when she shot him. If she was wearing them, she wouldn't have wiped it."

"Sure."

"Then she would have put them on before getting into the cab and setting the thermos inside."

"That makes sense." Meyer sat up.

"Could some of the Red Bull have gotten on the inside or the outside of the gloves?"

She stared over his shoulder and bit her lip. "It could, I suppose. That would be evidence, but there could be something else more important." Her eyes fixed on his. "Did they find gun residue inside the tractor, say, on the steering wheel?"

"Not that I know of," he said.

"If not, it supports your argument that she wasn't wearing gloves when she shot him, but she put them on before getting into the tractor. I know I've never shot with gloves on and can't recall people at the range wearing them while shooting, so having them off when shooting makes sense. She then picks up the thermos. She realizes her mistake and wipes it clean, maybe with the gloves or maybe with something else. Then she puts them on, picks up the thermos, and gets into the tractor. Once home, she washes her hands."

Taking his hand off her waist, O'Neill picked up his glass and stared at the red wine as it swirled in the glass. "I don't know what pair she used, but I saw some just inside her front door in her porch area. They were light brown work gloves. They might have been leather, cotton or some sort of synthetic fiber. Maybe that's what she was wearing when she drove the tractor." He finished his wine, placing the glass on the magazine. "She might not have gotten rid of them since she didn't get blood on them and she wouldn't have been worried about them having gunshot residue, since she wasn't wearing them when she fired the gun. Even the thermos. It would have appeared to have just been filled with water."

Meyer's grip tightened on his shoulder. "If we're right and she put the gloves on after shooting the rifle, then residue from her hands would likely transfer to the *inside* of the gloves."

O'Neill smiled. "Gunshot residue can transfer like that?" He grasped her waist and pulled her close.

"Sure. It comes off easily. For instance, if someone puts their hands in their pockets, some could wipe off the hands and into the pockets. It's been roughly four days since she shot him, but residue is likely in the gloves if she hasn't worn them again or washed them."

"I'll call Ryder."

"Yes, definitely." Meyer pulled him close and kissed him. "If they buy our argument, they may try to get a search warrant yet tonight. They need to beat any chance of her wearing or washing those gloves. Also, if they find Red Bull on the gloves, the sheriff could argue that it connects them with Vernon Cooper. But it's the residue that would be most persuasive. It would give the sheriff's office evidence that connects Marcie with firing a weapon."

O'Neill let go of her and dialed his phone.

"Yes," Ryder said as he answered. "What do you want? I'm busy."

"Has the Sheriff's Office searched the Ring property yet?" Meyer tilted forward so their foreheads touched. O'Neill inclined the phone so she could hear Ryder's response.

"They likely will tomorrow. Becker thought he'd get approval late tonight or tomorrow to request a search warrant for the place and to access phone records, but it likely won't be issued until sometime on Sunday. We're doubtful there will be any evidence at their place, but Becker intends to search it and to search for the body south of where we found the rifle. Deputies will, however, keep tabs on the Rings tonight."

"How about Roman Cooper? Or even Jenny?"

"Becker says Jenny's alibi is airtight. She was not only at the conference she mentioned; she was the check-in and check-out person. So she was there the whole time. She was still in Madison when the tractor started down the road."

"And Roman?"

"We can't see him pulling it off," Ryder said. "Becker says they verified Roman buying something at the hardware store just ten minutes before the disappearance. Like we said earlier, he could have driven past and picked up the body, but he would have needed an accomplice. Roman and his wife have two vehicles, but the daughter took one to work and he took the other into town. So the wife was home with the son. The only possibility is that Roman's family and his employee are lying. That's unlikely, so we're assuming Marcie shot Vernon and Bobby hid the body."

"Have they gotten access to Marcie's phone records yet?"

"No. That will come with the search warrant."

"I'll feel better if we see who Marcie was in contact with. I'm assuming it was Bobby but, in theory, Roman could be her accomplice. He could be the one who picked up the body."

"That doesn't make sense," Ryder said. "Roman working with Marcie?"

"Yeah, I don't think so either, but it's still possible. And if they were involved together, you'd think they'd take the opposite roles with Roman pretending to be Vernon. Either way, Erin and I were talking things through, and one thing that came up was Marcie's gloves." O'Neill filled Ryder in on their idea.

"You may have a point," Ryder said. "Neither Becker nor I thought about the inside of the gloves. It's possible she's disposed of or washed them but, as you said, she may not think about residue on the *inside* of the gloves. And she probably doesn't know the thermos had red bull mixed in with the water. If they find Red Bull, Marcie could argue she just had some herself, but having both would be hard to explain. It's worth looking for. I'm assuming Meyer doesn't want me to mention her name. Correct?"

Meyer shook her head.

"Course not," O'Neill said.

"Okay. Let me talk to Becker. I doubt he'll want me involved in any search, but he might want you to identify any gloves they find that have gunshot residue or Red Bull on them. But they won't need you tonight. I'll call you back after I talk with Becker."

O'Neill hung up the phone. "They don't need us. Guess we can go on with our date."

She leaned forward and kissed him. After a few moments, he ran a hand along her back and onto her hips. She pulled away, picked up both glasses, and walked into the kitchen area, returning with two half-full glasses. "Sorry if I am touchy," she said as she returned to her spot. "I'm a little out of practice. You see, I haven't been alone with a man in an apartment for ages. I'm...not used to it."

"No problem. I get it." He picked up a jigsaw piece. "Should we just finish this? Two detectives should make quick work of a five hundred piece puzzle."

After another hour, they had nearly finished the puzzle. Meyer put the leftover pizza into the refrigerator and rinsed out the empty bottle of red. Meyer's phone rang as O'Neill claimed the last of the white wine.

"Mom," she said. "It's good to hear from you."

As he listened to her conversation, his phone rang. He got to his feet, hurried into the bathroom, and closed the door.

"Seamus, it's me," Ryder said. "I just got off the phone with Becker. They have a search warrant, have collected phone records, and intend to serve the Rings tonight. The bad news is that neither of the Rings are home and Bobby's truck is not in their garage. They could be at a local bar or a friend's place, or they could be up to no good. We don't know."

"Let's hope they aren't moving the body," O'Neill said. "Or making a run for it."

"If they get caught with the body, it could solve everything. While there's not much you and I can do about it, I wanted to keep you in the loop."

"I'll update Erin." He opened the door and put the phone into his pocket.

Meyer was still on her call, but her eyes locked onto O'Neill's as he stepped out of the bathroom. "I'm still talking to my mom," she whispered, then turned away and spoke into the phone. "Can you repeat that, Mom?"

He listened to the conversation, learning that Meyer's younger sister, Jen, just announced she was pregnant. He also inferred that the grandmother-to-be was surprised her daughter had not yet heard the news. The conversation continued for a few minutes, and her attempts to end the discussion were unsuccessful.

"Mom, I have to go. Really. Yes. It's just that I'm on a date." There was a pause. "Yes, a date. We're working on a puzzle and I can't just ignore him. I need to go." Meyer covered the receiver and looked at O'Neill. "That will get her to hang up." She turned her attention back to her mother. "Okay, thanks. Yes, I'll tell you about him. Yes. Sure, you can tell Dad if you want to. I love you too. Yes. And when I get home, I'm sure I'll find a voicemail from Jen on my landline. Thanks. Bye." She hung up.

"When she asks about me, tell her I'm nice," O'Neill said, bracing himself against the counter.

"I couldn't get rid of her, and figured that would do the trick. I wanted to find out what Ryder told you, but my mom was so excited about my sister being pregnant that I had to let her talk." She pointed at O'Neill's phone. "What did Ryder have to say? Are they searching tonight?"

"Yeah. But the Rings aren't home and the cops don't know where they are."

"That's bad." Meyer took two steps and glanced at the front door. "I was going to head out as soon as we finished the puzzle, but it would make sense for me to stay the night."

"Just what I was thinking."

"Not for that reason." She feigned a punch to his stomach. "I just want to make sure I'm around if something happens; there are killers on the loose."

"And you need to protect me?"

Meyer smiled. "I wouldn't go that far, but you never know what they'll do. They may know about your role in this. There's always a chance they'll come after you. It's remote, but it's real."

"Very remote, but if it keeps you here for the night, I'm fine with needing your protection."

"But we're just sleeping. We're not fooling around. Okay?"

"Too bad, but okay." He put the window shade down and sat on the bed, where he struggled to slip his sock off without pulling off the bandage. He flipped on the television. *Nash Bridges* was on, and someone was shooting at the detective. "Must admit, I am exhausted. Being in that river was more work than I imagined."

The faucet turned on and she stuck a wine glass into the sink. "You should go to bed."

He nodded his agreement. "Okay if I take my pants off and sleep in my boxers? Sleeping in jeans isn't all that comfortable."

"You don't have any shorts?"

"They're wet." He had sweatpants, but didn't mention them.

"That's fine, since there aren't other options."

"How about you?" O'Neill tossed the two pillows onto the bed. "You're not going to sleep in your jeans, are you?"

"No." Meyer turned off the water and set the glasses on a towel. She checked the front door, then turned off the overhead light. The only illumination came from the television. "You want the side toward the wall or the outside?"

"Whatever you don't want," he said.

"I'll take the outside. You get in first."

He slipped off his pants, opened the sheets, and crawled in. Once he was inside, Meyer came closer. She unzipped her jeans, and they fell to the floor quicker than he thought possible. He glimpsed white bikini underwear as she stepped out of her pants and into O'Neill's new full-sized bed.

"Now we're here to sleep," she said. "No spooning."

"Darn." His voice was hardly audible. "You know what would be awesome?" He waited until she turned toward him. "If I wake up to you fighting off Marcie Ring in your underwear."

She kissed him. "Dream on."

"Will do."

Chapter 35

Daylight penetrated the window shade. O'Neill was alone in bed and the television was off. Twisting sideways, his foot touched the cold wood floor. A car horn brought his attention to the window, then he heard rustling outside the door. For an instant, he imagined it was Marcie and Bobby Ring, but when the door flung open, Meyer came inside.

"You're up," she said.

He glanced at the clock, which said 10:12. "Yeah. Must've slept a good twelve hours. I was out cold. How'd you sleep? Thought I remembered hearing you moving around at one point. You said something about socks."

"I didn't quite fit in the bed and my feet were cold."

O'Neill looked at the bed and realized she had pushed the sheets through at the bottom. The bed was not long enough for her. "Oh, sorry about that."

"I brought you a bagel and a bottle of Diet Mountain Dew." She left both on the kitchen counter.

He carried his pants into the bathroom. After relieving himself, he brushed his teeth and stared at the short-haired man in the mirror. Then he stepped into his jeans. The bandage was coming off, so he put down the toilet lid and called Meyer in. As she took off the remains of the bandage, O'Neill's phone rang.

"Seamus, it's me, Ryder. Can you come to the office right now? There's some news. I want to talk to you. It's important."

"Erin and I just went for a run," O'Neill lied. "Suppose she could give me a ride."

"Sure. Bring your girlfriend along, but no one else. Get here as soon as you can."

"Everything okay?"

"Yeah." The line went dead.

O'Neill grabbed Meyer's elbow. "Either Ryder got news on my PI test, or...something's wrong."

———

Traffic was light, and Meyer's Lincoln careened down the street at forty-five miles per hour. She pushed on the gas pedal and they sped through a yellow light. The car slowed as they turned onto Regent Street, pulling into a lot near Ryder's office. O'Neill searched through the parked vehicles, but didn't see a black Chevy S-10.

O'Neill finished his bagel and got out of the car. He held a half-full soda bottle, and Meyer carried an empty Styrofoam cup. They hurried to the building, slowing as they approached Sal's Subs.

As he started up the stairs of the detective agency, he moved his Sweetone tin whistle into his back pocket, making sure the mouthpiece aimed upward. Before reaching for the door, he took a gulp from his flask and offered it to Meyer. She shook her head. Then he pointed at the sign on the door which said, "Sorry, we're closed." He grabbed the handle, and the door opened. He exhaled and walked inside.

Ryder was behind his desk. On the opposite side, sitting in a chair, was Marcie Ring. Her hair was down and uncombed. Black eyeliner was smudged around her left eye. "Morning Seamus," Ryder said. "Come in."

"Morning, Boss." O'Neill maneuvered past the step that so many customers tripped on. Mcyer followed closely behind. His gaze bounced from Ryder to their visitor. "Good morning, Marcie."

"No, it's not," Marcie said. "Who the hell is she?"

"This is Erin. She's my girlfriend."

"Isn't she a little tall for you?" Marcie said.

"Sure," O'Neill replied. He didn't see a weapon, but as he came closer, he noticed she was shaking.

Ryder pointed at a chair next to Marcie's. "Take a seat, guys. Marcie and I have been talking, and after considering things, she decided to turn herself in. You can relax."

Marcie stared forward as O'Neill slid into the wooden chair beside her. Since there wasn't an open seat, Meyer leaned against the front of Ryder's desk.

"The police have arrested Marcie's brother." Ryder fixed his gaze on her. "The Rings spent the night in Watertown at a hotel. They took a truck owned by one of Bobby's friends, but that friend apparently told the police about it. The police found the vehicle and had the hotel room surrounded early this morning. Becker called me. He said they went in and found Bobby, but not Marcie."

She laughed and shook her head. "Bobby and I had gone out for a drink and I met some guy." She spoke as if in a trance. "Bobby went back to the hotel first. The cops weren't there, but when I arrived, they were everywhere. I spent an hour trying to decide what to do." She paused, and for the first time, she looked at O'Neill. "We hadn't gotten rid of our map, so I knew we were screwed. The cops knew everything, and they'd be able to determine where we had been and would eventually find the body." She shook her head. "Fucking Eric Sather."

"He's Bobby's friend," Ryder said. "The one who lent them the truck."

"I'm screwed." Marcie looked into O'Neill's eyes. "You know what happened. You know what I did."

"Yeah."

"There's no walking that back, ya know? There's no changing it and I'm okay with that since fucking Vernon Cooper got what he fucking deserved. But it's Bobby I worry about. I thought about making a run for it, but I couldn't because of Bobby. He didn't do anything except what I told him to do. If they want to come down hard on me, that's fine. But I want them to be easy on him. As easy as possible."

"So she's turning herself in," Ryder said. "I already contacted a guy I know at Banks and Fowler. They're some of the best criminal lawyers in town. He's hooking her up with someone who's got a clue and is affordable. She's already given me her weapon." Ryder paused, and they all looked at Marcie, who was staring forward. "Marcie is hoping that her cooperation will help to get a favorable result for her brother. She says they'll lead the police to the body and she'll confess to everything. She'll admit to killing Vernon Cooper, providing it gets leniency for Bobby. Her brother was only following her direction and helping her."

"Why did you call me?" O'Neill asked. "Sounds like things are all set."

"Ms. Ring wanted to understand how I figured everything out. I talked her through things, but I told her you puzzled most of it out, and that I was more the..."

"Figurehead," she said.

"Sure," Ryder said. "The figurehead."

"It surprised me that someone figured it out," Marcie said. "Becker wasn't even in the ballpark." She continued to stare out the front window. "Then I heard about you finding the rifle. I knew we were screwed unless we got the body buried where no one would ever find it. Bobby switched trucks with Eric for the night, and we went and dug it up and drove up north past Horicon. I hated driving that far with a body, but we thought that, if we had car trouble, we'd bury it off the road. But we got it hidden. They know the area where it is, but it will take them time to find it, unless we lead them to the spot."

"I told Marcie that the body's location would give her leverage," Ryder said. "It might not help in her case, but it could help in her brother's."

"I agree," Meyer said. "Any prosecutor worth their salt won't give in on a murder charge, but when someone abets a homicide, there are several routes the DA could take. They could go anywhere from first degree intentional homicide to hiding a corpse. If your brother and you cooperate, it could make a tremendous difference."

O'Neill raised a hand in the air. "Should have mentioned that she is also a detective. She knows about this shit."

"Your boss says you think I pulled the trigger," Marcie said, looking at O'Neill. "Is that right?"

"Yeah. I figure you laid down in the field and when Vernon got out of the tractor, you shot him. You then continued to ted the hay until well after the body was gone."

"Yeah," Marcie said. "I got my revenge. It was sweet. But now I'm screwed. I had to do it. No fucking regrets."

O'Neill lifted a hand slightly in the air, as if asking a question in school. "Why now? It's been five years since your mother's death."

Marcie's lips curled over her teeth. "When it happened, I swore I would get revenge." She glanced at Ryder before turning her attention back to O'Neill. "But Bobby was afraid. He said everyone would know it was us that killed him. I agreed to wait a year. But after a year, it was still too soon. The same thing happened on the second anniversary, but I made myself a promise that he wouldn't live five years past Mom's death. Zero percent chance. Eventually, it occurred to me that, if we made it look like Vernon ran away, people might look at his own family's history, rather than mine. Even Bobby knew I was right. I figured him disappearing right around the anniversary would make it look as if Vernon had some guilt. Though I doubt the piece of shit had any." She wiped an eye, and a tear dripped down her cheek. "What do you think Bobby's role was in this?"

"He took the body from Cooper's Chance and brought it back to your place," O'Neill said. "He got rid of the gun and buried the body after he got home from work. Got to admit, I wasn't a hundred percent sure it was him. I thought you might have worked with Roman Cooper."

"Kaiser?" Marcie laughed and wiped her eyes.

"Becker got phone records," Ryder said. "It's clear that Marcie and Bobby were in contact at the time of the disappearance. Neither of them had a phone conversation with Roman."

"I'm still surprised you figured it out," Marcie continued. "Your boss says the lack of prints on the thermos bothered you. You're smarter than you look, you know? I spaced-out, I guess. Fucking Vernon had it in his hand when I shot him. He dropped it and it spilled on the ground. I picked it up as a reaction. Just my fucking luck that a detective who doesn't have his head up his ass sees the fucking tractor crash. What are the fucking odds?"

"Fortune brings in boats that are not steered," O'Neill said. "That's mangled Shakespeare, I think."

"I fucking hate Shakespeare."

There was a knock at the door, and a man called in, saying he was a lawyer. Meyer let him in and after twenty minutes of conversation, Marcie, Ryder, Meyer, and the lawyer drove to the Dane County Sheriff's Office.

O'Neill was left in the office by himself.

Chapter 36

It was nearly noon on Wednesday and there was still no angry email notification from O'Neill's landlord. He slipped on shoes and walked to the Echo Tap. Inside, he waited in line behind an old man in Wisconsin Badgers gear. The ATM charged a fee for making deposits or withdrawals but allowed patrons to see their balance for free. Once the man stepped aside, O'Neill stuck in his card, fearing he would see a negative balance. Instead, the balance was positive. He did the math and realized that, not only did his rental payment go through, but he had one hundred and forty-five dollars more than he had expected. He dialed The Johnson as he walked outside.

"Johnson, it's O'Neill."

"What's up?"

"Did the royalties from the Bang Shoot thing come through? Someone deposited maybe a hundred and forty-five bucks in my account. Did you get your share?"

"Could be. If it is, I should also have my sixteen dollars and nine cents. Just a second while I log into my account. I do all my banking online now." There was a brief silence. "Yeah, I got my sixteen dollars deposited last night. So that's got to be it."

"Cool. Outstanding timing. My rent was due yesterday, so I was banking on this. Otherwise, it would bounce, or the bank would charge me a twenty-dollar overdraft fee thing."

"Sometimes, things just come together."

"Not often enough. Thanks again for your help. You're the best agent I've ever had."

Sticking his phone into his pocket, he leaned against a streetlight. A hundred and forty-five-dollar royalty payment wasn't exactly a step forward, but it told him that music could still positively impact his life.

O'Neill was a few minutes early for his meeting with Ryder at the Main Depot. Blatz was in his blue Blatz shirt. He lifted his hat high in the air, waving O'Neill over. There were only a few other patrons and, while he recognized them, he didn't know their names.

"They found that fishing boat in Lake Michigan," Blatz said as O'Neill sat at the counter, a single stool between them. He pointed at the television. "The Linda E, that is."

Channel 3's coverage shifted between the Navy minesweeper that located the fishing boat and a news conference that included the United States Coast Guard. The story showed black and white photos of the three men that went down with the boat.

"Are you surprised they found it?" Blatz said.

"The Linda E? Not surprised they found something, but I'm surprised they found the exact boat they were looking for. They must have known where to look, and having a minesweeper had to help. Suppose those things are good for finding something underwater. The keys are knowing where to look and having the right tools."

"The Coast Guard guy who was on said they're going to send a little sub or something down there to look to see what kind of damage there was."

"They wouldn't have located it without the minesweeper," the bartender said as she approached. "What can I get you? We're out of the Blonde Doppelbock. Capital replaced that with their Fest beer."

He sat a manilla folder on the counter. "I'll take a Fest."

As the drink slid in front of him, Channel 3 shifted to a "Breaking News — Update." The screen flipped to a wooded area. The crawl at the bottom of the screen said, "Body of Verona farmer found in rural Dodge County."

O'Neill took two gulps.

"You know anything about this Verona guy?" Blatz asked.

It had been three days since Marcie Ring had turned herself in to the Dane County Sheriff's Office. Earlier in the morning, O'Neill had gone for his run with Meyer and had made it even further than the prior Wednesday. She filled him in on the search details.

"Yeah, a little," O'Neill said. "I know they arrested two siblings, one for killing the farmer, the other for hiding a corpse or something like that. The suspects cooperated, which is probably what led the cops to the body."

"Horicon Marsh area," the bartender said. "Don't know how they found it so quickly unless the killers led them there."

They watched silently, and when the station showed Marcie's mugshot, one patron said she looked too innocent to be a killer. The door opened and in stepped John Ryder. "Hey, Seamus." He pulled up a stool between O'Neill and Blatz. "You make your run this morning?"

O'Neill nodded. "Made it almost two miles before I had to stop." He pushed his empty mug forward. The bartender snatched it up and set it under the tap. "Erin got called into work, so I walked home and went back to sleep. You want one?"

"Sure," Ryder said. "Did you make your Two for Tuesday?"

"Yeah." O'Neill laughed. "That's two weeks in a row. The bad thing is, she wants me to run with her on Saturday morning too. That's her other normal day off."

"A Two for Friday?" Ryder laughed and slapped a knee. "Will you be able to do that?"

"Don't think I could do two on a Friday. I mean, it's Friday. I'm going with Two for Tuesday and Five for Friday. We'll see how that goes."

It wasn't a big step. But it was a step.

Ryder shook his head. "Did Erin tell you?" He paused and lowered his voice. "Marcie and Bobby led the police to Vernon's body?"

O'Neill pointed to the television screen. "They just had something on the news, but the sound wasn't up."

"Yeah, what's up with that body they found?" Blatz asked.

Ryder glanced at Blatz, then turned back to O'Neill, dropping his voice to a whisper. "Becker called about an hour ago with an update. As you know, on Saturday night, the Dane County Sheriff's office searched the Ring property and tested the gloves. They got gunpowder residue from the inside and found traces of Red Bull on the outside, just as you and Meyer had suggested. While this went down, the Rings moved the body. Marcie says they had always planned to move it to a better spot once things cooled off. But when they heard about the gun being found, they switched vehicles so they could move the body right away."

"I wonder if it was near that boat landing that the rangers talked about."

"Becker didn't tell me." Ryder took a sip of his beer, then pulled O'Neill closer. "The DA is playing nice with Bobby. He'll end up serving about five years. They will convict Marcie of first degree intentional homicide. She'll probably get life, but she might be eligible for parole at some point."

"Got to admit I feel a little sorry for her." O'Neill sipped his beer and shook his head. "What a waste."

"Yeah, the Cooper kids were pretty forgiving as well," Ryder said. "They urged the DA to go easy on Bobby. I saw a draft of the Dane County Sheriff's office press release. It mentions the Ryder Detective Agency. Also, I've got two interviews tomorrow for a secretary. We need help to manage the fallout from the publicity. I'm hiring part-time, estimating fifteen to twenty hours a week. Also, I got your test results." Ryder pulled a sheet of paper from his jacket pocket. "You passed."

He took the sheet from his boss' hand and Blatz leaned closer. O'Neill didn't bother to read it, other than noting the score. "Eighty-seven percent. Not as high as I expected."

"You needed eighty-four percent."

"Thought you said I needed seventy."

"It used to be seventy. They moved it up, I guess."

"What test did O'Neill pass?" Blatz asked.

"Private investigator exam," Ryder said, his voice rising in volume.

Blatz reached around Ryder and touched O'Neill's shoulder. "I thought you already was a PI?"

"Now it's official," Ryder said.

"Drinks all around?" Blatz suggested.

The big detective looked about the bar. There were only four customers. "Sure. Why not?"

There was a roar and two older women came out of the bathroom.

"I passed," O'Neill said. "What's next?"

"There's a formal review of your application, but my contact told me you're already through and it's just a matter of paperwork. I'm guessing you'll be licensed within a week." Ryder laughed and slapped an open hand on the counter. "He said they've spent more time on your application than on any he can recall. Everyone's on board with it, and our involvement in the Cooper case will only help. Unless you get arrested, he says it's a given."

"Believe me, I won't get arrested. We should celebrate."

"Definitely. But don't overdo it. We have to make money, you know? And I want you to help me, so we can finally decide which cases we take."

"I take one case and you take one, right?"

"Exactly. Then, when it's official, we can have a bigger celebration. You want to invite anyone to join us?" Ryder asked.

"Erin, definitely. And The Johnson and Topper. Is this a plus one?"

Ryder laughed. "Sure. But I'm only buying your drinks. I'm not buying for everyone. Maybe I'll buy a cake too, but I'm not buying drinks for your music buddies."

"Cake, huh? Either way, they're the only ones who know what I do. I don't really tell anyone else about my job besides the crew here." He motioned toward Blatz and the bartender. "So that's it."

"How about Garcia? After all, he gave you that letter of support and got one out of Bobby Leidel."

"Garcia's okay, but Leidel's Erin's boss. Don't think she'll relax if he's there, unless maybe we invite Penny Jefferson. She thinks Erin shouldn't date me, but maybe I can charm her a bit. I should probably invite Lena too, though I doubt she'll go since everyone will be drinking. Just more offering, ya know. I'd invite Randy Cooper, but he's probably not old enough to drink, and Jenny and Roman might be pissed that we thought they were suspects. Speaking of which, have you talked to any of the Coopers?"

"No, but Becker told me that Roman isn't taking the land his brother gave him. Instead, it's going to Randy and his sisters. We can talk to them this weekend at Vernon's funeral. We can go to the wake and pay our respects."

"You think Mabel Purcell will be there?"

"You mean *that Purcell woman*?" He laughed. "How the hell should I know?"

"I got something I want to share with her." O'Neill tapped the manilla folder. "Think I found out what happened to Stephen Cooper."

"He's the one who disappeared a hundred years ago, right?" Ryder pulled the folder closer and opened it.

"There are databases and stuff available nowadays for genealogists and historians. I went to the Wisconsin State Historical Society and did some searching. I didn't find a Stephen Cooper in Walla Walla, Washington, but I found a Stephen Slatter, who had the same birthday as Cooper. And Slatter was Stephen's mother's maiden name. He first shows up in a 1906 Walla Walla city directory. It all makes sense."

"You even got a picture of him," Ryder said after opening the folder. "This is Stephen Slatter?"

"Yeah. And he's a dead ringer for the picture Mabel had of Stephen Cooper."

Blatz grabbed the photo. "O'Neill solved yet another mystery, eh?"

"Yes," Ryder said. "Two in a row where we didn't make any money."

"I was just curious," O'Neill said. "It only took a few hours. Course the guy's dead now. But he had kids, so Mabel may have some cousins she doesn't know about."

Ryder returned the photo to its folder. "Bring it to the wake. It will give the old lady something to talk about. You going to invite anyone to go with us?"

"Erin and Lena. Don't know if Erin will be free, but my sister will go for sure."

"Let me know whether we're going together or whether we're meeting in Verona."

"Will do. But for now, let's just have a drink for poor Vernon Cooper."

"Is Vernon the dead guy?" Blatz asked. Ryder nodded, so Blatz and everyone in the bar held their glasses high.

"To Vernon Cooper," O'Neill said. "May he be driving his tractor through that great hayfield in the sky!"

Acknowledgements

T hanks to all who supported me in writing this book and in providing help and feedback. Special thanks to Dannielle Breen, Dianna Breen, Matt Breen, Sue Krumenauer, Dan Birrenkott, Kelsey Breen, Dave Greenwell, Mike Rhiel, and Linda Rhiel.

About the Author

Paul Breen plays guitar poorly and spends far too much time on genealogy. A native of Columbus, Ohio, Paul grew up in Madison, Wisconsin, and worked at the University of Wisconsin-Madison. Paul enjoys running, biking, music, sports, history, and visiting brewpubs. He lives with his wife and family in Madison.

Printed in the USA
CPSIA information can be obtained
at www.ICGtesting.com
LVHW040635160924
790969LV00002B/153

9 798986 208374